GIDEON'S LOT

J.J. Marric

GIDEON'S LOT

STEIN AND DAY/*Publishers*/New York

FIRST STEIN AND DAY PAPERBACK EDITION APRIL 1986
Gideon's Lot was originally published in the United States of America in
hardcover by Harper and Row, Publishers, and is reprinted by arrangement
with Harold Ober Associates.
Copyright © 1964 by John Creasey
All rights reserved
Printed in the United States of America
Stein and Day, Incorporated
Scarborough House
Briarcliff Manor, N.Y. 10510
ISBN 0-8128-8258-X

1

Three Calls

The telephone on George Gideon's desk at New Scotland Yard rang a hundred, sometimes it seemed a thousand, times a day. A call might come from the room next door or from ten thousand miles away; there was no way of telling at the first *ting!* or the first buzz. Most of the calls brought some news of crime. They might be of crimes solved or crimes committed minutes ago. They might be trivial or significant, sensational or pedestrian. They might presage a tremendous upheaval at the Yard, a manhunt which would affect every man and woman there, from Gideon's few superior officers down to the newest office girl in the secretary's office. No week went by without tidings of murder being carried along those lines, no week passed without news of robbery, violence, blackmail, forgery, theft by holdup or smash-and-grab. All these and all other crimes had their accompaniment of shock and grief, loss and despair for the victims, brief moments of triumph for most of the criminals, deep satisfaction for those among them who had become professional, expert and virtually safe in their calling.

These things were part of the warp and weft of modern society, whether one liked it or not.

Gideon did not like it, but as the chief executive officer of the Criminal Investigation Department of London's Metropolitan Police, it was part of his job; over the years it had become part of his being.

Like so many things, the telephone was taken for granted. Each of the three on that flat-topped desk with its built-in trays marked *Post In—Post Out—Pending—Urgent—Closed* had a different ringing sound. The telephone nearest his right hand was the internal one; it had a low-pitched call, more buzz than ring. The second one, a little farther away, was from the Yard's switchboard; it had a muted ring and seldom rang more than once. The third, for which he had to reach over the others, was his outside line. This was the least predictable of them all.

On an afternoon in May, a fine warm day with full promise of summer, Gideon was sitting at his desk which was at right angles to the window, studying a report of a police court hearing at Bow Street. He was frowning because there were aspects of the case he did not like from a police point of view. Benito Dolci Lucci, of Milan, had been committed for trial on a charge of procuring, and released on two sureties of 5,000 pounds each, put up by a business partner and his solicitor. The fact that Lucci was wealthy did not mean that he was a ringleader even by proxy in London's vice, and Gideon had some doubts about the testimony of two of his departmental managers, although it damned Lucci. He had agreed to the charge because Vic Parsons, one of the Yard's shrewdest C.I.D. superintendents, had pressed for it. Parsons' latest report was quite objective, and Lucci had impressed him favorably in the dock; one of the witnesses had not.

Gideon looked at his second-in-command, Lemaitre.

"Lem, is Vic Parsons in?"

"Old Dog's Collar?" Lemaitre looked up, a pale, bony-faced man with slightly prominent eyes, thinning black hair which he brushed sleekly back from a shiny forehead. "Shouldn't think so. Last I heard he was having another go at the Lucci job." Lemaitre, deeply involved in reports on a North Country post office robbery with murder, gave a mechanical tug at his red-and-white spotted bow tie, and looked down at the papers.

Gideon made a note on his jotter: "Check if P's in, 4:30." It was now a little after three.

As he finished, the Number 2 telephone bell rang. Automatically he reached out for it. A truck growled past on the Embankment outside the open window, and although he heard the operator speak all he caught was the last word—York. There had been some sabotage to machinery in two Yorkshire woolen towns recently, and the Yard had sent a man to consult with the local police. Gideon took it for granted that this call was from York.

"Put him through."

There was a longer delay than usual, and squeaky noises on the line were followed by sounds which were loud one moment and faint the next.

"Hi there, George." Unexpectedly it was an American, his accent clear and loud. "Good to be talking to you again." The voice was somehow familiar, but Gideon could not immediately place it. What American would be calling him from the north of England?

"Hallo," he said, putting vigor into his voice. "Who's that speaking?"

The man began: "What—" and then the Yard's operator interrupted hastily.

"It's Captain Nielsen of New York, sir."

New York!

"Good lord!" exclaimed Gideon. "What are you doing in London, Kurt?"

"I certainly wish I was there, I wouldn't mind what I was doing," Nielsen said, sounding as if he meant it. "I'm tied to my desk here in New York, and that's where I'm likely to stay and swelter all summer. George, there are two things I can do for you and one you can do for me. How about a deal?"

Gideon was over the surprise, and thinking rapidly about outstanding matters which had any connection with New York. At least one of the things Nielsen wanted to talk about must be urgent, but Gideon could think of nothing on the files.

"Tell me what I can do for you, first." He covered the mouthpiece quickly and called across the room: "Extension, Lem." Lemaitre looked blank, then snatched a telephone off its cradle.

"There was a bank job in Brooklyn last night, and a night watchman was injured. He says he heard two of the thieves talking, and one of them was British." Nielsen half-laughed. "He said a limey! It was a very smart job. They opened the safe without blowing it, and we don't have anyone in New York at this time who could do it so well. Can you find out who could do it on your side, and is out of the country?"

"Do you want to hold on?" asked Gideon.

Nielsen laughed. "I don't believe even you could do it that fast, George. Cable me with descriptions and teleprint photographs, will you?"

"Of course," Gideon said. He saw Lemaitre put down his receiver gently, and get up from his chair. "What else?" he asked, puzzled by Lemaitre's action, even more puzzled when his assistant started for the door on tiptoe.

"That's all I need from you right now," Nielsen replied. "Any word about those Rite-Time watches?"

"Not yet," answered Gideon.

Lemaitre was already out of the office.

"I've got a feeling about those watches," Nielsen went on.

"Twenty thousand were stolen from a railroad truck in New Jersey, and none of them has been found over here. I think they've been shipped to Europe in large quantities, but are not being released to retail outlets yet."

"Haven't any been exported by the manufacturers?"

"Not to Europe, except to PBX stores. Any you come across are almost certainly stolen. Keep your eyes open, won't you?" With hardly a pause, Nielsen went on: "Now here's some really bad news for you. I've just been told that Abel Schumacher is on the *Queen Elizabeth* which is due at Southampton tomorrow afternoon. Abel is just about the best con man on this side, and he wouldn't cross the Atlantic for chicken feed. He flew over to London about three months ago —we didn't know until he flew back into New York a week later, and we wondered what he'd been up to. Now he's gone back again. I wouldn't be surprised if he was preparing the ground the first time. He's probably working on some innocent on board, and planning to make his killing soon after he reaches London. He's booked in at the Bingham Hotel, and that's money."

Gideon made another note. "Thanks. I'll cover him. How about a photograph and a description?"

"Both on the way."

"That's fine."

"There's another New Yorker in London already, and I wish I'd known it before," Nielsen continued. The tone of his voice changed, and Gideon sensed that this was the primary reason for the call. "He's a Frank S. Mayhew, suspect on a rape-and-murder job in Connecticut last month. We knew he'd skipped but didn't know where. Lives in an apartment with his mother on the East Side. She's just gotten a postcard from him, telling her he had a good flight. It was mailed in London two days ago—the 7th. One of my men saw the postcard before it was delivered."

"Do you know the exact postmark?" Gideon asked.

"S.W.1."

Gideon jotted that down.

"Thanks. Just a suspect, you say?"

"Don't quote me, but he did the job, George. Girl of nineteen, sexy little tramp but no harm in her. She'd known him for about ten days, and her body was found in Central Park. He'd done just about everything. But Ma gave him an alibi and we couldn't break it. That's why we're watching her—she knows what he's done all right. We'd have booked him eventually, and he knew it. So he skipped. Try to find him, George."

Gideon said, "Want him for extradition?"

"Not yet," answered Nielsen. "We haven't enough on him. This is just a warning. I wish it could be more."

Gideon also wished it could be. Unless he was virtually certain of his facts, the New York chief would not have telephoned, but Gideon could do little on the strength of such a warning. He could have a poster done for Divisional and Home Counties Police in the hope that a policeman would notice and identify Mayhew, and once the man was found he could have him watched in London—but even that precaution would be hard to justify for long.

"How about his photograph?" he asked Nielsen.

"I put a full report and pictures in the mail to you last night," Nielsen answered. "When I got to thinking about it I decided to call you. We've had medical reports on him, and two psychiatric reports. He's a psycho, don't make any mistake about it."

"I won't," said Gideon. "Is that the lot?"

"Isn't it enough?"

"Enough to be going on with," Gideon agreed mildly. "Thanks again, Kurt, and—oh! Hold on a moment." His door had opened. Lemaitre had come in brandishing three forms from the Criminal Records Office, eyes aglow with excitement, breathing, *"Hold him on!"* Now Gideon realized what he had been doing, and had to suppress a chuckle. Lemaitre slapped the forms down in front of him, and cocked a thumb. "Hallo there," Gideon went on. "I can name three of our top safebreakers who are out of the country, as far as we know. Ready?"

"Okay, okay, you're the quickest," Nielsen said. "Go ahead."

"George Snider, five feet eight, dark-haired . . ." Gideon read out the names and descriptions of all three, and went on: "We'll put copies of the records including fingerprints in the post tonight. I hope we've helped."

"I hope I've helped with Mayhew," Nielsen said. "See you, George."

He rang off.

Gideon put down his receiver and looked at Lemaitre's grinning face. Lemaitre would crow like any cockerel for days over this. He lived in the absolute conviction that there was no police organization in the world as good as the Yard.

Such pride would have mattered little but for his equal conviction that the American police were second-rate. This wasn't the moment for arguing with him, although the time would probably come.

"Nice work," Gideon said. "We've got a couple of new jobs on our hands." He told Lemaitre about Abel Schumacher and Frank S. Mayhew, and was not surprised at the way Lemaitre scowled and said with obvious feeling:

"Why the hell can't they keep their psychos at home?"

"We having enough of our own," retorted Gideon dryly. "We'd better get busy. First, a reminder about those Rite-Time watches, then check with the Cunard Line to try to find out which passengers on the *Queen Elizabeth* due in Southampton tomorrow are booked at the Bingham Hotel. Also check with the hotel. We want Information alerted to send out a poster about Mayhew as soon as Nielsen's report arrives in the post, too."

"That's if he's *in* London," Lemaitre said skeptically.

Mayhew was in London.

On that calm, pleasant afternoon he was in Regent's Park, a beautiful open space with the Zoo in one section and the canal running through another. He was on the bank of the canal, fifty yards or so from the road behind him and high above the canal in front. This was a clearing, surrounded by trees and bushes.

· Alice Clay was with him—pretty little, foolish little, sexy little Alice Clay. She lay on her back, her head pillowed on her hands which were linked behind her, for she knew that this posture gave an upward thrust to her breasts which fascinated men. Although she was so foolish and too keenly aware of her body, Alice was a pleasant enough person, nicer than most, generous, kindly, free of malice and of spite. She never went out with a man unless she liked him, either; it was the conquest and control that mattered most to her. She had enough money to live on, in fact almost too much for her own good. She did not need to work unless she wanted to, and most of the "work" she toyed with was for charitable causes.

Just now her head was turned a little to one side. The hem of her skirt was inches above her knees, showing legs which were too full in the calves but very small at the ankles, unexpectedly small just below the knees. Lying flat, like this, her hips looked wide, her waist tiny and her belly flat, so that the rising mounds above had greater prominence.

Frank was half-smiling at her.

He puzzled her a little because he was looking at her neck, not at her bosom. He was *ever so* handsome, dark-haired, sun-tanned, with fine flashing eyes and long, upswept eyelashes. She liked the way his nostrils were pinched in slightly, and the shape of his lips, which might have been carved from pink marble.

He kept on moistening them, and she thought she knew why.

She smiled at him.

"Like it here, Frankie?"

"It's just right," he said. "Wonderful." He was lying on his side, facing her. The air was still and warm, and apart from traffic noises muffled by the trees the only sounds were the buzzing of insects. "Just great," he added, and edged closer to her. "Are you okay?"

"Oh, I'm *fine*."

She knew she was tantalizing him, that here in broad daylight there was nothing he could do, nothing serious he dared attempt; she *knew* men. She was twenty-one, and in some ways thought and behaved as if she were seventeen. She imagined the desire that was heating his blood, but it did not occur to her that there was anything wrong about such tantalizing. Her flat was not far away, the moment he so longed for would soon come. It was a good thing to keep a man waiting for a while.

He edged nearer, still looking at her neck. She could feel his breath on her cheeks, and he was panting a little. She wished she could push her fingers through his glossy hair, but that would mean taking a hand from beneath her head. She showed her beautiful teeth in a smile.

"Like me, Frankie?" she whispered.

"*Like* you. Why, I—"

She was taken absolutely by surprise by the speed with which he moved, the ferocious strength of his body upon hers, the pressure of his lips on her mouth, on her teeth. It seemed only an instant from the moment she had whispered, "Like me, Frankie?" to the moment when she felt as if he would crush the breath out of her body. She could not breathe because of the fierceness of his mouth on hers, and the pressure of his hands about her neck.

She tried to cry out but could not, tried to struggle but could hardly move, tried to turn her head away but was imprisoned. The sky went dark as the blood strained against her eyes, and in that moment she understood what he was doing and felt the fear of death.

They did not see the dog, a wire-haired terrier, which came frisking.

They did not hear the man calling, "Snip, come here."

They did not see the man push aside the branches of a tree, which concealed them, or hear him gasp, "My God!"

Mayhew was aware only of the yielding softness of the girl's body, of the sharp grating of his teeth on hers, of the way his fingers sank into her plump white throat. He knew what he was doing and meant that she should die, and yet he did not know what he was doing, and when she was dead he would cry.

He had to go on. He could not stop himself. He—

He felt a blow on the side of his head, another and another, hard and painful, bringing him back into the world about him. The light of the sun and the green of the grass and the barking of a dog, which stood nearby, all merged together. A man's feet and legs were just in front of him, and there was a grip on *his* neck as the man dragged him away. He yielded. He was only just aware of Alice, lying motionless, arms by her sides and fists half-clenched, eyes closed and mouth slack.

Then realization of his great danger came to Mayhew's mind, driving away all thought but of escape.

Swiftly he calculated the odds. There was the man, still heaving at him, and the dog, barking, showing shiny, bared teeth. No one else was in sight. He let his body go, and eased himself up to his knees. The man said:

"If you've killed her you'll hang for it."

Mayhew shuffled farther away on his hands and knees, as the other man bent over the girl, his back toward Mayhew. Still unsteadily, his body trembling but his mind as cold as ice, Mayhew got to his feet. Now the dog set up a frenzied growling.

"Watch him, Snip," the man said. He was straightening out Alice's legs. "Don't let him go."

Mayhew staggered forward a pace, the dog still growling, then jerked himself up and kicked. The force of the kick drove the breath from the terrier's body, and lifted it three feet into the air. The man half-turned, and began to scramble to his feet, but Mayhew kicked him in the small of the back, and he collapsed, suddenly sick with pain.

Mayhew turned and raced away, half aware of a bargeful of people passing on the canal and staring toward the scene.

2

Lucci

Gideon's Number 3 telephone, the direct line one, sounded at the same time as the door opened and a messenger came in with some reports, one marked: *All Divisions and Scotland Yard—URGENT*. The messenger dumped these in Gideon's In tray and nodded to Lemaitre as he went out. Gideon said "Gideon" into the mouthpiece, trying to read the urgent message upside down. R-A-P—

"George, I'm sorry to worry you. Is it a bad time?"

"Hallo, Kate! No, perfectly all right." Gideon stopped at R-A-P to give his full attention to his wife. She had already made it clear that there was no cause for alarm, so this was some domestic trifle. "One of the youngsters coming home, or something?"

"No, nothing like that," Kate replied. "Helen Hobbs would like me to go to a wives' group meeting at her house, there's a special speaker on Hong Kong. But if you're likely to get home early I'd rather stay in."

She meant it.

"As a matter of fact I might be late," Gideon said. He could spend some time going over those files and weighing up the problems of liaison with New York, and Kate need not know that until that moment he had had no intention of staying. "You go and hear all about the Crown's ideal colony. Likely to be late?"

"Elevenish."

"I'll be home by then," Gideon promised. He was already at the next letter in the message. R-A-P-*E*. Suddenly, Kate's voice seemed to fade and Nielsen's was superimposed.

". . . -by, dear," Kate said. "Make sure you have a good meal."

Another phone was ringing.

" 'By," Gideon said. "Have a good time." He rang off almost brusquely and stretched out for the report. His middle telephone was ringing, the one from the switchboard. He let it ring, and read:

Teletype Message from A.B. Division
Rape and Attempted Murder—Regent's Park

At 4:30 p.m. approx. a Mr. *Charles Hislop* interrupted a man attempting to strangle a young woman named *Alice Clay* by the canal in Regent's Park. The assailant escaped while *Hislop* went to *Clay's* assistance. *Clay* is in Marylebone Hospital unconscious. We have an officer by her bedside. *Hislop* has been most cooperative. Latter part of attack and rescue was observed by occupants of a barge on pleasure trip on Regent's Park canal. *Hislop's* description of assailant is appended.

Gideon's second bell had stopped ringing; Lemaitre was holding a telephone and looking across the room.

"George, can you take this?"

Gideon was reading the description of the assailant: *Dark hair, blue-black eyes, lean features* . . .

"Who is it?"

"Old Dog's Collar."

Gideon's mind switched from the story of the attack in Regent's Park to the problem of the Italian, Lucci. At this stage in a case Parsons wouldn't call unless it was an unexpected development, probably an important one, but the rape case investigation was vitally urgent. What Mayhew would do twice he might do a dozen times if given the chance. Gideon picked up the divisional report and rose to his feet.

"I'll take it. Get busy on this, will you? General call, all divisions, the lot." He met Lemaitre halfway across the office, and after a single glance at the sheet, Lemaitre exclaimed:

"Blimey!"

As his assistant went out, Gideon stretched across his desk and picked up the telephone. It was so often like this: a period of comparative quiet followed by a burst of activity which allowed no time for thinking, hardly time to distinguish one case from another in his mind. The fact that he could keep a dozen quite separate, and call the details of each to mind at will, explained why he was commander.

"Yes, Vic?"

"George," said Vic Parsons, "you're not going to like this."

Benito Dolci Lucci was baffled and bewildered, even frightened, when he stood in the dock at Bow Street. He had never been in a court of any kind before, had not known trouble with the police since his early youth, when he had been rightly suspected of giving aid to English and American airmen shot down over northern Italy. In those days he had been a rebel against all authority, simply because he was a townsman, unfamiliar with the country, where his parents had sent him to be safe from the bombing of the great cities of the north, Turin, Genoa and Milan.

He had lived and they had died.

In his early twenties, back in the Milan of his boyhood, he had inherited two million lire from his parents, as well as a small bicycle shop and repair depot. He had been quick to see the prospects for motor-propelled bicycles and started his own factory, giving work first to a dozen, finally to a hundred returned soldiers, girls and youths. Bitterness about Il Duce and fascism was short-lived in those days when obtaining work and food was the all-consuming problem. His "factory" was a collection of dilapidated huts once a German prisoner-of-war camp, his early machines were made of scrap metal, parts from war-damaged jeeps, tanks and cars. In ten years he increased ten-fold the fortune his parents had left him.

He sold out to a manufacturer of motor scooters, becoming then a wealthy man in his early thirties with nothing to do. He married a girl he had known since childhood and they had soon become the proud parents of two daughters and a son, his precious Antonio. Lucci, wanting to occupy himself and have a business for his son to inherit, bought a small publishing house with a dozen trade magazines—including one ostensibly for the photography trade and one for the art world. These two became phenomenally successful, although there was nothing pornographic about them. Eventually the circulation of the arty magazines became so big that he could no longer keep the business in his own hands, and he relied more and more on managers and assistants. They built up a big export trade, and also widened the scope and extended the range of pictures, mostly nudes. But nudes did not shock an Italian with a love of art in his blood, and in any case he seldom studied the magazines himself; he traveled widely, generally with his wife.

He opened branches in big cities in Europe, usually in partnership with a national from the country concerned. One of the most flourishing branches was in London. He had heard rumors that his partner in London was in some kind of difficulty, sent a representative from the Milan office to investigate, and after a week received an urgent cable:

COME AT ONCE: GIOVANNI.

So he had flown here, leaving his wife, his teenage daughters and his ten-year-old son in Milan.

"I will be back in two or three days," he had promised them.

In three days he discovered a little of the truth. His partner was doing much more than publishing magazines filled with photographs and color prints of nude men and women. He was doing much more than distributing these pornographic photographs and magazines undercover in London, where they were sold to pimps and prostitutes, to the prurient young and the lecherous old, and where they were used by prostitutes to excite even their most regular clients.

The worst was very bad in England; bad anywhere, but especially in England.

Lucci, through his partner's actions, owned many of the houses which were let off to the girls, room by room. Through a resident manager of each house, the partners took a percentage of the girls' earnings. Two of the managers were Italians who had lived in London for years, but who visited Milan regularly. These two had given evidence that on each trip they smuggled two or three thousand pounds out of England, and delivered it in person to Lucci. Lucci, they said, knew about everything, Lucci made them take money from the girls.

Most of this Lucci had heard for the first time while in the dock at Bow Street, through a solicitor who translated quickly and unemotionally from English into Italian.

Lucci's partner had denied all knowledge of the letting-off of the rooms to prostitutes and of the financial transactions. The two managers had exonerated him in their testimony, blaming only Lucci.

"But I know nothing of this!" Lucci had cried.

The cry had seemed to fall on deaf ears; there had been no one to believe him.

Now Lucci stood, immaculate in his beautifully tailored suit, black hair shiny with pomade, face slightly powdered, dark eyes shimmering with fear and bewilderment and the beginning of hatred for his "partner," an Englishman named White: Percival White.

There had been no trouble in raising the money for bail, of course.

There was anguish in his mind. Until today he had believed he would be found not guilty, that there was a chance to keep this beastly story from his wife and family, but now he knew it would be in the Milan newspapers, *Il Giorno* would carry his photograph—it was terrible, terrible.

He went back, alone, to his hotel apartment, still only half-aware that it was owned by his company, and that many of the rooms were used for what the police had called "immoral purposes." His living room was beautifully furnished, on the fourth and top floor, overlooking a narrow street which seemed to be as full of restaurants as the arched *gallerias* which led off the Cathedral Square in Milan. There was nothing to indicate that in the ceiling there was a one-way mirror, through which one could peer down into this room.

A man was watching him from there. A microphone carried every sound he made to the watcher.

Lucci walked about the living room, then went into the bedroom, where a photograph of plump Maria, his daughters and Antonio stood on the dressing table.

Beside the photograph was a newspaper which he had not seen before and had not placed there himself. He picked up the photograph, and tears stung his eyes until he could hardly see. When he could, he picked up the newspaper and opened it. It was *Il Giorno*. A copy of this same family photograph was on the front page, with an enlarged photograph of him.

The headlines seemed to scream:

LUCCI ACCUSED OF VICE
SCANDAL IN LONDON

Hearing Tomorrow

In Milan, when she had seen the same edition the day before, Maria Lucci had said very simply to her daughters and her servants:

"I must fly to London quickly. Signor Lucci is in need of me."

She was flying over the Alps at the exact moment when Lucci saw the newspaper.

Lucci felt as if the world had crashed down on him. Maria now knew the worst, as did his friends, his priest, his staff, everyone who sold or distributed the magazines. He could never recover from this shame; never.

He picked up a bottle of brandy from a table by the window. As he poured out the sound of glass on glass quivered all the time; and the man above smiled down on him. Lucci

tossed the drink down, picked up the photograph, stared, put
it down, picked it up again. He went almost blindly to an
armchair with a high back and dropped into this, despairingly.

Soon a kind of quiet came over him.

Soon he slept.

When he was fast asleep, the door opened and a man came
in. This man replaced the brandy in the bottle with some
which was free from poison, replaced the stopper, then pulled
the sheets off the bed and stuffed them round the doors. Next
he drew the heavy curtains at the windows, stood looking
round for fully a minute, and finally bolted the door and
turned on the gas fire. Then he went back into the bathroom.
He closed that door firmly, and climbed out of a tiny window
into an airshaft, and onto a ladder which had been placed
there for him.

Maria Lucci was now flying over the valley of the Rhône.

Since the hearing, Superintendent Parsons had been very
uneasy indeed. Obviously Lucci had been in abnormal distress
in the dock; the guilty sometimes brazened a situation out, or
sometimes feigned distress, but Lucci had not been pretend-
ing. If he had told the truth, then Percival White had been
lying, but White had left London "for a rest" after the com-
mittal. He had left his address behind, wasn't on the run as
far as Parsons could judge. As he couldn't question White,
Parsons decided to have another talk with Lucci.

Parsons was a man with a conscience, but not one who
often questioned his own competence. He traded on his quite
natural but rather unctuous manner, his rather soft-looking
lips, his habit of pressing the tips of his fingers together as if
at heart he thought that all times were times for prayer.
Stored up in the brain behind the broad, rather wrinkled forehead, which gave an impression of constant perplexity, was a
remarkable store of knowledge about human vice, perversion
and frailty. He was the Yard's expert on vice, and his attitude
toward the beastliness he dealt with was coolly objective. He
could use four-letter words and the worst obscenities with absolute detachment, but except in the way of business he neither swore nor spoke obscenely.

He knew he was right about the vice ring built around
Lucci's businesses; he was now far from sure about the Italian's personal involvement.

He went to the beautifully appointed private hotel in Soho,
a place where orgiastic parties were thrown as often as it was

safe, where for a large enough sum one could become a Prince of Peeping Toms, and where Lucci had the most luxurious suite. Outside the hotel a divisional sergeant said:

"He's still here, sir."

"Good." Parsons went in, determined to test his own new doubts on the Italian, but there was no answer to a call to his room. A girl receptionist with enormous brown eyes gave him a timid smile.

"Perhaps Mr. Lucci, he is out."

"I'm going up to his room," Parsons said. He turned on his heel and strode to the self-operated lift. By the time he was banging on Lucci's door, and calling out, a youthful porter, also Italian, came bounding up the stairs. Parsons stood back, showed his card, and said:

"Open the door."

"But, sir, I cannot——"

"Open it or I'll break it down."

The youth tried a passkey, but although it turned the lock the door did not open. Parsons went to a landing window, thrust that open, beckoned the divisional detective and waited impatiently until he arrived. With the porter protesting as if in anguish, the two detectives put their combined weight against the door.

On the third assault the bolt gave way.

". . . Lucci was lying in an easy chair with the Milanese newspaper spread over his paunch and his knees. He was as pink as a cherry—must have been dead for half an hour," Parsons told Gideon over the telephone. "I think we ought to consider murder but we might put White and some others at disadvantage if we pretend we've bought it as suicide. I thought you might make up my mind for me about that, George. I don't want to make any more wrong decisions."

3

The First Wife

Gideon read the implication in that bitter remark but did not comment immediately. The decision could be important. In fact two decisions were involved, the one which Parsons wanted him to make and a consequent one: whether to give Parsons carte blanche to go ahead with an investigation which might be costly in time and manpower, and might also be ill-timed. Percival White and whoever worked with him would be on their guard by now; in vice investigations it was usually better to catch the suspects by surprise.

Parsons waited patiently.

"What are the indications of murder?" Gideon asked at last.

"A few scratches on a bathroom window opening onto an airshaft show that someone's been in that shaft lately and could have escaped by the shaft, leaving the door locked. There's a peekaboo window in the ceiling, and I had a look through it. Fresh cigarette ash shows that someone's been up there in the past few hours, though the hotel staff say the room's not been used for a week."

"I think I'd soft-pedal, Vic," Gideon decided. "Dig as deep as you can into Lucci's past. Ask Milan to help. Let the newspapers take suicide for granted if they will, and encourage them toward it if they don't go of their own accord. Take a couple of days on the job—nothing else on your desk, is there?"

"Nothing I can't pass on to someone else."

"Pass it, then. Concentrate on this, and we'll have a session together over a noggin soon."

After a long pause, Parsons said with feeling, "Thanks, George."

Gideon put down his receiver slowly, feeling very thoughtful, and in a way nostalgic. Parsons was now working in his, Gideon's, square mile, that part of the West End which was probably the gayest, the brightest, the ugliest, and the most sordid part of London. In Soho he had cut his teeth as an officer on the beat, and later as a plainclothes C.I.D. man. It hadn't changed much. Some new anti-vice laws had created some ingenious variations in the selling of sex and vice, that was all. Here the pimps and the prostitutes met the wide-eyed youth and the round-eyed countryfolk, and it was surprising how little of the corruption rubbed off onto the simpletons. Every now and again some natural leader took over the vice racket, organizing the girls, controlling the premises, going too far with strip shows, and it seemed to Gideon, with his thirty years on the Force, that it would always be so. Behind the conventional side of the vice, however, there was always the danger of drug trafficking, and drugs could do such shocking things. In any case the innocent had to be protected as far as the law could protect him.

If there was any indication of traffic in drugs, Parsons would soon find out.

If there wasn't, and if Lucci had been murdered, it was probably a bid on Percival White's part to take over his partner's share of the legitimate and the illegal business.

At one time Gideon would have been shocked by much of his own dispassionate analysis of the situation; now he felt a kind of unease, a vague reminder that it ought to affect him as a human being as well as a policeman.

It was almost a relief when Lemaitre came in, perky as ever. Seeing Gideon's preoccupation he went straight to his desk, but before he had settled down Gideon's expression changed, he squared his shoulders as if preparing a physical attack on the day's problems.

"How's the Clay girl?" he asked.

"Still in Marylebone Hospital, getting over it."

"No serious harm?"

"Only worse than death."

"Know anything about her yet?"

"Had a bitta luck." Lemaitre rubbed his hands together. "She's got a bachelor flat in Marylebone Street, and often goes to the Park. One of the A.B. chaps knows her by sight. Bit of a tramp but nothing nasty. Inherited about thirty thousand quid from Ma, four years ago. Some people have the luck."

"Has she made a statement yet?"

"Says the chap was an American who called himself Frank Mason. F. M., George. She's known him about a week. This was the first time he tried anything, she says. The chap who saved her life—Hislop, remember?—got a good look at

Mason, and the description fits Mayhew to a T. We shouldn't be long picking him up."

This was Lemaitre, the perennial optimist who always jumped to conclusions—his one restricting weakness as a detective.

"I hope you're right," Gideon said.

"Oh, I will be. George, I'll tell you what. I'll take these papers home tonight and give 'em the once-over there. Can't concentrate in this atmosphere." He was referring to the North Country post office murder. "I'd better send those reports to New York, and get a report on this rape job. I haven't talked to the Bingham Hotel or the Cunard Line yet, either. Cunard offices will be shut if I don't get a move on." He pushed the post office murder file away from him, and picked up his telephone.

Gideon looked through his own Pending tray.

The call from York Minster hadn't come although he had expected it hours ago; it looked as if there was no new development in the sabotage case. He had two requests for information from Interpol, which he had to supply to the Assistant Commissioner in the morning. One was about some forged West German marks being distributed in England (and the rest of Europe) and the second was an inquiry from Australia about a small private banking company in London; he had everything ready for that, too.

Lemaitre was taking down names over the telephone. When he had finished he looked up and said briskly:

"Three couples are booked in at the Bingham off the Q.E., George. Lord and Lady Melroy, and they'll only stay overnight. Mr. and Mrs. Albert Henderson from Atlanta, Georgia, and Mr. and Mrs. Carpenter, from Winnipeg. Like me to have a talk to the Q.E. by radiotelephone?"

"To say what?"

"Ask our contact man to find out whom Schumacher's been softening up."

"No need to hurry," Gideon said, and immediately saw the disappointment in Lemaitre's eyes; then suddenly he became sharply aware of something that had been simmering in his mind for some time. Lem was tired. He had not had a holiday of more than a few days at a time in the past year, and badly needed one. Meanwhile, a day out of the office would do him a lot of good. On impulse, Gideon added, "Why don't you go down to Southampton to meet the ship tomorrow? You can go aboard with the Immigration chaps, and have a talk with our man. Give Schumacher the once-over, too."

Lemaitre leaned back in his chair, pulled slowly at the ends of his tie and said:

"I could take my wife down for the run, couldn't I?"

"It would be silly to leave her behind."

"Do just one more thing for me," pleaded Lemaitre. "Pray for a nice warm day."

Gideon grinned—and his Number 2 telephone bell rang. This time there were no deafening noises from the Embankment, and he heard the operator say clearly:

"Mr. Ormeroyd from York, sir."

At last.

"Put him through." There was a click on the line. "Hallo, Jake," Gideon said. "Thought they'd taken you lambing on Ilkley Moor."

"No such luck," Superintendent Ormeroyd retorted. He made "luck" sound almost like the word "look" with long vowels; a kind of drawn-out "Luke." Thirty years in London had not changed his accent or his dialect. "Eh, George, it's a bad business up here."

"How bad?"

"It's sabotage, there's no doubt of it."

"I half-expected that," said Gideon.

"That's right, you did, but you didn't expect me to find out that it fits in nicely with that machine trouble they're having in Birmingham, did you? Same method—same corrosive acid — same knowledge of machinery. When you come to think, George, it's much the same as the trouble they had in Northamptonshire in the shoe factory, or in Macclesfield over the silk. Take it from me it's a countrywide job. What I'd like to do if you've no objection is go up to Glasgow, where they had some damage in the biscuit factory, and then visit Macclesfield, Birmingham and Northampton on the way home. Allow a week or ten days, say. Will that be all right with you?"

"Try and finish it this week," Gideon urged. "If you're right we ought to get cracking."

When Ormeroyd rang off, Gideon reflected almost subconsciously that if there was a connection among crimes committed in these different parts of England and Scotland, the first thing to look for must be a connecting motive. He jotted down the names of the cities concerned, and added: *Expect to hear by Monday.* He put this into the Pending tray.

As he did so he became aware of a mood almost of apprehension. He was not unfamiliar with it, for he had known it all of his working life but had never really analyzed it to his own satisfaction.

It was an oppressive, at times almost intolerable, sense of responsibility. Crimes of which he knew nothing were being committed every minute of the day—and some would be serious enough for him to be consulted. He could do absolutely nothing to prevent them and yet he felt he should. If the man Mayhew killed again, then he, Gideon, would have a share of the blame because the Yard had failed to catch the man.

He knew that this was utterly wrong, yet could not overcome that all-pervading sense of guilt. The feeling would go, of course, but sooner or later it would come back. Today the burden of it was very heavy. There was the combined weight of disquiet about Schumacher, Mayhew, Snider in New York, and added to these the sickening realization that if Mayhew struck again, his victim would probably be unknown to him at this moment—a happy girl who did not dream of her impending fate.

There were so many unsuspecting victims of all manner of crime.

There were so many criminals—Americans and Englishmen, Italians and French, people of every nationality—that to Gideon it sometimes seemed that London was a clearinghouse for them all.

He could understand Lemaitre's resentment about imported criminals, but it was difficult to explain to Lemaitre about the way he was feeling.

It was a strange fact that he, George Gideon, Commander of the Criminal Investigation Department of the best-known police force in the world, who had had so much experience in fighting and preventing crime, felt a need that was almost hunger to talk about these things with another man. The only one who might even begin to feel as he did was Vic Parsons, whom Lemaitre had recently dubbed "Old Dog's Collar"—partly because of his name, partly because if he were to turn his collar around no man could pass more easily for a cleric.

The internal telephone rang, and drove these preoccupations out of Gideon's mind.

Michael Dunn was a man hovering on the brink of crime.

He was in his shop, checking on supplies of typewriter ribbons, when he heard his wife cough. It was a terrible cough which made her catch her breath and then retch as if she could not breathe at all. It had been going on for months, on and off for years. It made him feel as sick as it made Cynthia.

"Get her away," the doctors urged.

But where could he take her?

"Get her more help in the house," they said.

How could he afford to pay for help with his debts piling up and the threat of bankruptcy drawing nearer day by day?

"There's no way of curing these bronchial troubles while she's in London."

Cynthia had been away once, spending three months in Bournemouth. That period had been the beginning of Dunn's financial worries. She had hated being at the seaside alone but had been much better for it; there had actually been color in her cheeks when she came back. Then after a few weeks the cough had started again, and now it was as bad as ever.

But, "It's no use talking, Mike. I won't go away without you," she would insist.

She didn't know, because he dared not tell her, that he could not send her away again; that he rushed to get the post in the morning to make sure she should not come upon a peremptory demand from his bank or from some pressing creditor. He had to protect her, yet he could not. The situation was ten times worse because it was his own fault; he had bought the business from the widow of the owner after working as compositor for ten years, and had believed he knew it inside out.

Now he owed nearly 3,000 pounds, which was for him an enormous sum.

He heard Cynthia coughing on and on. Suddenly she stumbled and he thought he heard her fall. He rushed into the little living room between the shop and the printing works. She was standing by the side of a chair, gripping the back, face drained of color, mouth open as she fought for breath. It made her look so awful, so near death.

She gave a strange grating whine of sound; the paroxysm was passing; but for an hour afterward she would be limp and exhausted on the couch.

She looked at him with anguish in her eyes.

"I'll have to go away again, Mike," she said hoarsely. "I'll have to."

She *would* have to, and he could not afford to send her unless he committed the crime he had been contemplating for months. He had been restrained by conscience, by his religion, by all the principles he had ever been taught and still believed in.

"It's no use," he said to himself when Cynthia was quiet. "I'll have to do it. I'll have to."

It looked so easy.

In this small stationery and printing business in Brentford, not far from the Great West Road, he had one big customer, the only profitable one on his books—Kismet Cosmetics of the Great West Road, the English subsidiary of an American firm. He printed labels for boxes and bottles, supplied office stationery, typewriters, even some packing material for them. His was only a tithe of Kismet's business, of course; he was their local printer who got them out of difficulties when stocks ran unexpectedly low or main suppliers were late.

In the past two months Dunn had made a significant discovery; there was a flaw in Kismet's accounting methods. They had paid him twice for the same goods. On checking this with the assistant accountant he had realized that there was only a nominal check between the buying office, which placed the orders, the warehouse where goods were delivered, and the accounts department, which paid the bills. Moreover, they had allowed him to see the way the buying office and the warehouse passed an account for payment; a small rubber stamp was marked "O.K. to Pay" and initialed in both office and warehouse.

He had actually ordered the rubber stamps for each department, without realizing their significance. He had a facsimile of the stamp in his own books, in case another supply was needed. He printed some of the official order forms for the firm. He repaired typewriters for them. He could overprint some order forms, have a rubber stamp cut, type out false orders, and initial "O.K. to Pay" impressions. Even the initialing caused no problem, because he was familiar with it on notes from the Kismet Company.

He could easily put in fake invoices, and be virtually sure the account would be paid. If he added 300 pounds a month to the amount really due he would be out of immediate trouble and would be able to do everything needed to help Cynthia back to health. All he required was the courage to make the decision.

Barney Barnett had a different problem and a different kind of decision to make: when to do the job in hand. He had the place in mind, and the bricks ready. Maggie was as nippy at the wheel as any driver in London, and the police seldom thought of suspecting a woman driving a runaway car. Barney knew the habits and the timing of the police patrols in

Soho, and a few hours earlier he had discussed the job with Maggie—his wife.

She was as good a cook as she was a driver, and that day it was roast leg of lamb, with rich thick gravy, roast potatoes, done to a crisp golden brown, and cauliflower.

"You'll have to get me some cash, Barney, if you want to eat tomorrow," she said.

"Like that is it?" Barney was a wizened-looking man in the late forties. "Can't you get something on tick?"

"Never have, never mean to. Cash and carry, that's my motto. What's the matter with you these days? Gone lazy or just soft in the head? You haven't brought me home a decent pay packet for a month."

Barney ate in silence for a while, and Maggie, a well-preserved, well-rounded forty without a gray hair, kept pace with him.

"I know a place," he announced suddenly.

"Where?"

"Soho—in Frisk Street."

"I know the one," Maggie reflected. "On the corner by that shoeshop."

"That's right—Klein's place. It's one-way traffic into the Avenue, and you can lose the whole bloody Flying Squad at Cambridge Circus. How about it?"

"Suits me," Maggie approved. "After I've done the washing up and had a nap, then. Okay?"

"Okay," agreed Barney. He grinned, leaned across and dipped his finger down the V of her dress. "Do a dinner and a show tonight, eh? Some place where they can cook."

She slapped his hand away.

4

The Second Wife

Barney strolled along Frisk Street, cheerfully aware that two policemen who did not know him had passed him at the corner opposite the Grandi Hotel. He looked as he always did when he was on a job—a man just up from the country; all he needed to complete the illusion was a haystalk in his green porkpie hat. There was even dried mud on the soles of his brown leather boots, the uppers of which shone like mirrors. What he did not know was that two plainclothes policemen were now outside the Grandi Hotel and that the police with Superintendent Parsons in charge had taken over Benito Lucci's front suite.

Barney reached the corner where a jeweler's shop was next to a long narrow shoeshop. Round the corner, parked only three cars along, Maggie sat in an old Austin taxi with a cloth covering its "For Hire" sign. Except for those in a hurry, no one ever took any notice of a parked taxi; and Maggie was so mannishly dressed that one had to scrutinize her to see that she was a woman.

Only two cars were coming along the street where Maggie was parked, and only one in the intersecting street, where a right turn was permitted. Barney took a cloth-covered brick out of his capacious left-hand pocket and hurled it at the window. Before anyone within sight realized what had caused the crash of sound, he took a second cloth-covered brick and broke off three long splinters of glass, to make a gaping, danger-free hole. He grabbed two trays of rings and one of watches, skillfully slid them into his pocket, and then yelled:

"Thief! Stop thief!"

A little shiny-haired man appeared at the doorway.

"There he goes!" yelled Barney, pointing.

He rushed past the man toward the corner. Maggie was already pulling out, and he jumped between the taxi and the car behind it and scrambled into the cab with Maggie holding the offside door open. He hooked the door to with his foot. Maggie started off. Barney knew that from this moment on she would be in her element. Driving was second nature to her, and she could weave through traffic skillfully enough to make a taxi driver applaud.

Absolutely confident in her ability to get them to safety, Barney wriggled out of the big tweed suit and kicked off the boots; underneath he wore a shirt, flannels and thin canvas shoes. He folded the suit and pushed it and the boots into a space under the back seat of the taxi, then he took a black jacket off the seat and shrugged himself into it.

Maggie was squinting at him over her shoulder. She winked. Good old Maggie! he thought happily. She had shamed him into doing the job, and as always she was seeing him safe.

That was almost the exact moment that Michael Dunn put seven invoices in the post to Kismet Cosmetics, all genuine; and put three more, all forged, into his brief case to take to the factory when he next called there.

He was trembling.

Cynthia was coughing.

Parsons heard the crash of glass as he passed the window of Lucci's apartment. The body was now on a stretcher, ready for the waiting ambulance. Two photographers and a fingerprint man had been over the flat with great thoroughness, and Parsons was sure he had missed nothing. There was a scraping of cigarette tobacco and paper from the carpet, now in a plastic bag; someone had carried it in here on the sole of his shoe, it would never have squashed so flat on a carpet. He had photographs and scrapings from the scratches on the airshaft, too, and felt positive that a man had climbed out the bathroom window recently. He had talked to a tall, middle-aged Italian, Giovanni Mancelli, who had flown from Milan a few days earlier. Mancelli professed to be shocked by the whole affair.

"What his wife and family will say I cannot imagine," he had said. "I must fly back to them as soon as possible. Is it in order for me to leave now?"

Parsons had raised no objection.

Parsons went to the window and looked out, and one of the photographers joined him.

"Car crash?" he suggested.

"I only heard glass," said Parsons. "What's going on at the corner?" A crowd had gathered, and a little man in the middle was gesticulating wildly. One of the divisional men had left his position outside the hotel, and two policemen were among the crowd.

"See that window?" asked the photographer.

"Smash-and-grab," decided Parsons. "Nip along and take some pictures. I'll be there in five minutes."

The photographer was a middle-aged, prosy man, heavy featured, stocky and gray clad.

"Two birds with one stone, eh?" He picked up his camera and plodded out.

The ambulance men took the stretcher toward the small lift; Parsons wondered how they would manage in there. He turned back to the apartment. There were the dead man's clothes, a few of his better magazines, some cigarettes—and the newspaper and photograph. Parsons studied the face of Maria Lucci, then wondered who would look after Lucci's things here. He reminded himself that he could treat this as murder, in which case the apartment could be sealed off for as long as he wanted—or he could release it in the hope of convincing White and everyone else concerned that the suicide theory was accepted.

It was one thing to leave the decision to Gideon, another to shelve the responsibility for carrying it out. Gideon knew that he had really wanted to soft-pedal; had he thought a murder charge would stick, he would have made it.

"Two days George gave me," he mused aloud, and stepped toward the door. As he reached it the telephone bell rang. He went across to the instrument which was by the side of the bed. "Parsons."

"Mr. Parsons, please." It was the girl of the reception desk. "There is a lady here."

"Well?"

"She has come to see Signor Lucci."

Parsons said again, "Well?"

It might be any one of a dozen women who habitually used this hotel, but something in the girl's voice made him wonder.

The girl said, "It is—the signora."

"Signora who?" asked Parsons, but before she answered he realized whom she meant.

"Signora Lucci. Please—what shall I do?"

Parsons said heavily, unhappily, "Where are the ambulance men?"

"They are gone now."

"Did she see them leave?"

"No, sir, I do not think so. Please, sir—"

"I'll come down," Parsons said.

Lucci's wife was very short, five feet at the most, plump, but not plump enough to be dumpy. In her dark-eyed, olive-complexioned way she was quite a beauty. She was dressed in a smooth-textured chocolate-brown suit trimmed with mink.

She looked at him apprehensively with huge brown eyes. He was relieved to hear her speak in English, even with a marked American accent. He became the "parson," the man of understanding and sympathy.

"Please, I want to see my husband. Where is he?"

"Mrs. Lucci," Parsons said, "I am sorry that I have bad news for you."

"You have bad news about my husband? You have sent him to prison, then? But that is wrong, my husband knows nothing about such evil things as it says in the newspapers. Please, you must believe me. He is a good man."

That was the moment when Parsons felt a sense not only of responsibility but of guilt, and the moment when he drew nearer to Gideon in his concept of his work. When he had pressed for Lucci's arrest, believing he should seize the opportunity of one of the man's rare visits to London, he had created the conditions which had led to his death.

"Please, I tell you he is a good man."

Parsons said humbly, "I think we would have proved that, if only—"

Her eyes flashed.

"I must see him. Please, take me to him." She took his hands and gripped tightly. He was aware of her perfume as well as of her terrible intensity. Even then, even with that sense of guilt in his heart, he felt ill at ease because of a kind of theatricality in her manner, common to so many Southern Europeans. There had been nothing at all theatrical about Lucci; he had behaved as if he had been in a state of shock from the momtnt of his arrest.

"Please, I wish to see him!"

Parsons wished Gideon were here to cope with the dead Lucci's wife.

"Signora, you cannot see him," he said slowly, and the tips of his fingers touched. "I have very, very bad news for you!"

Signora Lucci's eyes appeared to become huge and luminous. Obviously comprehension grew in her mind and slowly her expression changed to one of horror. For a moment he thought that she would become hysterical. Her lips trembled and she began to cry. Softly, the little Italian girl came forward and began to talk in Italian, and a tall man in a black cassock came in; obviously the girl had sent for a priest.

He also began to talk in Italian to Signora Lucci, and suddenly she turned from Parsons as if he were unclean.

In a way he would have felt better if she had stormed at him and blamed him.

He went out glumly, but soon perked up, for dozens of newspapermen were waiting for him, and he had to "sell" the suicide story. He hoped to God he was right to.

"How much did you get?" Maggie Barnett asked her husband.

"Who wants to know?"

"*I* want to know."

"Money and fair words. How about the Ritz, ducks?"

"So it was a good haul," Maggie said with satisfaction.

"Good enough for the Trocadero, anyway," confirmed Barney.

"How long will it keep us in comfort and ease?"

"A month, if my wife doesn't start throwing the dough about."

"I never have and I never will," said Maggie. She was sitting in the kitchen, a cup of tea in her hands, slippers on, flowered dress opened at the zip-fastener side for comfort's sake. "Give, Barney."

Maggie held out her hand, rosy palm uppermost. Barney played a little game of indignation, then took a wad of notes from inside his jacket and slapped it into her hand.

"That's my boy. How much?"

"One hundred and forty," declared Barney.

She widened her blue-green eyes.

"Say, you're learning. Those sparklers must have been worth a thousand quid." She counted out the notes, some fives, more ones, and tucked some back into his pocket. "Forty for you," she announced.

"Ought to be seventy," Barney argued.

"Barney," said Maggie, as if she hadn't heard him, "how do you know old Adam didn't cheat you? How do you know there wasn't *two* thousand quids' worth in that loot? Did you get another price?"

"Didn't have time," said Barney loftily.

But there had been time, and Maggie was right; he had been in too much of a hurry to sell. Maggie, sensing his mood, planted a kiss on his lips, and said:

"What about a little drink, ducky?"

He had two, but he was thoughtful and quiet when they got ready for the trip to the West End from the little house in Fulham, near the Eelbrook Common. It wasn't until he had had his second glass of champagne at the Trocadero, not a quarter of a mile from the place he had robbed, that he began to enjoy himself. Next time he would make old Adam pay through the nose.

Among the other people in the Trocadero dining room was Detective Sergeant Lacey, there to watch a man and woman who were believed to be planning to defraud an old man from the country. The prospective victim hadn't yet shown up, and the suspects were at the bar. Lacey watched Barney and his wife dancing with the expertise of ballroom professionals. Maggie seemed to have magic in her feet; it was almost possible to forget that she was portly and middle-aged.

On his general report next day, Lacey wrote:

Barney and Maggie Barnett were living it up at the Trocadero last night. They had two bottles of champagne between them.

Cynthia Dunn lay up on her pillows, fighting for breath after another bout of coughing. The television was turned on low, and Michael was watching it and thinking of what he had done.

"Mike," she said with an effort.

"Yes, Cyn?"

"Mike, can we afford it?"

"Afford what?"

"Bournemouth, of course."

"Of course we can! And if all goes well we'll move down there, lock, stock and barrel, before you can say knife."

"I'd love that," she said. "I'd just love it."

She did not raise the question of the expense again, appearing to be fully reassured. Dunn, so sensitive because of his guilt, could not understand why she had raised it at all.

Alice Clay lay awake in the General Ward of the Marylebone Hospital, a little scared and at the same time glad of the shadowy figures in the other beds, the sound of many people breathing, one woman snoring, one whistling reedily. Every now and again she seemed to feel the pressure of Mason's hands at her throat, and his body on hers, and she felt tears flood her eyes and a kind of panic rise up in her.

She would never go with a man again.

Frank Mayhew, alias Mason, was almost asleep in a small hotel in Kensington. He had moved here from his Mayfair hotel during the period of panic that had followed his flight from Regent's Park. A newspaper with the story in headlines and with a picture of the Clay girl was on the floor by the side of his bed. One of the subheadlines read: *American Wanted for Questioning*.

That was his great hope, the cause of his confidence that he would not be found. He had assumed an Australian accent, which he had acquired on the ship. No one would know he was an American, but no one would be surprised that he didn't speak quite like an Englishman.

He was safe enough.

It was a funny thing though. In the hotel there was a girl who was remarkably like Alice Clay, in the same way as Alice had been like Juanita Candless in New York. Face, breasts, wasp waist, legs—she was almost a carbon copy.

He wondered what room she was in.

Her name was Florence Foster. She was fast asleep, in Room 97 of the Rosemount Hotel, one floor down and along a narrow passage. She was alone in London for the first time in her life, which wasn't so remarkable as she was not quite nineteen years of age.

Gideon slept soundly, with Kate beside him. She had come home vivacious and talkative, thrilled with the pictures she had seen and the stories she had heard of Hong Kong. The speaker had been a woman C.I.D. officer from the island colony, and the hostess the wife of one of the few ex-public school and university men—Superintendent Hobbs. Gideon had listened with half an ear, while going over the events of the day in his mind. He had stayed late at the office, had a meal at the pub in Cannon Row, two hundred yards away, and walked home through his beloved London, although the word "beloved" would never have occurred to him.

He had done more.

He had geared his mind for the tasks of tomorrow which would be born out of the events of this day. The feeling of responsibility for preventing some threatening crimes was still on him. He was afraid that he might have missed a key factor in the day's reports, and had fallen asleep wondering about the man Schumacher on the *Queen Elizabeth*, hoping that his subconscious mind would succeed where his conscious mind had failed.

Lucci's widow did not sleep at all.

She had been comforted, but felt no comfort. Her grief was so great that it stifled the other emotion within her—one of anger. Now and again it burst out in an anguished cry: "*Not my Benito!*" Her Benito had been a good man, a religious man. He would never have taken his own life. He would never have trafficked in young girls, the thought was hideous. It was a wicked lie. Yet he was dead, and shame smeared his memory.

A thought flashed across her mind. I must not allow it, I must clear his name!

5

Dockside

"What a sight!" exclaimed Lemaitre. "They can say what they like, but the old *Q.E.* is still the finest ship afloat. Ain't she a beauty?"

"Lovely," said Chloe, his wife.

"They knew how to make ships when they made her. These postwar crates—just sheets of metal riveted together."

"The *United States* looks lovely, too," Chloe ventured.

It was one of those days when two great transatlantic liners passed close by each other in the Solent. The fastest and the largest passenger ships afloat, each in its way majestic, steamed through a sea as calm and blue as the Mediterranean on a day when the South Coast of England and the green slopes and tall cliffs of the Isle of Wight looked as serene as if no gales had ever whipped the sea to dark-gray fury.

The Lemaitres were standing in the thwarts of the cutter taking the port medical officer, the immigration and customs officials aboard. Most of the work for both immigration and customs departments had been done on the ship but there was no end to formality. The sides of both ships were lined with passengers, the *United States* was bedecked with a thousand flags, the *Queen Elizabeth* flew the Union Jack on the foremast, the blue ensign, the Cunard Line flag on the aftermast, and pilot's red and white flag between the mast and the nearer funnel. The sirens boomed out across the water, the passengers waved almost frantically.

As the cutter drew near, the ships passed. The white side of the *Queen Elizabeth* loomed huge over the tiny ship. Lemaitre looked at his wife, half afraid that clambering up the rope ladder would scare her. She was his second wife, married three years ago after long years of marriage to a harridan. Chloe was like a dream wife. He was apprehensive that something might smear the marriage, some accident, some trick of fate, some idiocy of his own. She was very blonde, very small, big-breasted, slim-legged. He kept on making new discoveries about her. He made one now. She swung herself onto and up that ladder with the agility of a cabin boy. At the ship's rail she turned to ask:

"Want any help, Lem?"

"Just carry me." Lemaitre grinned. In the grand hall he was anxious again. "Don't lose yourself, Chlo-ee. This is a big ship."

"And I'm a big girl now," Chloe retorted.

He left her at the windows of the closed shops, already wistful.

Lemaitre knew the liaison man on board the liner, Jack Simmons, who had once been at the Yard but retired early to take up this job with the steamship company. He was nominally assistant chief steward, and yet his work had more to do with the master-at-arms. He kept a watchful eye on the passengers of the ship much as a hotel detective did in a hotel. Like many men trained at the Yard he had an almost photographic memory; it was he who had reported that George Snider, the cracksman, had traveled first class on this ship to America.

Lemaitre met him in his cabin.

"Don't give you much room, Jack, do they?" He looked round, only half-approving.

"Room enough for a bottle or two," retorted Simmons. He was young-looking for his fifty-six years, sleek, well-groomed, tubby. He poured out whisky, added soda from a small bottle, and raised his glass.

"Here's a toast to getting the man you're after."

"A Yank named Schumacher."

"Not surprised," said Simmons promptly. "He's got a funny look about him. I thought he was card-sharping, but my tame budgerigar could beat him at anything from penny-nap up. Hangs around the middle-aged socialites but they don't like him much. He's seen a lot of one American couple—the Hendersons."

Lemaitre said, "Rich Americans?"

"Rolling in it, they say."

"Sounds right," said Lemaitre.

"What's his line?"

"Conning."

"Conning," echoed Simmons. "I wouldn't know but if I wanted to fleece anyone it wouldn't be Elliott Henderson. He's as sharp as a needle, and his wife isn't so blunt."

"Has Schumacher paid much attention to anyone else?"

"Can't say he has."

"The Melroys, or—"

"Stow it," interrupted Simmons. "Melroy's in a wheelchair, his wife's his nurse."

"The Carpenters?"

"Not much more than boy and girl on honeymoon. He's over here on a two-year term at the High Commissioner's office."

"Then if it's anyone it's the Hendersons. May be a lot of hot air. Nielsen of New York told George he was worth watching."

"When Nielsen blows hot air the sky will fall in," declared Simmons. "That man's the coolest customer I've come across —including Gee-Gee. Want to take a look at Schumacher?"

"Suits me."

"Another tot?"

"Not when I'm on duty," said Lemaitre virtuously. "Anyone else on board worth watching?"

Simmons took an envelope from his pocket.

"Here's the lot—seven of 'em. Three cardsharps, a homo, a dip who kept his fingers clean this trip, a shoplifter who didn't —I've tipped off Customs to open all his cases—and a watchmaker who might present a suspiciously big paunch to Customs. Sure about that drink?"

"Tell you what, you can give my wife one when we've finished upstairs," said Lemaitre.

As it happened, Schumacher was talking to the Hendersons in the huge main lounge. Lemaitre took one good look and would forever be able to remember their names and their faces—and associate one with the other. Elliott Henderson was a dapper man of medium height, with clean-cut features, iron-gray hair, a decisive manner even at that moment. His wife Felisa was perhaps fifteen years younger, in the late thirties, beautifully dressed in a dove-gray velvet suit, pale-green shoes, pale-green gloves. Schumacher was so different not only from them but from Lemaitre's preconceived mental picture that it was hard to believe he was the man under suspicion.

He was middle-aged, rather careless in dress, with untidy gray hair and a face vaguely like a good-humored spaniel's. The one noticeable thing was his eyes. Although his eyelids drooped, the silvery brightness of the irises was very noticeable. They seemed wrong in that homely face.

As Lemaitre and Simmons passed, he was saying:

"Yes, as I say, I know London as well as any American can, I guess—apart from New York it's the greatest city in the world."

Lemaitre almost warmed to him.

". . . and if you can make your daughter believe it's worthwhile, I'll gladly show her around."

"The daughter is Mrs. Henderson's," Simmons said. "She was a Mrs. Pallon before she married Henderson. Nina Pallon is traveling cabin class, don't ask me why. Seventeen or so. If Schumacher is going to chaperon her around there must be an ulterior motive."

"Maybe he just wants to earn a fee as a baby-sitter." Lemaitre kept a straight face.

"Lem, don't let anything fool you," Simmons said earnestly. "If Nielsen says a man's worth watching, watch him. Maybe Schumacher thinks this is a way to become one of the family."

Abel Schumacher didn't hear Simmons' remark; had he done so he would probably have had difficulty in repressing his laughter—except that he was a past master in the art of concealing his real thoughts and his feelings. He was a clever, shrewd and very successful man, but he lived high and gambled heavily. He urgently needed a large sum of money, and knew that it would be fatal to attempt another confidence trick. He did not know how they had achieved it, but he knew that the police these days suspected him and watched him closely whenever he was associating with possible victims.

So he was not as usual going to attempt to defraud Henderson by trickery.

He was going to try a fresh approach. He was going to kidnap Henderson's seventeen-year-old stepdaughter, which was hardly the way to become one of the family.

Gideon woke that morning without any sense of reassurance. Over breakfast, Kate was still a little starry-eyed about Hong Kong, until the post brought letters from Malcolm, their youngest son, at a school camp in the Swiss Alps, and their married daughter, Prudence. Then she became starry-eyed at the prospect of becoming a grandmother soon.

The newspapers did everything but use the word "suicide" over Lucci's death. One of them, the *Globe,* had a scoop with a picture of Signora Lucci outside the Grandi Hotel. The stories of the attack on Alice Clay had little impact; *Girl Attacked in Park—American Sought,* was the most graphic. Had the Clay girl died she would have rated front page. Once she had identified her assailant as Mayhew, Gideon should be able to do more about the investigation. In that morning's paper he heard for the first time of the smash-and-grab in Frisk Street. An hour later, after a squad car had called and taken him to the Yard, he read Sergeant Lacey's comments about the Barnetts, a comment put in to bolster up a divisional report on a night empty of sensation.

Gideon gave a half-grin; one day they would catch Barney Barnett red-handed again. He had kept out of their hands for over three years. Everyone who knew anything about him knew that his wife was really responsible for his success, since Barney had plenty of nerve but little common sense. It would be worth checking him about the Frisk Street job.

The Assistant Commissioner was called to a conference and Gideon sent written notes about the West German marks and the banking house, both reassuring. The day continued much as it had started, not dull but not exhilarating. It was late afternoon before Lemaitre phoned with his report on Schumacher.

"That won't set the Thames on fire, will it, George?"

"You be careful in Southampton water."

"Okay," said Lemaitre. "Thanks for fixing the weather."

As soon as he rang off, Gideon arranged for a man to be at Waterloo Station, to follow Schumacher, and for another to watch for the Hendersons at the Bingham Hotel. There was always a possibility that Schumacher would make his play quickly, and Gideon did not mean to be caught on one foot. The readiness of the con man to ingratiate himself through Henderson's stepdaughter seemed incidental; certainly Gideon did not give a thought to the possibility that there might be any danger to the girl. He looked through notes which had come in about Henderson, who was a collector of paintings and was likely to visit one or two private exhibitions.

Art thefts? Gideon half-wondered.

Now that Schumacher was actually being watched, he felt better.

At seven o'clock the boat train steamed into Waterloo Station from Southampton in two sections. It brought 1,703 passengers from the liner, nearly half of them citizens of the United States, although there was a strong contingent of British, a smaller one of Canadians, and groups from Japan, South America, Australia and New Zealand, as well as the odd families and individuals from thirty different countries.

Nina Pallon was one of the Americans. By most masculine standards she was not one of the most attractive, but on the trip she had been one of the happiest. For five long days she had been in cabin class, second class of the big ship, mixing with a heterogeneous crowd of teen-agers, none of whom seemed to have the slightest idea who she was. That was exactly as she had hoped and planned, but she had never believed that it would be possible.

The Americans, English, French and Italians in the group had played, swum, danced, sun-bathed, eaten and drunk their fill, and had a wildly enjoyable time without causing offense to the older passengers, almost without causing any raised eyebrows.

Now Nina was tired, although no one would have thought it to judge from the brightness of her blue eyes and the near-radiance of her expression which made her much more attractive than usual.

But the radiance gradually faded.

Her acquaintances from the ship passed her, all of them in a hurry.

" 'Bye, Nina." "Don't forget, British Museum, tomorrow at five." "Sure you're all right, Nina? You mustn't get lost in London!" "See you, Nina." " 'Bye, Nina."

As she watched them hurry out of her life sadness fell upon her like a shadow. They were different. They had been different since morning, although they had the same faces, the same voices, the same looks. It was as if they had put on a new personality with their going ashore, going-home clothes. The hilarity of the night before, the glowing vitality and burning protestations of friendship had all gone. What had they sung? *"We'll meet again, don't know where, don't know when, but I know we'll meet again some sunny day."* She had never heard the song before; an older man had said something about the Forces Sweetheart, and she still didn't know what that meant. But last night it had brought tears to most people's eyes.

These were yesterday's tears.

Today there were none. There was casualness from those whom she had felt to be close friends.

The newly-wed Pommeroys came up, Jill from Southern California, John from Chicago. John was to take up an assignment with a cosmetics factory somewhere in West London. Would they pass on, too?

"Nina!"

"We thought we'd missed you," John said as if in genuine relief. He was round-faced, round-eyed, curly-haired. "Aren't your folks here yet?"

"No. They came to London by road, and they were on the way hours before the boat train left."

They had arranged to go straight to the hotel, and her step-father had promised to be here to meet her; her mother had flatly refused to let her make her own way to the Bingham.

"They must have been delayed," Jill said. She was elfin, heart-faced, slant-eyed, very very slightly Japanese-looking, with a complexion as beautiful and lustrous as the best china. "Come with us, honey."

"Oh, no, I—"

"But you must," said John. "Why don't we all go to their hotel, anyway? What's the name of it?"

"The Bingham, but—"

"Only millionaires stay at the Bingham," John remarked. "I didn't know you had rich relations."

"They're planning to have a good time on their first European vacation in years," Nina said hurriedly. "I'm sure Elliott will be here."

"We can't just leave you waiting," Jill protested.

"We can stay here with her." John picked up her valise. "Where's the rest of your baggage?"

"The others took it on." It was good to feel that the Pommeroys were so ready to keep her company, so friendly; Nina felt a needle of guilt because she had hedged about her step-father's wealth; he must be fifty times a millionaire. A train came in, slowly chug-chugging, and all three watched as it stopped by the buffers just beyond the iron gates. Here the tracks came right up to the main hall of the station, very different from big city stations in the States.

The man with the hooded silver-bright eyes approached the trio, obviously with purpose. He was middle-aged, wore his gray hair overlong, but had rather a nice, homely face. His tweedy herringbone suit was a little too large for him, baggy at the knees.

"Miss Pallon?"

"Why, yes." Nina was surprised.

"I hope I'm not a disappointment to you, but I've come to escort you to the Bingham Hotel." He had a suspicion of a drawl, like many who had been born in the Deep South but had been away for years. His drooping eyelids made him look tired, even lazy, but the silvery eyes were alert. "Your father had some urgent long-distance calls to make, and your mother has a bad headache. I was on the ship with them and I'm also staying at the Bingham." He smiled at the Pommeroys. "I'm Abel Schumacher."

The Pommeroys introduced themselves.

"You're very kind, Mr. Schumacher," Nina said.

She was a little confused but not at all surprised, for her mother was always fussing over her. She exchanged addresses with the Pommeroys, who then took their place in a taxi queue. When Nina glanced round at them, Jill was waving, John talking to a porter.

Abel Schumacher was saying:

". . . traffic is very heavy at this time, Miss Pallon. As you have only hand baggage, would you like to walk across Waterloo Bridge? There is perfect visibility today, and that isn't always so. From the bridge there is the finest panoramic view of London. On one side you can see the Houses of Parliament, on the other St. Paul's against the skyline."

"I'd love to walk!" Nina cried.

He took her travel case and they walked off together. They were on the bridge approach when a square black taxi passed, with the Pommeroys waving from the open window.

It was nearly half past six when Gideon locked the control drawer in his desk, stood up, and went to the window. The rush-hour traffic was over, and cars were moving fast along the Embankment and over Westminster Bridge. The sun was making a yellow shimmer on the unrippled surface of the Thames, and he craned his neck to see how far he could see across London. The low, pale span of Waterloo Bridge interrupted much of it. London had never looked more mellow or more peaceful.

He turned to go, and the door burst open.

"Hi, George!" Lemaitre strode in, beaming, not only with good will but with excitement. "Can't stay long. Chloe's in the car, but I couldn't sleep on this one without letting you know."

"Schumacher?" asked Gideon, almost eagerly.

"There's nothing urgent about Schumacher. George, I saw Quincy Lee come off the Q.E. He'd traveled cabin class. Bit gray, but doesn't look a day older. It's twenty-six years since he slipped through our fingers. I'd been here six months and you were only a sergeant. How about that!"

Gideon said slowly, "Quincy Lee. Well, I'm damned." The name carried him back over those years, to the days when he had first begun to establish himself as a man headed for the top. Quincy Lee had actually helped him, for Quincy had tipped him off about a fence whose shop had been chock-full of stolen goods. Quincy's tip had not been spiteful, for the fence had also been a moneylender, squeezing every penny he could out of his debtors, and setting off ludicrously small sums against valuable jewels.

Quincy had had a record, and was known as a smash-and-grab thief. One day soon after the fence's trial there had been a smash-and-grab raid in Hatton Garden which had been the sensation of the day. Forty-five thousand pounds' worth of diamonds had been stolen. Lee had disappeared soon afterward, and although there had been no proof, Gideon had felt sure he was the thief.

"We never got a sparkler back, and never saw Quincy again," Lemaitre said nostalgically. "What are we going to do?"

"Do?"

"Can't let him run around loose, can we?"

Gideon was rubbing the shiny bowl of the big pipe he often carried but seldom smoked.

"After twenty-six years?"

"A leopard doesn't change its spots, George!"

"Really want to pick him up?" asked Gideon.

Lemaitre laughed. "You know damned well I don't. Just wanted to see how you'd react. We ought to tip our chaps off, though, in case he's come to try his old tricks again."

"We'll think about it," Gideon said.

"Oke. Anything new on?"

"Nothing much," Gideon answered. "It's been quieter than usual. We've had the autopsy report on Lucci. It was death by coal-gas poisoning. Some indications of veronal in the stomach, just enough to make him sleep, and it may have been in the brandy he drank just before death. He had veronal tablets with him. They'll bring in suicide at the inquest, and Signora Lucci is going to have the body flown back to Milan."

"Mayhew?"

"Nothing."

"Funny if everything Nielsen told us about fades out."

"Yes, wouldn't it? One thing's cropped up, I'd forgotten it. Some Rite-Time watches."

"Well, what do you know!"

"There are thirty-eight of them over at Jerry Klein's in Frisk Street. Luther's always suspected Klein of doing a quick turnover in hot stuff. He seized a chance to look over the stock before Klein had got his breath back after the raid. Luther hasn't talked to him yet, he's checking the other stuff on the stock list."

"Ought to charge Klein while we've got a chance," Lemaitre said. "Before you know it he'll do a Quincy Lee on us!"

Gideon found himself chuckling.

6

The Third Wife

Jerry Klein was a curious little man.

He was honest by nature and honest at heart, but somehow he could never get along by straightforward methods, and he succumbed to temptation far too easily. Most of the stock in his shop in Soho came from bankrupt businesses and discontinued lines, and he did a good, often brisk trade. Every now and again he had a chance to pick up a line of bargain price goods, knowing them to be stolen, and although he always protested his honesty he usually took the risk.

Even these days he took risks he could have avoided, despite the harsh lesson he had learned years ago when he had first bought watches and clocks, costume jewelry and trinkets from the Orlova Watch Company, knowing them to be stolen. Some goods had been too hot, and he had wanted to refuse them. His determination had been weakened with the loss of a tooth, and two broken ribs.

Now, whenever Orlova wanted him to buy, he bought.

He had not wanted forty-four Rite-Time watches, even at a low price—he preferred to turn stolen goods over quickly. But he had no choice. The one favorable thing was that Orlova always kept their goods until the heat was off. He had not thought seriously of risk, but he had not wanted to increase his stock by over two hundred pounds.

"You'll make two hundred per cent, Jerry," Darkie Jackson had said. "Just gimme the cash."

In three weeks Jerry Klein had sold four watches at 17 pounds 10 shillings each; it was going to be a good deal after all.

Because of his association with Orlova he had always felt secure in the shop. (None of the regular smash-and-grab boys ever troubled him. Once an amateur had tried to make off with a tray of rings but he hadn't got far.) So the raid on Monday afternoon upset him very badly indeed, and was the more upsetting because two of the stolen watches had been Rite-Times. The police had arrived before he had collected

45

his wits, and had found the empty watch boxes. They had insisted on going through his stocks with him, on the pretext of
making sure nothing else was missing, and he knew they
would not have taken such trouble unless they suspected him
of stocking stolen goods. On the Monday night he had been
edgy and nervous with his wife and children, and put it down
simply to the shock of the smash-and-grab. Actually he was
afraid of Darkie Jackson's reaction if he realized that the police had checked his stocks. No one from Orlova called or telephoned on the Tuesday, though, and until he reached his
home in Islington on Tuesday night he felt much more secure.

He let himself in with a key, as usual, and called out, "I'm
here, Annie," also as usual. There was no answer, which was
surprising. Annie had taken the kids somewhere and had left
a note in the kitchen. He reached the open kitchen door, and
Darkie Jackson said:

"So you're here."

Darkie had a touch of color—not much, not enough to be
noticeable unless one looked for it. He had a lean, swarthy
face and a domed forehead, with very close dark curls. He
was quite a slick dresser; he was also slick with a knife.

Klein gasped, "What are you doing here?"

"Waiting for you."

"Where's my wife?"

"Taken the kids to the pictures."

"But she's always in when I come home!"

"I persuaded her to disappoint you tonight, daddy. I said I
had some important business to discuss with you. Don't look
so sick—I gave the kids their ticket money."

Klein was still standing in the doorway. He was as angry as
he was frightened, and he was very frightened indeed. He and
Darkie were the same kind of build, the same height, the
same age, but Darkie was hard and tough, and physically
Klein was flabby and weak.

His voice grew shrill.

"You've no right to come to my home!"

"No *right*, Jerry?"

"No, you haven't! I won't allow it!"

Darkie did not move out of the chair, but he moved his left
hand from his pocket; in it was a flick knife, the blade hidden.

"No *right*, Jerry?" he repeated softly.

"You can't scare me! Get out of my house." Klein knew
that he had to make a stand, that if he gave in now he would
never be able to assert himself; he knew it in the same way

that he always knew it was crazy to buy stolen goods, yet always did. "You heard me!"

"I can't believe I'm hearing you right," Darkie said. "I just want a little talk."

"We can talk at the shop."

"But the shop's being watched."

"That's a lie! That's a damned lie!"

"It's the truth," Darkie asserted. "Ever since that smash-and-grab yesterday the cops have been hanging around inside or outside. Why didn't you telephone me about the raid?"

"Why should I?"

"You know how worried I get about your profit margin. Were you insured?"

"Yes, I was. Do you think I'm a fool?"

"I think you're a very nervous type of individual, and pretty forgetful. It was a mistake not to call me, I had to discover what happened through a pal—a real pal, not a weak-livered rat like you."

Jerry gasped, "Don't talk to me like that! Don't—"

Darkie leapt out of the chair. There was a sharp click as the blade stabbed out from the sheath, and Jerry backed away, a scream on his lips. The blade seemed to shimmer in front of his eyes as Darkie gripped his throat with his free hand, and squeezed the scream to gurgling silence. He kept Klein pinned against the wall for fully two minutes, while Klein struggled for breath but made no attempt to free himself. All his nerve had gone, as if slashed with that knife.

Then Darkie let him go and he almost fell forward, clutching at his neck, gasping for breath. Darkie watched him sneeringly, suddenly pushed him into a chair. Klein collapsed into it.

"Why didn't you telephone me?"

"I didn't—I didn't think you'd want to know."

"I want to know everything that happens if you have the cops in your shop. How many Rite-Times were stolen?"

"Two—*two*."

"Only two?"

"I swear it!"

"If you lie to me, I'll—"

"I tell you I swear it!"

"How many watches were stolen?"

"Two, only two."

"The flicking dicks—why were they so long in the shop?"

"How—how should I know?"

"Did they check your stocks?"

"Yes—yes, they did."

"They check the Rite-Times?"

"Yes."

"Why didn't you stop them?"

"It would only have made them suspicious if I had."

"As if they weren't suspicious," Darkie said. He touched the side of the knife, and the blade snapped back; the click of sound made Klein flinch. "They ask where you got them?"

"No!"

"Didn't they check stocks against invoices?"

"I told them I'd lost a file of invoices a month ago."

"I hope you're always as smart," sneered Darkie.

"I—I try to be. I don't want any trouble."

"Jerry," Darkie said, "did they see Orlova's invoices?"

"I swear they didn't!"

"Okay," said Darkie. "Okay." He stood over Klein, playing with the knife. *Click*—out. *Click*—in. *Click*—out. *Click*—in. The bright steel dazzled Klein, and the movement of the blade became so swift that it made him dizzy. *Click-click-click-click-click-click.* "They aren't going to find out where those watches came from, are they?"

"Not from me."

"Not from anybody."

"I—I'm the only one who knows."

"That's right," said Darkie in a tone of surprise. "So if you're the only one who knows you're the only one who can tell them, aren't you?"

"I won't tell them."

"Jerry," Darkie said, "I want to tell *you* something. You listening?"

"Of course I'm listening."

"You love your kids?"

Klein almost screeched, "Yes!"

"You love your Annie?"

Klein began to gasp and fight for breath again, before he managed to ask, "What—what have they got to do with it?"

"If the cops find out where you got the Rite-Times, you'll know what they've got to do with it," Darkie said. He held the knife upward, the blade glistening bright and cruel, and the needle-sharp point was only inches from Klein's sweaty cheeks. "How'd Annie look with her face laid open, eh? How would the kids—"

"No!" gasped Klein. He thrust his hands out and Darkie could not withdraw the knife in time. It sliced through the heel of Klein's left thumb, but he hardly noticed the searing pain. "Don't touch them, don't touch them. If you ever touch them I'll kill you, I swear I will. I'll kill you!"

Darkie actually drew back a pace, as if the intensity of the threat stabbed him with fear. Then he slapped Klein across the face with a force that sent the jeweler lurching against the wall. Blood dripped from his hand to the spotless, rubber-tiled floor and made big red blots against the pale green.

"Don't ever threaten me again," Darkie said. "And don't squeal about those watches. You know what will happen if you do."

He turned and stalked out, and the door slammed.

Klein stood for a few minutes by the sink, blood dripping onto off-white porcelain and onto the pointed toe of his shoe. He kept catching his breath, almost sobbing. At last, slowly, fearfully, he held his hand under the cold-water tap, and the water turned to crimson. It ran up his sleeve, staining the starched white cuff of his shirt. It dripped to the floor. It ran along his fingers. He dried it with a tea towel which smelled faintly of coffee, then wrapped the towel round his hand and went unsteadily into the bathroom and across to the first-aid cabinet. He took out a patch of medicated adhesive plaster, pulled off the tea towel, and pressed the plaster on the clean cut.

He kept moistening his lips.

When he took a whisky and soda his hand throbbed so much it almost drove him out of his mind, but it was better when the family came home at last, the children excited over a wild West film.

Annie Klein gasped, "What have you done to your hand?"

"I cut myself," Klein lied. "It's not much—I just cut myself."

Annie stared into his bloodshot eyes. She was a tall woman, too thin, so flat-breasted and narrow-hipped that some people were surprised that she was the mother of three big and bois-terous children. Klein tried to outstare her, but could not, and he knew that she did not believe him. She made him pull the plaster off the cut, bathed it in antiseptic, put on a quick-healing salve, and made a better job of taping it. It was not until the children were in bed that she asked flatly:

"Did that man who came here do that?"

"What—what man?"

"The man who was here when you came. The man who said he had important business with you."

"I—I didn't see any man. What—what was he like?"

"He was a redhead with a bruise on his chin. You saw him all right."

A redhead? A bruise?

It hadn't been Darkie; someone else had come to see Annie, not Darkie. They were really ganging up, they really meant business. Klein found it difficult to breathe again, but when he could speak he said with whispering vehemence:

"Don't ask any questions. Don't ask anything. Understand me? You're not to know a thing."

That was about the time when Nina Pallon stepped into the apartment in the Bingham Hotel, overlooking the beautiful green grass of Bingham Square. She hugged her mother, gave her stepfather a much more fervent kiss than usual, and said ecstatically:

"I'm going to love London. It's wonderful—it's beautiful. Why didn't anybody tell me what it was like before? It's so *huge*—it seems like everywhere!"

"Where did Abel Schumacher take you?" asked Henderson, obviously pleased with her reaction.

"First of all we walked—"

"Walked!" echoed Felisa Henderson.

"Yes, it's the only way to see London, absolutely the only way. And Abel knows it so well. He's promised to take me to the East End tomorrow, and Kensington the next day, and . . ."

"That was certainly the right thing to do," Felisa Henderson said when Nina had gone to shower and change. "In a way it's better than if she was going around with a gang of teenagers."

"It's just right for a day or two, anyhow," Elliott Henderson agreed.

Alice Clay was alone in her flat for the first time since the assault. She locked the doors and shot the bolts, made sure that the windows were secure, and kept the television set on low, for fear of missing sounds. She had never been so nervous. She *never* wanted to see a man again.

Florence Foster wasn't at all afraid. She had never been of a nervous disposition, and although the enormity of London had overawed her for a few days, she was used to it now. She did not know how long she would stay, and it didn't matter, because her time was her own. Six months ago the widowed aunt with whom she had lived since childhood had died, leaving her with a house, 3,000 pounds worth of furniture, and nearly 25,000 pounds in money and securities. She had been both housekeeper and secretary to her aunt, living in an obscure village in Wiltshire. Now she had let the house furnished to an army officer and his wife who needed it for a year, and in that year she meant to travel.

But London intrigued her, and she might stay here for months.

If she did, she would want a small flat, or even a bed-sitting room with a kitchenette and her own bathroom and W.C.; she was too thrifty by nature to stay in a hotel for long. The cooking here was good, though, and a few days wouldn't hurt.

She refused to admit it to herself, but she was intrigued not only by London but by the handsome man sitting at a table opposite her. He was an Australian, or so she had heard him tell another guest. He had a rather full, dark mustache which made him seem old-fashioned, and his manners had an Old World courtesy too.

He was a Mr. Frank Matthews, who had been here only a day.

She went to the lounge for coffee, and Matthews came in a few minutes later, to see that nearly all of the red plush chairs were occupied.

She gave a rather timid smile.

He approached her.

"Is it all right if I sit here?"

"Of course," she said, and hoped devoutly that her smile had not been too brazen.

In the little house in Fulham, Barney Barnett was clapping his hands together and saying over and over again:

"So Quincy's back, who'd ever believe it! Old Quincy here, large as life. Bless his old cotton socks, won't it be good to see him?"

"You be careful with Quincy Lee," cautioned Maggie. "The police might know more about him than you do."

It was a funny thing, but since the decision to send her to the coast again Cynthia had looked brighter and had coughed much less. Michael Dunn told himself that everything had been justified. Kismet Cosmetics would never miss a few hundred pounds; it was their own fault to allow such flaws in their accounting system.

He did not really convince himself but he stilled the voice of conscience for the time being.

Out for a stroll with Cynthia that evening he passed another couple, strangers, getting out of a car in a house which he knew was owned by Kismet. It was rented to new members of the staff, often those from the American parent factory, until they found a permanent home. Dunn had no idea that these were John and Jill Pommeroy, and that Pommeroy had come to make a secret time-study and investigation into the manufacturing and accounting systems at the factory, where profits were far too low.

Maria Lucci and Giovanni Mancelli were sitting in the back of a car being driven toward London Airport. All the arrangements had been made for Lucci's body to be sent home, and now Marie was anxious to rejoin her children. Giovanni glanced at her set face from time to time, and when they were stopped at traffic lights on the Great West Road, he said:

"What are you thinking, Maria?"

"I am thinking that those people lied about my Benito," she answered. "And I am thinking that if you are a man you will stay in England, and find the proof."

"If only I could!"

"You must try," Maria declared fiercely. "You must talk again to this man White. I do not trust him—do *you* trust him?"

"No," answered Giovanni. "No, Maria, but I will be honest with you. I am frightened of him."

7

Reports

On Wednesday morning the face of London had changed. A drizzle of rain concealed the skylines and dulled the river, smeared windows and coated roofs and walls, made pavements slippery and slowed traffic down. It was 72 degrees Fahrenheit and muggy, as unpleasant as a summer day could be. Gideon and most Londoners accepted this without conscious thought, not even with resignation. The visitors, especially those who had arrived in yesterday's golden sunshine, were very disappointed, for it hardly seemed the same city. Street noises were muted, umbrellas were dotted about like sinister black mushrooms.

Gideon's desk was as dull as the day, yet piled with reports, some long, some short, some typewritten, some penciled. He looked through them before his daily briefing with the superintendents, to make sure he was abreast of all the latest developments. If he didn't, if "Gee-Gee's losing his grip" or "Gee-Gee's slipping" began to go round the Yard, a little of his authority would be lost and might be impossible to win back. The others, senior men or beginners, could disagree with him, argue with him, feel angry with him, even resentful and even vengeful; none of that mattered much. It was vital to know exactly what was going on. It had taken years to develop a system and to discipline his own mind to this need; now it was automatic, even though it sometimes took a great deal of effort to switch on.

He read those reports dealing with pending matters first.

Report from L2 Division: two Rite-Time watches seen in window at Allen's, High Street.

Report from CD Division: Barnett spent most of the day at home, went to cinema in afternoon, alone.

Report from Supt. Parsons: Signora Lucci flew back to Milan. Giovanni Mancelli stayed in London to look after

interests of Signora Lucci. Body to be flown to Milan
May 12 subject our approval.

Report from Chief Inspector Luther: Jerry Klein, jeweler where 39 Rite-Time watches found, injured left
hand. Cause of injury unknown. Appears very nervous.

Report from Leadenhall Street: Office of Thos. Cook &
Son Ltd. report that twenty-seven West German marks
changed for a German student yesterday appear to be
forgeries.

Gideon made a note on this one: "Today—job for Oliver."

Report from Central: Abel Schumacher still at Bingham Hotel. Also Nina Pallon.

There were the new cases, dozens of them, but none of any
known importance, certainly none of any size.

There was a sharp ring from the switchboard.

"Yes?" Gideon was studying the case of the suspect marks.

"There's a cable for you from New York, sir, reported by
telephone."

"Read it to me."

"It begins: 'Snider booked today fingerprints make him a
certainty. Thanks.' The signature is Nielsen."

"Good!" Gideon was gratified into an ejaculation. "Have
them send the confirmation to me, will you?" He rang off on
the girl's: "Very good, sir."

Her voice was comparatively new at the Yard but she did
her job with minimum fuss and, as far as he could judge,
maximum efficiency. The report from New York was a good
start for the day and his mood was bright when Lemaitre arrived, wearing a trilby with a plastic rainproof cover, and
carrying a dripping mackintosh. Lemaitre's smile was more
than bright, it was merry.

"Morning, George! Bit of all right, getting a day like this
today instead of yesterday." He took his hat off. "Ought to
nip along to the cloakroom with these. What do you think of
the Tottenham job?"

"What job?"

"Haven't you heard? Busted a bank during the night, got
away with forty thousand nicker. I looked in on my way here,
that's why I'm late. Clean as a whistle. Looks like a Snider
job to me."

"He can't be in two places at once," said Gideon.

"Eh?"

"Nielsen's booked him."

"Well, how about that?" rejoiced Lemaitre. "Bit of smart work that was, George, even though I do say it myself." He opened the door. "Old Uncle Charley at Tottenham's had quite a night. There was a break-in at a jeweler's in Edmonton High Street, the thieves got away with about seven hundred quids' worth of loot—*including* six Rite-Time watches. How about that?"

Lemaitre ducked out.

Gideon made a note on the report about the report from MX Division, which was in the north of London. These American watches had now been found in three places, which suggested general distribution. He went to the files and took out one dealing with this: it contained a photostat copy of the request for information from Nielsen back in March, and details and descriptions of the watches and the factory in Buffalo, New York, from which they had been stolen. The inquiry had been handled on this side by Superintendent MacPherson, a Scotsman fairly new in seniority and who had been promoted very rapidly; he had had the breaks, and Gideon believed that a lucky man should be given every chance to play his luck.

MacPherson had reported after two weeks. "No Rite-Time watches appear to be on the British market." Two weeks later he had sent in a similar report. A month had passed before a laconic note had come in: "Rite-Time still negative." The last time the Scotsman had put in a negative report was two weeks ago, just before he had gone on holiday.

Lemaitre came in, dry, spruce, smiling.

"When's MacPherson due back?" Gideon asked.

"Next Monday."

"By then he should have quite a file waiting for him on Rite-Times," Gideon said. "Who's waiting?"

"Dog's Collar."

"No one else?"

"Not yet."

"Anything reached you about Mayhew alias Mason?"

"Nope," answered Lemaitre. He seemed just to prevent himself from adding "Not likely to, either." "Want Parsons in?"

"Yes," said Gideon.

Parsons came in, wearing his almost habitual clerical gray.

His forehead was puckered, but he gave Gideon a quick smile
and raised a hand to Lemaitre.

"Sit down, Vic," Gideon said.

"Thanks." Parsons sat on the arm of a green leather chair.
He took it for granted that Gideon would be *au fait* with the
situation. "Can you see any objection to letting Mrs. Lucci
have her husband's body flown home tomorrow?"

"Not if you can't."

"The autopsy was positive. We don't need the body even if
we do find enough for a murder charge. The woman looked
like death when she left for Milan last night. Mancelli was
going with her, but changed his mind for some reason. I've
seen Percival White," added Parsons. "He came straight back
to London when he heard Mrs. Lucci was here, and they had
a session together—not very friendly, I'd say. I saw White immediately afterwards, and he was properly on edge. The
whole case bothers me, George."

"Any particular reason?" asked Gideon.

"At first sight I thought White might have murdered Lucci
so as to be able to blame him when the case broke. He hasn't
blamed him for anything, only the managers have. They could
be lying to try to save their own skins, but the thing which
gets under my skin is that White seems genuinely shocked and
surprised. George—" Parsons was pressing the tips of his
fingers together.

"Yes?"

"I'd like to go to Milan."

Lemaitre glanced up and asked:

"Who wouldn't?"

"Now?" asked Gideon. He began to think about other cases
related to northern Italy which might justify a visit there,
while he waited for Parsons to answer.

"Yes," Parsons said.

"For the funeral?"

Parsons wrinkled his forehead again.

"Right in one," he confirmed. "And I'd like a word with the
Milan police, tell 'em exactly what happened, and find out
what they can tell us about Lucci's local reputation and ac-
tivities. I've been doing my damnedest to think up a good sup-
porting reason for going, but I can't. Mind you, we go good
and hard for Italians in Soho, and once or twice I think the
Milan chaps have resented it. This could be the time for a bit
of rapprochement."

"Backslapping, you mean," interpolated Lemaitre.

Parsons was looking hard into Gideon's eyes, ignoring the

second-in-command, who rolled his eyes resignedly and turned back to his desk.

Gideon said: "All right, Vic. Authorize the removal of the body, and fly to Milan. Handle it as a public relations job. Take the attitude that we're all worried about the murder of a man we now believe to have been innocent. Don't be more than three or four days. How about some traveling money?"

"If you'll okay the chits when I get back I'll draw on my own account," Parsons said. He was already on his feet, looking like a highly gratified cherub. "Thanks, George!"

"Give my regards to Nocci and Angelo," Gideon said.

Parsons nodded from the door. Lemaitre waited for it to close, then blew his cheeks out like a balloon, leaned back, exuded a long, slow breath, and said:

"Your week to play Santa Claus, George?"

Gideon felt a flash of annoyance. What did Lemaitre think? That he'd been sent to Southampton and Parsons was going to Milan solely for the good of their health? He saw Lemaitre's grin fade and knew that he had realized his gaffe. So he should. The good mood inspired by the news from New York had passed, but before either man had time to speak two telephones rang on Gideon's desk simultaneously—the internal and the outisde line. He lifted the outside one, and grunted, "Hold on." He picked up the nearest telephone. "Gideon."

"Hallo, George." The voice was that of Ray Fox, the Deputy Commissioner of the Uniformed Branch. "Doesn't sound the right moment to ask you a favor."

Gideon forced a laugh.

"Try me."

"Will you present the prizes at the Annual Sports Day next month?" asked Fox. "The Commissioner can't get there, and if we pick any one of the Assistant Commissioners we're bound to cause mortal offense."

"How about the other commanders?"

"That's easy. You're senior."

"If you really want me, count me in," Gideon said.

"You're in," declared Fox, sounding not only pleased but elated.

The invitation was gratifying, for Sports Day was one for wives; Kate would love it. Gideon was back in a better humor when he picked up the second telephone.

"Gideon."

"*Commander* Gideon?" The voice was American, but with a curious overtone of Cockney.

"Yes."

"Risen in the world, Gee-Gee, haven't you?" the man said.

"Who's that speaking?"

There was a pause; then: "I didn't mean to be rude, Mr. Gideon. As a matter of fact I wondered if you could spare me half an hour some time. I expect you'll remember me. My name's Quincy Lee."

By the time Lee had announced himself, Gideon had realized who the caller was; and he had to smother a laugh.

"What do you want to do?" he asked. "Give yourself up?"

"Always one for a joke, weren't you?" Quincy Lee retorted. "You wouldn't hold anything against me for a quarter of a century, even if I'd done anything I shouldn't—which of course I never did. Don't mind me calling you, do you?"

"Glad to hear from you," Gideon said. "I was told you were in town."

"Eyes all over your body, same as always," Quincy remarked. "How about that half hour, Mr. Gideon?" He paused. "Just a social chat over a pint. Be my guest."

Gideon chuckled. "Tonight suit you?"

"Just name the place."

"The pub in Cannon Row?"

"Now show a bit of imagination, Gee-Gee," protested Quincy. "That place has unpleasant associations for me."

"I daresay," Gideon conceded, and then suddenly realized the obvious thing to do. "How about coming to my place in Fulham, Quincy? Eight o'clock, say. We'll have more time."

"Now that's a real gent speaking." Quincy, like Fox, was delighted. "I'll be there. Same place?"

"Same place."

"Eight o'clock on the dot," said Quincy. "See you."

As he rang off Gideon saw Lemaitre's expression before his assistant averted his face. But for the flash of annoyance Gideon had shown a few minutes ago, Lemaitre would have made some crack. Instead, he tried to pretend he had heard nothing.

"Lem, how about coming to my place tonight and having a drink with Quincy Lee and Santa Claus?" Gideon invited.

It was Lemaitre's turn to sound as pleased as Punch.

"Tell you what, Goerge—Quincy might be able to tell us something about the man Schumacher," he said later. "There were a hell of a lot of crooks on that ship."

"Yes. What's in about Schumacher?" Gideon was suddenly and acutely conscious of the fact that he had not given the American much thought.

"I had a word with Central," Lemaitre told him. "Schumacher and the Hendersons are as close as two fingers, but I don't see what we can gain by having Schumacher watched. If he finds a way of robbing or defrauding Henderson, we know who to go for. We can keep tabs on him if he moves from the Bingham, but I can't see any point in having him followed. All he's done so far is show Nina Pallon the sights of London."

Gideon deliberated; and then he made a mistake he was going to regret very, very much.

"All right," he said. "Get the hotel detective to let Division know when he leaves and when he comes back."

"That ought to be plenty for Schumacher," Lemaitre said with deep satisfaction.

8

Three in Danger

Nina Pallon had not been particularly pleased that morning, believing the rain would spoil sightseeing, but soon after breakfast in the suite, Schumacher had telephoned.

"I think this is a day for the picture galleries and maybe some museums," he had suggested. "Would you like that?"

Nina hadn't felt sure.

"Why don't you tell him you'll call back?" her mother had advised. When she had done so, Felisa had added: "Would you like to come shopping with me, honey? I'd love to have you along."

"I'm not sure that would improve her education," Henderson had said dryly. "Which would you prefer to do, Nina?" He would prefer her to go to the exhibitions, but didn't say so; he was going as a prospective buyer to Sotheby's, where there were two sixteenth-century Dutch collections for sale, and for that he wanted to be alone.

Nina dithered. She knew what a day in the salons with her mother would be; fun for an hour, boredom after that, although Felisa's enthusiasm would last all day—all week, for that matter.

"I think I'll go and see the art galleries," she decided. "Dad, do you think there *is* any modern art in London?"

Henderson laughed.

"Picasso fetches better prices here than in New York."

Nina's dark eyes brightened. "That sounds wonderful!"

"That's wonderful!" said Abel Schumacher when she called his room. "Shall I come up for you or meet you in the lobby?"

"I'll be in the lobby in fifteen minutes," Nina promised.

When she met him, she thought it was a shame to make him go out, he looked so tired. But apparently he knew the London art galleries well, and took her straight to the Tate, where there was an exhibition of paintings by Ritschl and abstracts by Baziotes. It enthralled her.

"You certainly like the abstracts," Abel remarked.

"The form and the color certainly get me," Nina said.

"You obviously know a lot about them. Don't you like them?"

"I can have too many," Schumacher said. "Would you like to see some by up-and-coming Continental impressionists who haven't reached big exhibition stage yet? You'll like the coloring if nothing else."

"It sounds interesting," Nina said. "Surely."

"We can walk or we can take a cab."

"How far is it to walk?"

"Twenty minutes, I guess."

"Let's walk," decided Nina.

The drizzle had slackened by the time they left the Tate Gallery. It was almost impossible to see across the Thames, and tugs hooted, as if smothering London in melancholy doom. At least a dozen people were waiting for taxis, and a policeman was controlling the traffic. Nina was glad they had decided to walk. She went with a spring, hardly aware of the fact that Schumacher had difficulty in keeping up.

Soon, they approached a small shop in a narrow street in a part of London which seemed as depressing and gray as the weather. A milkman with an electric float was a little way along, and an elderly man was approaching from some distance off.

Half a dozen indifferent impressionist paintings were in the shop window. Schumacher smiled at Nina's expression.

"They're better inside."

"Is this the place?"

"There's a big shed at the back—an old studio turned into a gallery," Schumacher told her. He opened the shop door, and a bell clanged. They went into a shop smelling of oils and paints; more indifferent abstracts and a few third-rate impressionist paintings hung on the walls. The street door closed. A girl about Nina's build, a little taller and with a fuller figure but with the same kind of glossy dark hair which fell to her shoulders, came out of a back room.

"All ready?" asked Schumacher.

That seemed to Nina a strange question to ask, and it puzzled her. The girl's answer puzzled her even more.

"You're late."

"A few minutes won't make any difference," Schumacher said.

Nina hadn't the faintest idea why, but quite suddenly she felt scared; perhaps it was the way the other girl looked at her—almost as if *she* was frightened, too. Nina turned to Schumacher.

"Isn't the exhibition open all the time?"

"Why, sure."

"I don't understand," Nina said. "Why does it matter what time we arrive, then?"

"It doesn't matter at all." Schumacher took Nina's arm. "Lucy's talking nonsense." He thrust Nina toward the inner door through which the other girl had come."

Nina pulled herself free.

"Please don't do that." She stood outside the door, looking from Lucy to Schumacher; in those few seconds she felt dreadfully sure that something was wrong. Schumacher's eyelids no longer drooped and his light-gray eyes seemed almost sinister. "I don't think I want to see this exhibition. I've a headache, and I would rather go—"

Schumacher's left hand dropped to her arm, twisted, and thrust her forward. She screamed—a cry of sheer panic, not of pain. Schumacher swung his right arm and clapped his hand across her mouth so savagely that her lips were bruised against her teeth and tears of pain nearly blinded her. There was only terror in her mind.

Two people in Gulliver Street, Chelsea, heard the scream. One was an elderly man, walking at leisure, who had paused to glance at the paintings. The other was a young milk roundsman a few yards ahead. They stared at each other, and then at the shop.

"Did you hear that?" the elderly man asked.

"Heard something," said the milk roundsman. "Dunno what it was, though."

Then a woman came hurrying from a doorway, calling him shrilly, and he grinned.

"Sounded a bit like her." He went toward the woman, a crate of milk bottles rattling in his hand.

The older man stared at the curtain behind the paintings, which cut off the inside of the shop. Then he walked on.

Nina Pallon still felt absolute terror.

There was pain at her mouth and pain at her arm, and tears stung her eyes. There was the awful realization that some dreadful thing was happening to her. There was the violence with which Schumacher hurtled her into the room beyond, while keeping his hand over her mouth.

There was another man inside.

"What the hell are you playing at?" he demanded.

"Where's that needle?"

"If she screams again—"

"Give me that needle!"

Nina kicked wildly, caught Schumacher on the shin and heard him gasp with pain. Another voice sounded suddenly: Lucy's.

"*There's a man outside.*"

"The little bitch!" Schumacher rasped.

"Quiet!"

Nina struggled wildly, fear giving her strength. Suddenly Schumacher snatched his hands away, only to fling his arms round her, one at the waist, one at her breasts, hurting terribly. He squeezed. He seemed to mean to squeeze the life out of her. She could no longer struggle or kick, she could hardly breathe. She was aware of the man in front of her. His hands moved, something glistened.

The needle!

In her brain, Nina screamed, "No, no, no!" but no sound came from her bruised and swelling lips.

The girl muttered, "He's gone."

"Take her arm."

"Can't you——"

"Take her arm!"

Nina was half-fainting, only just aware of all that was going on, yet sufficiently aware for terror to reach a new peak. The girl pulled her arm straight and pushed up the loose sleeve of her sweater, the glittering thing sparkled, sharp pain stabbed in the crook of her arm.

Darkness came upon her, quickly dulling pain and fear. She did not know she was lowered to a couch, and her scarlet skirt and loose-fitting black sweater were pulled off. She looked so tiny in bra and lacy panties. Neither man seemed to look twice at her. They lifted her, one holding her feet, one holding her shoulders, and placed her into a coffin-shaped black chest. She did not know that the lid was closed on her, and secured with a padlock.

Lucy said fearfully, "Sure she can breathe?"

"She can breathe," the man with the hypodermic syringe declared. "I bored holes in it."

"She won't be here for long." Schumacher's eyelids were drooping again, and he was breathing more heavily. "Put her sweater and skirt on, and be quick about it."

"That sweater's a bit too small for me."

"Who cares if you show how big you are." Schumacher looked as if he would strike Lucy, but in fact he realized that he should have thought of Nina's slighter figure. It was too late now. "Get them on, quick." He watched as she took off

her wool-knit dress, and as she pulled on Nina's clothes he
went on: "When I talk to you at the galleries and the museums, you just say: 'Gee, that's wonderful' or 'Gosh, I like
that.' Don't try to say anything clever. Understand?"

"I could fool *you* with my American," Lucy said. She
pulled at the sweater, to prevent it from clinging so tightly.

"Don't try to fool anybody." Schumacher turned to the
other man. "Facey, get her away from here as soon as you
can, and when it's safe, open the chest."

"Don't you worry," said the man he called Facey.

Schumacher led the way into Gulliver Street, and no one
took any notice of him and Lucy. No one took particular notice of him in their brief visits to the National Art Gallery,
the Royal Academy, or the Victoria and Albert Museum in
Knightsbridge, but a great many people had a mental picture
of Abel Schumacher and an American girl in a black sweater
and a red skirt. Some of the younger men even carried a
mental image of the tight fit of the sweater.

Florence Foster thought that Frank was such a gentleman,
and obviously determined to get to know her better. It was
strange, but she knew surprisingly little about men. She had
not allowed herself to be particularly interested while she had
looked after her aunt. She seldom admitted the truth to herself, but years ago, when she had been a little under fifteen, a
very well-developed under-fifteen, she had allowed herself to
be taken for a walk in some woods near her home. Nothing
had "happened," but before she had scared the man into taking his probing hands away she had been nearly hysterical.
For a long time even the thought of sex relations had been re-
pugnant to her, and her aunt had been glad that she should be
so little interested in men. It had not occurred to Florence
that her aunt had been selfish and possessive, nor had it occurred to her that she was developing an unnatural antipathy
toward the opposite sex.

Two or three men had wanted to become friendly but had
cooled off when they saw the odds. Since she had been on her
own she had made herself think more about them, and had
actually been able to laugh at that early experience. Now she
was little more than shy.

It was impossible to be shy with Frank Matthews.

They were going to dine at a West End restaurant tonight,
and then go to a dance.

A detective officer from New Scotland Yard was at the restaurant, saw the couple, thought the man looked like the American Mayhew alias Mason, and steered his partner toward the pair. When he heard him speak he believed he was Australian, not American. Thereafter, he concentrated on his job: he was working for Old Dog's Collar, checking whether many of the hostesses here went off with the men who dined alone.

That same afternoon, about the time when Schumacher and Lucy left the Victoria and Albert Museum, where they had studied the Constables as well as some early English painters, Alice Clay was looking out the window of her tiny flat. She was beginning to feel lonely. She had never been one for solitude, and liked to be out and about, dancing, or at the pictures, or eating at restaurants—anywhere there were people. There were plenty of people in the street, cars, cyclists, school children, and everyone seemed happy.

"I can't stand *another* night stuck in here with the telly," she said aloud.

Then she felt that suffocating feeling come over her, and the idea of going out on her own was frightening. She stood by the window, hands clenching, when there was a ring at her front door.

"Who's that?" she cried.

Slowly, she approached the door, and touched the handle as the bell rang again. It made her jump. She put a foot against the door and opened it a few inches.

"Who's that?"

"Is that Miss Alice Clay?" It was a man with a pleasant English voice.

"Yes. Who wants me?"

"Miss Clay, I called on you once before, when you first came to live here. My name is Stephens, the Reverend Ronald Stephens—curate at St. Mary's."

"Oh, yes, I remember!" Alice opened the door wider and saw a fair-haired man of about thirty, with nice blue eyes. She knew he was married; he'd told her so and she'd thought what a pity. Now he was someone it was safe to invite in, someone to talk to. "Won't you come in?"

"May I?" When he had entered, and had refused the offer of a cup of tea, he said very quietly, "Miss Clay, forgive my frankness, won't you? One of my parishioners is an officer at the local police station, and he told me how deeply upset you were by the terrifying experience you had so recently."

Alice said, "It was *awful.*"

"I'm sure it was. I'm deeply sorry about it. I came along to see if I could help in any way."

"Help?" Alice echoed.

When the Reverend Ronald Stephens smiled he had quite a twinkle.

"If only to remind you that most people are very good and worth knowing. You haven't been out since the incident, have you?"

"I've been scared to," Alice confessed. "I know it's silly, but I've been scared to death."

"It isn't silly at all," declared the curate. "Do you like meeting people?"

"Oh, ever so!"

"I wonder if you'd be interested in a kind of club we run at St. Mary's. It isn't a church club, in fact many of the members never come to St. Mary's, although we hope they will one day. There's nothing we'd like better than to see you there, incidentally. But that's up to the individual. I won't try to describe the club, but if you care to come along you'll soon get a good idea of what it's like." When Alice didn't answer, Stephens went on: "One of our members would be happy to call for you tonight."

"Oh, would he?" Alice's eyes lit up.

So did the eyes of the curate of St. Mary's.

And about that time Elliott Henderson lifted the telephone in his suite at the Bingham, expecting a long-distance call. Instead, it was Abel Schumacher.

"Hullo, Abel. How did the art galleries go today?"

"Not too well, I suspect," Schumacher said. "In fact Nina gave up a couple of hours ago—she said she was going to see someone she knew from the *Queen Elizabeth*. I checked at the desk, and when they told me they hadn't seen her come in, I thought I'd better tell you."

"I'm certainly glad you did," Henderson said.

"It's my pleasure," Schumacher declared. Then he added ruefully, "I think the truth of the matter is that I'm far too old for her. Let me know how she talks about the day, won't you?"

"Surely," Henderson said. "Thanks for calling."

He rang off, without any cause for suspecting that Abel Schumacher had lied.

Felisa came in a little after half past six, before there was any word from Nina. By seven o'clock both mother and stepfather began to feel anxious, although not yet alarmed.

9

The Fourth Wife

Just before six o'clock, when Gideon was planning to leave for home, Oliver of the Fraud Squad came in. Oliver was a tall, glum-looking individual, who wore thick-lensed glasses "the better," he would say with his almost gloomy humor, "to see the forgeries with, Gee-Gee." He was a man with a vocation: that of distinguishing any kind of forgery; also a man with a cross: his eyesight, so essential to his work, was failing. He had always tried to keep pace with the scientific methods, using infrared rays and anything he felt was reliable. Just as some men had a nose for news, and others for luck, so Oliver had an eye for counterfeit currency and forged documents.

"Something about the look of it," he would say, then rustle a specimen between his fingers, and add, "And something about the feel of it."

Now he brought a transparent plastic folder with several pockets, each pocket containing West German marks. He also had a typewritten report.

"Spare five minutes, George?"

"Five?" Gideon echoed, and smothered a sigh. "I mustn't be too late. Won't it keep?"

"You said treat it as urgent," Oliver reminded him. "Just five minutes."

Gideon resigned himself to half an hour, lifted the internal telephone and dialed the sergeants' room.

"Sit down, Olly . . . Hallo . . . Stott, ring my wife, will you, tell her I'll be having three or four guests in *after* supper —emphasize the 'after'—and ask her to lay everything on."

"I'll do that right away, sir," said Detective Sergeant Stott. Gideon rang off.

"Beer session." Oliver sniffed. "Why can't I come?"

"Like to?"

"Can't," said Oliver. "That's if I can persuade my boss to spare me five minutes on a certain job. If he sees it my way, I'll be up half the night preparing a memo for tomorrow."

Gideon opened a cupboard in his desk.

"Like a Scotch?"

"Thanks, George, don't mind if I do." Oliver extracted four of the mark notes and placed them on Gideon's desk as Gideon poured. "Those marked with a red A—genuine, George. Ta. . . . The Black B—one of the forgeries Bonn sent us. The red B, one of those from Thos. Cook's, this morning. Nice drop of Scotch."

"Go on," said Gideon.

"The black B and the red B are identical," Oliver told him. "So some of the same forged notes are on this side—twenty-seven are at least. The forgery's as perfect as any I've come across. Paper's the same, dunno how they got it but that's Bonn's problem. Color's identical. There's one thing Bonn either didn't tell us or didn't know." Oliver sipped his whisky and soda again, but Gideon did not spoil his moment of satisfaction. "See red B?"

Gideon studied it, and saw a single pale smudge, rather like a spot left behind by liquid which had caused a slight fading.

"Yes," Gideon said.

"Found that out by accident, last night. I was having half a pint and a spot dropped onto that." He dipped his little finger in his drink and dabbed the note. After a pause he wiped it off, and there was a faint mark. "I'd like to ask all banks, including all tourist agencies who have foreign exchange facilities, to try the alcohol test on each one. Give 'em a couple of days and we should get some idea how many of the forgeries are here. Right?"

Gideon finished his drink.

"Right."

"I'll ask all the head offices to send to their branches and have the replies analyzed by the head offices. Save us a lot of trouble, and—"

"Go ahead," interrupted Gideon.

"Okay. Seven minutes," Oliver said. "Don't blame me if you're late home."

"If they're coming at eight you haven't much time," Kate said to Gideon when he reached home just before seven o'clock. "Who's coming?"

"Lem, and an old friend of yours."

Kate looked startled.

"Of mine?"

"You once said you wished you could have one hundredth of the diamonds he lifted in the way of business," said Gideon. He laughed. "It was a long time ago. Twenty-six years."

Kate stared at him, and then turned to the door.

"I must get the front room ready. You'll have to take the dinner out of the oven, dear. Just the two?"

"Just the two." Gideon took a steaming cottage pie out of the oven, the potatoes on top a crisp golden brown. The kitchen table was already laid. Kate liked her food cool, he liked his hot. He was half through his huge plateful when Kate came in.

"Give up," she said.

"Quincy Lee," declared Gideon.

"Quincy—" Kate actually shifted her chair back in astonishment. "The smash-and-grab man?"

"He's come to make sure all is not proven, if not forgiven."

"I'm not sure I think it's a good thing," Kate said.

When Quincy Lee arrived, at exactly eight o'clock, she was at her gracious best. Lee was a short, wiry man, with iron-gray hair, gray eyes, a weather-beaten complexion. He wore a shoestring tie, and the cut of his lightweight suit was unmistakably American. He shook hands with Gideon as if they were longlost brothers, and when Lemaitre arrived five minutes later almost crushed his hand.

After two or three minutes of "How are you?" "How've you been?" and generalities, Kate got up, saying:

"I mustn't stay here, I've some letters to write."

"Don't run away on my account," urged Lee. "I guess you'll get as much kick as the boys will."

Kate glanced at Gideon, who said easily, "The letters can wait, Kate, can't they?" He noticed the deliberation with which Kate sat down again; as if she were making sure she did not appear to be overeager.

"First thing I want to get off my chest is how much I owe to you guys—" Quincy began.

Lemaitre snorted. "For not nabbing you, you mean?"

"I didn't mean nothin' of the kind," denied Quincy. "You made it so hot for me I knew there was no future in little old England for Quincy Lee, so I emigrated. Worked my way across the Atlantic on a tramp steamer—"

"So *that's* why we never caught you," Lemaitre butted in. "Tell me something, Quincy. How much did you make out of that Hatton Garden job?"

"Easy, Lem," counseled Gideon.

"He won't incriminate himself after all these years!"

"Just to be on the safe side, why don't I put it like this?" suggested Quincy. "I managed to save up a little pile in England, and when I decided to emigrate I had enough to set myself up in a little business. Got up to Boston, and decided it looked too much like home, and New York wasn't safe, with C.I.D. men using airplanes like a ferry service. So I got a Greyhound bus—heard of them Greyhounds?"

"You bet!" Lemaitre's spirits seemed to rise higher all the time.

"Took a ticket across to Los Angeles, but liked the look of a place en route—Albuquerque. It wasn't until I'd lived there a month I discovered it was in New Mexico—always thought it was Texas, they were so pleased with their sand and their sun. Seemed big enough to get lost in and small enough to get out of quick," went on Quincy. "So I set up as a watch repairer and built up a nice business, then I started buying a few bits of costume jewelry and went on from there." .

"Anything hot?" demanded Lemaitre, almost hopefully.

"Take my word for it, Mrs. Gideon, I kept on the straight and narrow from the day I set foot in the old U.S.A. Never deviated—not by so much as a penny. I got fascinated in a different kind of rock—real rocks and minerals, semiprecious stones, that kind of thing," he explained. "They're scattered all over Arizona and New Mexico, up in Utah and Colorado too. In the winter I went into the mountains and dug the stuff out of the rocks, and made jewelry and sold polished rocks in summer. Happy as a sandboy, I was—never looked back and never regretted it."

After a pause, Kate said, "Did you get married?"

"You betcha! Girl came in to get her watch repaired. Fascinated by my English voice, she was, and that watch kept on going wrong. We were married in less than a year. She asked me what I did in England and I told her I was a rock collector there too."

Lemaitre snorted. Gideon laughed, Kate smiled broadly.

"So we hitched up. Had five kids, and they're all married now. Got eleven grandchildren, Mrs. Gideon—eleven, believe it or not." There was pride in his voice, yet sadness in his eyes. He pulled his bulging wallet from his hip pocket, and took out a wedge which proved to be a photograph holder. He flicked through several, stopped at one, looked at it solemnly for a moment, and handed it to Kate.

"There's my Liz. Wonderful woman, she was. Cancer got her, the end of last year. Wicked to watch her, it was." Quincy paused, while Kate studied the pleasant-looking face of a woman who had been in her thirties when the photograph was taken. "Never had any inclination to come back home while she was alive," Quincy confided. "But when she was gone I kinda had a hankering. Two of my sons are in the business. They go out and dig the minerals these days. Their wives help in the shop, and all of them urged me to come. Six months' vacation I've got."

He stared at Gideon.

"Why did you get in touch with us so soon?" asked Gideon.

Quincy replied simply. "I had to know how I stood. The Gee-Gee I knew way back would be okay, but people change. You're the top man now, and when you're at the top you look at things different, somehow. Six months okay, Mr. Gideon?"

Gideon hesitated. Kate looked at him as if she could not believe that he had any doubts, Lemaitre actually gaped. Quincy Lee did not once shift his gaze.

"As a top man, Quincy, I have to say this," said Gideon. "Keep out of trouble, and you can stay six years if you want to."

Quincy's eyes lit up. "I'll keep my nose clean—I swear it!"

Gideon grinned. "As George Gideon, I didn't even need to say it, Quincy. Now—"

The telephone bell rang.

Kate said quickly, "I'll answer it," and jumped from her chair before any of the others moved. Quincy Lee glanced at her as she went out, and then looked back at Gideon.

"Never had any real doubt what you'd say, Mr. Gideon. While she's out of the room—mind if I give her a little present? Navajo silver and turquoise work, the genuine stuff." He pulled a long narrow box out of his inside breast pocket. "Earrings, bracelet and a couple of brooches, not worth much and I got it wholesale. Okay?"

"Do something for me," asked Gideon.

"Just name it."

"Give it to her a day or two before you leave the country. She'll love it."

"Never miss a trick, do you?" said Quincy. "May I bring it in person?"

"Of course."

"It's a deal!" Quincy pushed the box back into his pocket quickly as Kate came into the room.

"It's Leslie Scott," she said. "He says it's to do with a man named Schumacher, and you would know about him."

Gideon said, "Oh. Yes, I know."

His mood and his manner changed with the words, and instantly he recalled his decision not to have Schumacher followed wherever he went. He stood up slowly, looked meaningfully at Lemaitre, and with a kind of massive deliberation went out. Kate's manner changed subtly too; she was always sensitive to his moods.

"Think I ought to go, Mrs. Gideon?" Quincy asked.

"No, of course not," Kate said. "Lem, pour out another beer for Mr. Lee, will you? I've some sandwiches and tarts in the kitchen." She went out, squeezing past Gideon, who hardly seemed to notice her as he said;

"Give me that again, Les."

Superintendent Leslie Scott, who was the senior night duty officer at the Yard, repeated what he had just said.

"Elliott Henderson called from the Bingham Hotel twenty minutes ago to say that his stepdaughter is missing. She was last seen by Abel Schumacher about four o'clock, leaving the Victoria and Albert Museum. Schumacher says she went to meet some friends she'd made on the *Queen Elizabeth*. You left a note to be told if there was any kind of trouble with Henderson or Schumacher, and I know Schumacher's reputation."

Gideon said, "Thanks for calling so quickly." Already he had decided what to do. It was too early to be sure that it had been a grievous mistake to take the watch off Schumacher but, mistake or not, he had to make sure this inquiry was handled well from now on. No one else knew much about the confidence trickster, while Henderson was not a man to be left to ill-informed subordinates. "Tell Henderson I'll be at the Bingham in about half an hour. Meanwhile, you check on anything we know about Schumacher's movements today."

"I can tell you he's with Henderson now," Scott said promptly.

That was a relief, in its way, and Gideon was a little less grim when he went back to the others.

10

Henderson's Wife

"I quite understand, Mr. Gideon," Quincy said. "You've got to take care of the bad men. I'll vamoose."

"Stay here, will you, and talk to Lem and my wife," Gideon interrupted. "If you don't I'll be on a sandwich and lemon-curd tart diet for a week. I'll call you when I'm through at the Bingham, Lem. You can drop Quincy on your way after that."

No one argued. Kate went to the door with Gideon, squeezed his hand, and asked, "Think you'll be long?"

"Shouldn't be too late," Gideon said. "Don't wait up, though."

He looked up at the stars as he walked to his garage round the corner. There wasn't a cloud in sight, and it was pleasantly warm, both for the law-abiding and for the criminal. As he drove toward the West End he thought about all he knew of Schumacher and the Hendersons. Henderson was in tobacco, cotton, real estate and citrus growing, fabulously wealthy, with commercial and business interests in most of the world, and a private collector of works of art. Three or four years ago he had married the widow of a Texas cattleman, who had one daughter. Nina Pallon was worth millions of dollars in her own right, while her mother had also inherited a huge share of Texas oil.

They're made of money, Gideon reflected.

The years of experience had taught him not to be ill at ease with any man; they had also taught him that it was almost impossible not to regard a millionaire as some people regarded film stars; as being in another world. The really worthwhile ones acquired more than money; they acquired judgment of people, understanding, a sense of responsibility.

He suspected this was true of Elliott Henderson as soon as they met in the sitting room of a luxury suite. Henderson had a fine-drawn look and there was anxiety in his eyes.

No one else was in the room.

"Good of you to come yourself, Commander. I greatly appreciate it. And I know I can be absolutely frank with you."

"I hope you will be," Gideon said.

"Be sure I will. Can I get you a drink?"

"Mr. Henderson," Godeon said, "minutes could make a difference."

Henderson eyed him levelly, and said, "You're certainly right, Commander, it's time I got straight to the point. The point is very simple. I made a mistake in sending for the police. I'm sorry."

Gideon didn't speak.

"Sure about that drink?" asked Henderson.

Very slowly, Gideon said, "Quite sure, thanks. So she's been kidnaped?"

Henderson didn't answer.

"And you've been telephoned and told not to report to us."

Henderson still didn't say a word. He was much smaller and leaner than Gideon, yet Gideon was unaware of it, knowing only that this was a man of great stature, whose will power matched and might well surpass his own. It would be impossible to browbeat him.

It was very quiet in the room. Gideon wondered whether Felisa Henderson had gone into the bedroom, to help maintain a conspiracy of silence; and he wondered where Schumacher was.

"Commander," Henderson said at last, "I'm really sorry I sent for the police when there was no need to."

"May I see your daughter?" asked Gideon.

"My stepdaughter is spending the night with friends," Henderson replied.

There was no mistaking the emphasis he put on the "*step-daughter.*" Gideon, trying to assess the situation with intelligence as well as detachment, considered the possible reasons for that. After a while, he said probingly:

"If she were your daughter, Mr. Henderson, would you act in the way you are doing?"

"There is no other way I can or wish to act at this juncture," Henderson declared, but Gideon thought he had been shaken by the question.

"Mr. Henderson," Gideon said flatly, "of the last five kidnapings of this nature, only two of the victims were returned safely to their families, although the ransom money was paid in every case. I can't make you tell me the truth, but I can and do emphasize the danger and the gravity of the decision you have to make. Whether it be from conviction or out of consideration for your wife—even at her insistence—it is both morally and materially wrong to try to buy off the kidnapers. Speed is vital. Unless we can find your stepdaughter quickly we might never find her at all."

Henderson's unwinking eyes were more green than gray. He moved to a table, and poured himself a whisky and soda; there were three glasses on the tray.

"You talk as if you expected Nina to be—to disappear, and if she disappeared, would know where to find her."

"I didn't expect it. I did expect you to run into some kind of trouble in London. When a man of your wealth makes the mistake of trusting a man on too short an acquaintance, trouble is as predictable as a hangover. As a matter of fact, sir, we have reason to believe that Schumacher is a confidence trickster."

The blood drained from Henderson's face; even his lips seemed to lose their color. He put the glass down, the drink hardly touched, and moved back to Gideon.

"Why didn't you tell me?"

"I didn't judge the time was right. If Schumacher knows anything about your stepdaughter's disappearance, he's changed a lot from being a confidence trickster." Gideon hesitated, and then went on with a bitterness meant only for himself, "But, after all, he did win your confidence."

Henderson hesitated, still pale, giving the impression that he could not decide whether to blame Gideon or not. The decision was taken out of his hands. The communicating door opened and Felisa Henderson entered. Gideon, used to all kinds of people under stress of anxiety, had never seen one make quite such an entrance. It wasn't stagy, it wasn't artificial, it did not even seem rehearsed. Yet there was a veneer of unnaturalness about it, perhaps because of the woman herself. She was tall, slim, and strangely beautiful, strangely in the sense that her skin seemed to be burnished with a layer of polished perfection on features which were a little too thin and too sharp in themselves. Spanish, thought Gideon. Her hair was raven-black. She was sheathed in a dress which looked as if it were of beaten gold, and yet it did not seem ostentatious.

"No," she said to Gideon, "Abel Schumacher won my confidence, not my husband's."

Nine out of ten men would have been quick to deny that. Henderson made no attempt to. His color was better, his eyes brighter.

"Felisa, this is Commander Gideon of the Criminal Investigation Department at New Scotland Yard."

"I wish I were happy to know you," Felisa Henderson said, with a quiver at her lips. "I'm sure you know what I mean. Does a confidence trickster customarily resort to kidnaping?"

"Seldom."

"Then why do you assume the worst now?"

Gideon said bluntly, "Only you can tell me whether the worst has happened or not. Has it or hasn't it?"

Felisa moved across to her husband and touched his hand, an unexpectedly intimate gesture.

"Thank you for trying, darling," she said. "But I'm afraid Mr. Gideon is right."

"He may be," Henderson conceded very slowly, "but even he can't guarantee results. Can you, Commander?" There were challenge and defiance in his manner.

"No, I can't," Gideon admitted.

"Elliott, I still think he is right. Won't you handle the situation as if you thought so too?"

Henderson drew in a breath which seemed to hurt him physically. In the long pause that followed Gideon did not feel at all sure how this would work out. Then Henderson said:

"If you knew for certain this was kidnaping, how would you deal with the investigation, Commander? Would you immediately tell the newspapers?"

"I most certainly would not."

"Presumably you would tell me to go ahead and pretend to meet the kidnapers' demands and be ready to act when the money was to be paid over."

"It might come to that," Gideon agreed. "It might even come to making a deal with the criminals, but only if we can be absolutely sure your daughter is alive and will be returned uninjured."

Very quietly Felisa Henderson asked, "You think she may be dead already, don't you?"

Nina Pallon was not dead, but she lay on a small bed in a London suburb, as still as death.

Felisa's question seemed to hover about the big room. She did not look away from Gideon, who was trying to probe beyond the facade of calmness, but it wasn't easy. Only the dark-brown eyes seemed to have any expression; they seemed to smolder.

"Please tell me the truth," she said abruptly.

"We both want absolute frankness," put in Henderson.

There was only one possible attitude to take: be absolutely truthful.

"Yes, I think your daughter may be dead, but I don't see any reason to assume it yet," said Gideon. "I think the moment of greatest danger will come just before any exchange arrangement is concluded, at the time when the kidnapers think they can get the money *and* murder her."

"But why should they then?" Felisa's voice was almost shrill.

"She could describe and perhaps name the men," Gideon answered. "Money wouldn't be any good to them in prison. How much have they asked for?"

"A million dollars," Felisa announced, and somehow the amount did not sound out of place, she spoke so matter-of-factly. "Mr. Gideon, I want you to understand one thing. Compared with the safety of my daughter, a million dollars is insignificant. If we could absolutely guarantee her safety we would pay ten million. You will confirm that, Elliott, won't you?"

"Yes," Henderson answered.

He did not need a moment to consider; he could contemplate paying—*losing*—ten million dollars, without giving it serious thought. In all his working life, Gideon would not earn half a million dollars, less than two hundred thousand pounds.

He said, "I don't think I really grasp that, but I know what you mean. Mind if I use your telephone?"

Felisa started to speak, as if to ask him, Why? Henderson gripped her arm, and silenced her.

"The red telephone is a direct line," he said. "The other goes through the hotel switchboard."

"Thanks." Gideon lifted the red receiver, dialed his own number, and was not surprised when Lemaitre answered. "Lem, it's what we thought but it's not as straightforward as I'd like it. . . . Yes, Schumacher's probably involved but we can't be certain yet. I should think he had some local talent to help him, if he did lay it on. I want you to go to the Yard and talk to the Central Divisional superintendents. We want to find out if anyone's heard a whisper about a big kidnaping job, or heard if anyone who might play with this kind of fire has had any recent dealings with an American. You know the kind of thing. . . . No, don't send it round on the teleprinter, we don't want it to spread too far yet. We might pick up something quickly. Another thing: tell Photographs we'll want a big print job started tonight—I'll bring the original photograph over myself, about midnight. We may not need to use the prints but I want 'em ready. All clear?"

Lemaitre said, "I've got you, George."

"How are things at home?"

"Couldn't be better," replied Lemaitre. "Quincy said he'd forgotten what lemon-curd tarts tasted like. I—George!"

"Yes?" Gideon was aware of the Hendersons watching with increasing tension, but Lemaitre's tone meant that he thought he had had a brain wave.

"Quincy could put his ear to the ground. He'd pick up word about anyone with an American angle quicker than most."

Gideon hesitated.

"Come on! It couldn't do any harm!"

"It could do a lot of harm to Quincy," Gideon said.

"But he's going to see all his old buddies. You know how old pals open up when they haven't seen each other for years."

"Talk to him, tell him the situation, make it clear there isn't the slightest obligation," Gideon said. "I'll see you at the Yard."

He replaced the receiver and turned to the Hendersons.

"Sorry that took so long. One of our problems is that we can never concentrate on one job at a time. But I've no doubt you're familiar with that particular difficulty, Mr. Henderson."

"Only too well."

"Well, *I'm* not," Felisa said in a harder voice than Gideon had yet heard her use. "I want to make sure this case is given absolute top priority, Mr. Gideon."

This time Henderson made no effort to quiet her. Gideon saw her eyes flash, as if fire was breaking out of the smoldering. She drew closer to him. He saw her beautifully made-up lips quiver and her hands clench; perhaps no one would ever realize how hard it had been for her to prevent the anguish from breaking down her composure.

"Do you understand me?"

Gideon answered quietly. "Yes, this is something I can really understand, Mrs. Henderson. If a daughter of mine needed hospital treatment or an operation, I'd want her to have absolute top priority—and I'd get it if I possibly could. But this isn't our only case of urgent importance. At this minute we are combing London for a paranoiac killer who we know will kill again if we don't find him quickly. You asked for absolute frankness, Mrs. Henderson. This is it. I will give every minute I possibly can to searching for Nina. I will put the investigation in charge of one of the best officers on the Force, a man who can handle a case like this from experience. I will consult you and Mr. Henderson at every stage. I shall not attempt to stop you paying over the money if that seems the only chance to save your daughter. But—"

He broke off.

The woman's eyes were shiny with unshed tears, and it was Henderson who winced at that *"But—"*

Gideon seemed to be quiet for a long time, before going on:

"If this were a case with the same high emotional content, if the same portent of tragedy lay over a family who never knew what it was to have a full larder or a safe income, I would treat it in exactly the same way. And if I seem to consider other things and other people too much, will you try to remember this? Crimes are contagious. A successful kidnaping might well lead to others. If we at the Yard mishandle this in any way—any way at all—then some other parents and some other child might have to pay a terrible price. I can't handle this entirely for you, the parents. I must give absolute priority to Nina and to others who might suffer in the same way."

Felisa heard him out, then turned away and almost ran to the door; her shoulders were shaking and she had one hand at her face. She pulled open the door and disappeared; the door slammed. The sound still seemed to be echoing a long time afterward, when Elliott Henderson said:

"I think you can be sure we shall want you to handle this however you think best, Commander. But before I go to my wife, will you answer me one question?"

"If I can," said Gideon.

"How are we to deal with Schumacher?" Henderson asked.

11

London Night

Gideon moved across the room, without answering, and picked up one of the two empty glasses. He twisted it round and round in his big fingers, trying to make up his own mind about the way to deal with Schumacher.

"Was he here just before I arrived?"

"Yes."

"Did he know you'd sent for the police?"

"Yes."

"How did he react?"

Henderson said bitterly, "I didn't notice it at the time but I can now recall that he seemed shocked."

"Did he disapprove?"

"He questioned the wisdom, just as my wife questioned it."

"When did the ranson demand come?"

Henderson closed his eyes. In that moment he looked a man in his sixties; earlier, he might have been taken for one in his late forties. Without opening his eyes, he answered:

"Ten minutes or so after Schumacher left the apartment."

"Why did he leave?"

"He said that he wanted to make some telephone calls. One was to an acquaintance who had sailed cabin class on the *Queen Elizabeth,* a man who might know the people with whom Nina had associated on board. And—" Henderson opened his eyes, and it seemed to Gideon that there was almost unbearable pain in them—"I thought that sounded reasonable."

Gideon put the glass down.

"And it was perfectly reasonable, sir. No use blaming yourself because you can see so much more with hindsight. I'm going to see Schumacher. I'm going to appear to accept his story, giving no indication that I know his record. Will your wife be able to behave naturally with him tomorrow?"

"If it's necessary—yes."

"It'll be necessary," Gideon said grimly.

"Commander."

"Yes."

"Is there any good reason why I shouldn't tell Schumacher that you believed me when I said I had located Nina?"

Gideon said vehemently, "There are a dozen good reasons. The first and most important is that Schumacher would know that no police officer of experience would believe you, so he would expect the Yard to be working without your knowledge. Do you follow me?"

"So far."

"That would scare him badly. The one positive witness against him is probably Nina. If she were dead, he would have less to worry about—at least he would think he had. But if you tell him you told me that Nina was spending the night with friends but I wouldn't buy it, he'll believe you."

"How will it help?" asked Henderson.

"He will know that you will expect and will obtain close cooperation from us at the Yard. He will know that a man of your standing will want to be kept informed of developments and of what we're doing. So you will tell him whatever I tell you. He will feel secure for as long as he's in your confidence and believes he has your trust. That's why it is so important that both you and your wife behave naturally with him. For a start, ring and tell him I'm on my way to see him, will you?"

After a long pause, Henderson said slowly, "I see. Yes, I see. And this way we can at least feel that we're helping."

Gideon said, "Unless you convince Schumacher, I doubt if we can save your stepdaughter. Her safety depends on you much more than you may realize." After a pause, he went on: "Have you a good photograph of her?"

"Yes." Henderson went to a bureau and picked up a leather photograph folder. He opened this, slipped out a post-card-sized photograph and handed it to Gideon.

Gideon studied Nina's narrow, rather elfin face, and saw a promise of the same kind of beauty as her mother's. The huge dark eyes held a glow of warmth; she had a look of simplicity.

"Thank you." He put the picture into his pocket, and turned toward the door. "Can't tell you how sorry I am about this, sir."

"Commander Gideon," Henderson said, "I want to thank you."

He came across and shook hands.

Gideon, deeply thoughtful, went down two floors in the lift to the sixth floor, then walked along to Schumacher's room, Number 697. There were odds and ends of background information which lay buried in his mind, sometimes for years, and rose to the surface whenever they were needed. Now he remembered that all the 90 to 99 rooms on all floors at the Bingham were back ones, available at comparatively low rates. Either Schumacher had little money to play with or he thought it wise to put up a modest front. By the time he had tapped on the door Gideon had concluded that an expensive room would have suited the man's purpose better, so Schumacher wasn't too flush with money.

That might make him impatient.

Schumacher opened the door, and stood aside immediately. He was very like his photograph, and at first sight Gideon could understand why people liked and trusted him. The homely face and the rather untidy, grandfatherly appearance were most disarming.

"Mr. Henderson told me you were coming," he said as Gideon went in. "But I was puzzled by one thing."

The room was small and unbelievably old-fashioned, with a single bed in a corner, a hand basin, no door to a bathroom.

"Were you, sir?"

"He used the title 'Commander.'"

"That's right."

"A military rank?" Schumacher sounded more incredulous than he allowed himself to look.

"It's a rank at New Scotland Yard," Gideon said. "That doesn't make us a police state, Mr. Schumacher." He half-smiled, sat down in the only armchair while the other sat on an upright one at the dressing table. "I've talked to Mr. and Mrs. Henderson, who are very distressed and a little vague on some aspects of what you told them. I wonder if you will tell me everything you know, what museums you visited and the approximate times—anything at all which might help us clarify the picture."

Schumacher raised his hands.

"I only wish I could be of real assistance, Commander. As it is—" He told the story which Gideon had already heard with an earnestness and air of conviction which it was impossible to fault. When he finished the details he went on: "I cannot help feeling that someone among her shipboard acquaintances is responsible. I've been trying to call them to mind, and have talked with a friend of mine who might have helped. There was a young couple named Pommeroy, I remember, and . . ."

He named two more.

He seemed unperturbed when Gideon said:

"If Miss Pallon is still missing tomorrow I'll have to have one of my men come and take the details down as a formal statement. Will you be in all the morning?"

"I'll stay in the hotel until I hear from you," Schumacher promised.

There was no glint in his eye, no change of tone, nothing at all to indicate any relief at the way the interview had gone. Gideon would have given a lot to see his face when the door closed, however.

Schumacher closed the door, and smiled, very slowly. Then he wiped the perspiration off his forehead. Next he put in a call to a Hammersmith number, he felt so sure of himself.

"I think it's all right," he said when Facey answered.

"Thank God for that!"

"How is she?" Schumacher asked.

"She'll sleep till morning," Facey said.

A stocky man standing at a telephone in the foyer of the Bingham brought Gideon up with a sense almost of shock that he could have overlooked so obvious and important a step: he should have told Lemaitre or Leslie Scott to arrange for all calls to and from the Hendersons and to and from Schumacher to be reported. There was nothing to stop Schumacher making a call, and he might be on the telephone this very moment. Gideon felt sick at his own fallibility. It was poor consolation that he could make some amends, but not necessarily enough: from the Bingham local calls could be dialed direct. All he could do was find out whether Schumacher had made any call at all.

He went into the small office used by the hotel detective.

"Give me five minutes, Mr. Gideon, and I'll have the information for you." The hotel detective, a big, hardy-looking man, left Gideon and went off; he was back in three minutes, apparently quite positive of his facts.

"Mr. Schumacher did make a local call, five minutes ago. It was automatically recorded, but there's no way of telling who it was to or what it was about. Now I have your request it will be a different matter. I'll see you get the information you want."

Gideon thanked him, and went off. He was still bitterly self-reproachful when he reached the Yard, but now there was a lot to do. Lemaitre was more than halfway through the task of telephoning divisional superintendents, most of whom were at home. Gideon helped finish the job. One of the most important factors in the work of the Metropolitan Police was the grapevine or gridiron system. All over London, the greatest concentration being in Soho and the East End, titbits of information about crimes planned and pending and crimes just completed seemed to float in the atmosphere—like a myriad short-wave radio communications. Everyone talked to someone; the cleverest professional criminals could not resist bragging of what they had done and boasting about what they were going to do. Hearsay wasn't evidence but many a man was behind bars because he had made a careless remark which had been carried from man to man, woman to woman, place to place, until eventually the police had heard. The police acted more or less like highly sensitive radio receivers, picking up odd statements, jokes, rumors, malicious gossip—all these and much more. They knew which criminal or associate of criminals was most likely to talk, for there were among them the garrulous and the gregarious as well as the surly and the solitary. The police were also quick to hear of quarrels between old friends, quicker to get their ears to the ground, for thieves who fell out were prone to insult one another bitterly.

The criminals and the police had one thing in common: they kept their eyes open and their wits about them. The most trivial unusual thing would warn the one and alert the other. A man might be hard up one day and flush the next—and this would automatically make him suspect if his kind of job had been done the previous night. Many approaches were less obvious. For instance, two men might have a drink in a pub away from the district they usually frequented, so: were they planning a job? Or a man might take his girl or his wife to a restaurant in an unfamiliar part of town, so: what place was he casing? Into this category of the less obvious would come such an observation as: X was talking to a Yank last night, what's on? Or: Y's rented a room for a girl who spends all her time there. They can't be at it *all* day.

Some fragment of gossip such as this could give the police their badly needed lead. Gideon and Lemaitre were alerting all the senior officers to give even closer attention than usual to some specific questions. The Yard was briefing the divisional senior officers, who would brief their junior officers, who in turn would brief their subordinates in the C.I.D. and also in the Uniformed Branch. Before the night was out all the divisions in London would be alerted, and the antennae of the Metropolitan Police would be at their most sensitive.

One young uniformed officer from the Kensington district had put a single short paragraph in his report that evening:

A milk roundsman named Wilson mentioned to me he thought he heard a girl scream as he was passing Geddos, an art shop in Gulliver Street, about eleven-thirty a.m. The assistant in the shop, a Lucy Green, appears to be a bit nervous and short-tempered. She was not on duty this afternoon but returned about five o'clock.

This item was in the report because a week ago the constable had overheard a quarrel between a man and his wife, and the wife had been found badly injured the following day. Had the constable reported the quarrel, the police would have worked on the husband at once. As it was, he denied the assault and a neighbor's report of the quarrel had been the first to reach Divisional H.Q.

The constable still smarted from the reprimand by the Superintendent.

". . . and if you ever want to become a policeman instead of a car park attendant, keep your ears and your eyes open, and put everything you see or hear in your report."

Hyde had obeyed that order to the letter.

He had also put in a great deal more, and the sergeant whose duty it was to read all reports and mark those he considered sending to the C.O. yawned his way through it.

He did not mark the milk roundsman's story for special attention.

With the Force alerted, the photographs of Nina Pallon in hand, and everything ticking over well as far as he could judge, Gideon did the inevitable: he checked what was going on in London. Every few minutes a report came through of another crime. Standing in the big new Information Room, watching the men at the telephones—line and radio—seeing the teleprinters moving as if by invisible hands, hearing and reading reports which were brought to the inspector-in-charge in a never-ending stream, it was easy to imagine that London's streets were running with blood, echoing to the cries of the assaulted, crackling with the breaking of window glass, reverberating with the roar of stolen cars, pulsating to the pneumatic drills of men invading the vaults of banks and business houses. In fact as Gideon drove home a little before midnight, London seemed to be sleeping as peacefully as any man tired by the exertions of the day. Few people walked, fewer drove their cars; there was only a background of noise.

But in a hundred, in a thousand parts of the somnolent city crime was being committed.

Somewhere Nina Pallon lay—alive, please God.

Somewhere Quincy Lee was talking.

Somewhere the man Mayhew was hiding, awake or asleep. Alone, wondered Gideon, or with some other girl who did not know how near she was to horror?

Jerry Klein, with his cut hand, was nursing his secret.

The killer of Benito Dolci Lucci felt absolutely secure.

The distributors of the counterfeit West German marks had no idea what the police were ferreting out, no idea that in three days Superintendent Oliver should know how many there were circulating in England.

There were these and other criminals, with the police more intensely active at night than during the day—a war of attrition was being waged all the time, as it had been since Gideon had first joined the Force.

The bedroom light was on, so Kate wasn't asleep. He locked the front door and went upstairs. She was sitting in bed, high on the pillows, with the evening newspaper. She wore a pink woolen bed jacket loose about her shoulders over a simple nightdress of the same color; she had not yet put on her hair net. As Gideon entered she switched on an electric kettle, so she had waited for their tea nightcap for him.

"How has it gone?" she inquired. When he did not answer, she seemed to comprehend the weight of the burden on his mind, and asked more earnestly, "How is Mrs. Henderson?"

Gideon talked as he undressed and had tea. It was good to confide in Kate, even though there was nothing she could do to help. When at last he stopped, she was silent for a while, until she said quietly:

"Lem telephoned just before you came in. He says he forgot to tell you that Quincy Lee promised to keep his ear to the ground. What a nice little man Quincy is!"

"What a lot of nice little men are in the cells tonight," said Gideon gruffly.

He found himself thinking what a lot of beasts there were not in police cells or behind prison bars: Schumacher, for instance.

Yet he was tired, and dropped off to sleep before Kate did; and she was very glad.

12

Of Many Wives

"Hey, Maggie!" Barney Barnett cried as usual as he pushed open the living-room door. "Old Quincy Lee! Fancy him back! You could have knocked me down with a feather, you could really."

"Who needs a feather?" Maggie scoffed.

"That's true enough. Come to think, I'm wasting away for want of some good food. Why don't you go to tech school and learn to cook?" He paused. Maggie's eyes called a truce, and he went on enthusiastically, "Done all right for himself, they say."

"Who says?"

"Some of the boys. He was with a dozen old pals yesterday. Don't know whether it's true or not but they say he's on the level."

"If Quincy's on the level, you watch your step. He was dangerous enough when he was in the business. What other breath-taking news have you collected, Barney dear?"

"Bit sarky this morning, aincha?" Barney moved forward, gave her a big bear hug and would not let her go. "You'd better be careful or I'll emigrate like Quincy did. I never heard nothing much else," he went on. "Oh—you know old Facey?"

"No."

"Go orn—old Facey, who paints lightning portraits for half a quid a time."

"Oh, him." Maggie sniffed. "Don't go getting mixed up with him."

"Just because he didn't flatter you when he did your phizog," jeered Barney. "He's doing a job with some Yank."

"What kind of job?"

"I don't know much about it, but they say it's fake pictures," answered Barney. "Who'd believe old Quincy Lee would be back? Must be thirty years. Precious close to thirty, anyway." He let his wife go, and moved to a kitchen chair, straddling it. "How about inviting him over to a bite of dinner one day?"

Maggie moved toward her husband, and her manner silenced him. She stared at him fixedly, and then spoke with great deliberation:

"Barney, I don't mind you having a drink with Quincy Lee, but don't get too friendly until you see what he's up to. The police aren't nits, and they've got a grapevine that never lets them down. They know Quincy's here, and they'll wonder if he's come to pick up some hot stuff cheap and take it back with him. You be careful."

"You're the boss," Barney said humbly. Then his eyes sparked. "God damn it, can't you trust my discretion?"

"No," said Maggie simply. "And don't do anything for that Facey, either. He's a queer, and I don't like queers."

"Old Facey," whose name really was Philip Facey, was in a small studio at the arches, in Hammersmith. This was one of the more thickly populated boroughs of London but quite near the better-class western residential suburbs. The arches were big arch-shaped sheds formed by a viaduct over which the railway line led to the West Country. Beneath the studio was a carpenter's shop, where among other things picture frames were made for the trade. Half a dozen men worked there, all of them acquainted with Facey, the "artist bloke upstairs." They had soon learned that Facey was useful with woodworking tools, and when in need of extra cash, or when the carpenter's shop was short staffed, he would lend a hand downstairs.

Adjacent on one side was a car-body work and repair shop; on the other a paint and oils warehouse.

No one at the arch had been surprised when Facey had brought a big tool chest in the back of his old station wagon. Two men had helped him lift it to the foot of the loft ladder, the only access to the studio. He had arrived at four o'clock, left the chest padlocked until five, at which time the others finished for the day. When the last had gone he had opened the box and lifted Nina Pallon out.

She had looked near death. Even like that she had been light enough for him to carry up the ladder without too much difficulty.

Now she lay in a little cubicle, too small to be called a room, partitioned off from the main section of the studio. It was in a corner, without a window and without a light. She lay on an old camp bed, wearing only bra, girdle, panties and stockings, covered with an old gray army blanket. She was still unconscious, and yet was beginning to become aware of outside influences.

One was a roar which seemed to make her whole body quiver until it faded, but it was never silent for long. It was the roar of the trains overhead; they followed one another very quickly, especially at rush-hour periods.

Facey had a bed in another corner, against the far wall of the partition. By the side of this bed was a telephone, the one on which he had talked to Abel Schumacher the previous night. It was not unusual for him to spend a night at the studio, working late; as far as he could tell there was no danger at all.

Yet Facey was ill at ease, almost afraid.

The unconscious girl was the chief cause of his fear, for if she was ever questioned by the police she could describe him, perhaps even name him. A corpse was so much easier to hide than a living person.

Maria Lucci also was thinking of a dead body: her husband's.

It was in a fine new mausoleum now, one he had had erected a few years ago. The bones of his mother and his father, two brothers and an aunt had been interred there, and their photographs, expensively framed, were outside for passers-by to see and perhaps to remember. In all the cemetery no one was better known, today, than Benito. The newspaper photographers had been here, and the reporters, asking question after question. There was one and only one good thing: it was rumored but not yet proved that Benito had killed himself, and the church did not refuse to bury one of its faithful because of rumor.

She, Maria, dry-eyed until the last awful moment, had held Antonio's cold hand tightly and had comforted her daughters too. Behind the crowd of black-clad relatives, far more of them than she had ever seen during Benito's lifetime, there had been Giovanni, arrived only just in time for the funeral. Among the mass of wreaths and crosses had been an enormous cross from Percival White. She had been surprised to notice the English detective, who had been at the hotel in Soho, studying the cross. By his side was a younger man, an Italian.

Maria made a detour among the graves and the carved headstones and the caskets and the burial places which looked like marble ovens.

"They lied, I tell you," she said as she reached Parsons. "My Benito was good, he did not do these awful things."

Parsons, taken aback, said awkwardly, "If he didn't, we will prove it, ma'am."

Maria went past without another word, watched by Parsons and his companion, a tall, dark-haired, sharp-featured detective named Nocci.

"You are not sure he did, are you?" asked Nocci.

"I'm here to try to find out if those managers lied," answered Parsons.

"I think you are here because Lucci's wife has persuaded you that she is right," said Nocci. "But Lucci would not be the first man to have deceived his wife."

"Florrie sweetheart, where would you like to go this morning?" Frank Mayhew asked next day.

The "sweetheart" seemed to be uttered from the core of his being.

"Anywhere," Florence Foster said gaily. "I don't mind at all." She almost added, "So long as it's with you," but that would be throwing herself at his head, and all her upbringing made her shy away from such boldness.

"London city or London parks?" he asked.

"Honestly, I don't mind."

"Why don't we go out of town to one of the parks, say, Hampton Court, or Windsor Great Park, or Richmond? I've been reading all about them." Then Frank's face fell. "Perhaps you know them already."

"No, I don't," Florrie said hastily. "I'm not a Londoner, remember. I've always wanted to see Windsor Castle and the park, too. I'm told they're wonderful."

Mayhew leaned across the breakfast table.

"*You're* wonderful," he said in a vibrant voice.

It did not matter what he said, only that she should not be too forward. If she was, she might lose him, and already he seemed part of her life.

She seemed part of the background of his life too; like the trees of the woods and the parks and the rustling which kept them company there.

The cashier at Kismet's was in his office, with a man whom Michael Dunn had seen out for an evening stroll; a young, pleasant-looking man wearing a well-cut suit, dark gray in color. Dunn wished the cashier, whom he knew well, was alone, but as it happened that made no difference.

"Ah, Mr. Dunn." The cashier was fussy and middle-aged. "I promised you a check this morning, and it's ready and waiting." He had the check clipped to une little sneaf of bills. "If you'll just sign the receipt . . . My goodness, though, you haven't met Mr. Pommeroy from our parent company, have you? Mr. Pommeroy, this is Mr. Dunn, who does all our emergency printing for us, and a lot of other things. I don't know where we would be without him."

"Glad to know you, Mr. Dunn," said Pommeroy.

"How are you?" asked Dunn formally. "I hope you're enjoying this country."

"I haven't had much chance to get around but I like what I've seen very much."

Nothing was said about his purpose here, and Dunn had no reason to feel any presentiment of trouble. He went straight to his bank and deposited a check for eight hundred seventy-four pounds, three shillings—two hundred fifty pounds more than it should have been. Then he hurried to the shop and sent a check in advance to the small private hotel at Bournemouth where Cynthia was going.

Cynthia, in the kitchen of the upstairs flat, was actually humming to herself; not coughing.

Jerry Klein stretched up for a box of mixed pendants in his shop and banged his injured hand. He winced. As he was holding his hand tight, to hold back the pain, the door opened. Klein caught his breath; even the opening of the shop door scared him these days.

A youth and a girl came in.

"I'd like to see one of those Rite-Time watches, like the one you sold to a friend of mine," the man said.

"I want to buy my fiancé a birthday present," explained the girl, "and he liked the Rite-Time watch ever so."

Nothing, absolutely nothing, seemed to allow him to forget Darkie Jackson, Klein thought miserably. These accursed watches had brought him nothing but trouble. He forced an apologetic smile as he said:

"I'm sorry, but we're out of them. There were just a few exported, that was all. Now, I've a very good Italian watch, much the same in appearance . . ."

For Gideon, that Wednesday started as if it were going to be one of those days. He woke with a very rare thing for him: a headache. It wasn't unbearable, but it took the edge off the morning. The postman brought two letters from their children, and as Kate scanned the one from Prudence he saw the narrowing of her eyes. Soon she looked up.

"Pru's having some trouble with her blood pressure. The doctor says she mustn't overexert herself before the baby comes."

Gideon grunted. "Meaning you ought to go to her."

There was one good thing: Kate was so preoccupied about their daughter that she did not notice the ungraciousness of his tone.

"I think I should, George, don't you?"

He hesitated.

"At least I ought to go over today and see how she is," Kate went on. Prudence now lived at Epsom, about an hour's journey by bus. "Knowing I'm able to go whenever it's necessary will ease her mind, if nothing more."

"Suit yourself," Gideon said. "Don't spoil her, though."

"If either of us ever spoiled Prudence, you did," Kate declared.

"Only one of the family I ever spoiled was you," Gideon retorted. "Don't worry about me, but phone the office if you're not going to be home tonight."

"Oh, I'll be back!" Kate assured him.

There wasn't a hope, thought Gideon, but at least he saved himself from sounding surly. He was edgy, hoping the telephone would bring news of Nina Pallon, but it did not. His good-by kiss to Kate was more perfunctory than it should have been, but she seemed still too preoccupied to notice it. It was a pleasant morning, the sort the Meteorological Office was fond of describing as "sunny intervals with occasional showers." He pressed the self-starter of his car, and didn't much like the repsonse: it grated too much. It was five minutes before the car started, and on the first mile it stalled three times. He told a constable to report the trouble to the vehicle maintenance department, and went on.

Lemaitre almost jumped when he thrust the office door open.

"George—"

"Anything in about the Pallon girl?" Gideon demanded.

"Not a thing. George—"

"I want Hobbs to drop whatever he's doing, and to go to see Schumacher, get a written statement, and then go in person to each of the art galleries and the Victoria and Albert Museum to check the story." It was then that Gideon faced a fact which he had rejected before: there was an outside chance that Schumacher was telling the truth, and the girl had been kidnaped by someone else. "I want to hear from Hobbs by four o'clock at the latest."

"I'll fix it, but, George——"

"Fix it first, and talk afterwards."

Lemaitre looked as if he would snap an angry retort, but instead he stretched out for his internal telephone, speaking to Gideon as he did so.

"The Commissioner wants to see you. There's some kind of a brouhaha going on. I canceled all your briefings, just told everyone to carry on."

Gideon sat back in his chair. Lemaitre dialed, and half-grinned, half-smirked across. Gideon forced a smile and an "Okay, Lem," and hoped it sounded conciliatory enough. He glanced through the reports on his desk and discovered that very little of importance had happened since his visit to Information late last night; the criminal liked his sleep as much as the next man.

Lemaitre finished talking to Hobbs, and rang off.

"He's on his way."

"No squeaks of any kind in?"

"Give it a chance," protested Lemaitre. "Most of the chaps haven't got the sleep out of their eyes yet."

"Time they had," grumbled Gideon. "Don't mind me, Lem. Know anything more about the Old Man's problem?"

"Nope. I do know Rogerson's had a relapse, though."

"Oh," said Gideon heavily. "I'll be back as soon as I can. Ask the Old Man's secretary to interrupt us if you get any word about Nina Pallon or Mayhew."

"Right," said Lemaitre. Almost at once two telephones rang on Gideon's desk. "You go, George. If either of these is important I'll catch you before you go in to the Great White Chief."

13

Prize within Reach

He was genuinely sorry about the relapse suffered by the Assistant Commissioner for Crime, Gideon told himself, but deep down his first thought had been: how will this affect me? If he had a load of administrative work to do as double for the A.C. he would be able to concentrate less on the two urgent jobs on hand. It was no use jumping his fences before he reached them but he was prepared for the worst as he stepped into the Commissioner's secretary's office. The Commissioner, head of the Metropolitan Police, was in a different building from the C.I.D.; somehow the atmosphere was different too.

"Morning," Gideon said to the middle-aged secretary, neat in gray with neat gray hair and silver-rimmed pince-nez.

"Good morning, Mr. Gideon. The Commissioner would like you to go straight in." As Gideon moved towards the door, she added, "Mr. Lemaitre asked me to tell you that the two calls were routine."

"Thanks." Gideon felt some of the gloom lift: at times Lem was maddeningly exasperating, but he was the old reliable. Gideon tapped perfunctorily on the door and went in as the Commissioner called:

"Come in."

Lieutenant-Colonel Sir Reginald Scott-Marle was alone in the severely furnished office. That was right for him. An ex-military man, he had a look, some thought a habit, of severity, even of aloofness. There were men at the Yard who had known him for years and yet did not feel they ever got near him. Gideon had once felt that way, and been ill at ease in the presence of this tall, lean, gray-haired man, ill at ease unless he was on his own ground, dealing with some specific case of which he had positive knowledge against the Commissioner's opinion. Once or twice they had clashed when Gideon had held stubbornly to the rightness of a course of action; once Scott-Marle had conceded the point, once he had insisted on a change of approach to a case, afterward admitting he had been wrong. Out of these things had grown a mutual trust and respect and the years were turning this into liking.

Had anyone else been present, Scott-Marle would have been formal. "Commander" or, at best, "Gideon." Now he motioned to a chair in front of his large, flat-topped mahogany desk.

"Sit down, George. I gather you've plenty on your hands without extracurricular matters, so to speak."

"I've two bad ones," Gideon said, sitting; and he was reminded of the way Henderson had kept silent when his wife had accepted the responsibility for trusting Schumacher. "Lemaitre tells me that Rogerson's had a setback."

"A bad one," Scott-Marle confirmed.

"Oh." It was almost superfluous to add "I'm sorry." Scott-Marle was looking at him intently, almost embarrassingly. "How bad?" he asked.

"I think we can be sure he won't return to the Yard," declared Scott-Marle.

Gideon said, shocked, "As bad as that?" Now his own emotions and his thoughts were in turmoil, because of what this could mean. "What's happened, sir?"

"He collapsed on Monday morning, was rushed to hospital, and operated on at once. They found that in addition to cardiac trouble there is the cancer, which has spread very rapidly. They give him between six weeks and six months."

Every word had the impact of a blow delivered with a hammer and chisel; cold, unrelenting, shocking. Even when Scott-Marle's dry, almost unemotional voice stopped, what he had said was hard to believe. Rogerson had been ill on and off for years; it had been easy to think he would die of old age.

He was two years younger than Gideon.

"What a damnable thing," Gideon said at last.

"It is indeed." Scott-Marle was still looking at him with that probing intentness. "We have two things to face up to, George—long-term and short-term policy. I think the short-term speaks for itself. I'll do all I can on the administrative side to help, but you'll deputize for the time being."

Gideon knew that this wasn't meant as an order, it was simply the acceptance of the inevitable. It would mean extra work, extra hours, extra responsibility—perhaps it was a good thing that Kate was needed at Pru's, it would be easier to spend more time at the Yard.

He nodded.

"And we can no longer leave the long-term problem in abeyance. While there was a chance that Rogerson would be coming back there wasn't such a problem. Now there is—the question of appointing his successor."

"Yes," Gideon said. "I know."

"This is what I want to know from you as soon as you can make up your mind, George," said Scott-Marle almost brusquely. "Do you want the appointment or not?"

Now that the question had been put into words, Gideon realized that he had expected it; yet, like the grim news of Rogerson, the question came as a real shock. He was aware that Scott-Marle was watching him intently, no doubt trying to judge his reaction. Scott-Marle knew as well as anyone that to become assistant commissioner for crime was to reach the zenith of hopes and ambition in the C.I.D. In a way, Gideon felt, the Commissioner knew that Gideon's whole life in the Force, from humble police constable to commander, seemed to flash in front of his eyes.

Scott-Marle let his question stand, and did not prompt Gideon by word or gesture.

At last Gideon said, "When do you have to know, sir?"

"Within a week, say. Ten days at the outside. The Home Secretary wants to make the appointment within the next month."

Gideon pondered before asking:

"If I say I would like it, what are my chances?"

For the first time this morning Scott-Marle smiled.

"If you would like the appointment I would recommend you, and I don't think a recommendation of mine in this context would be passed over. There would be some objections, of course, but only formal. The day has come when the man, not his social background, is the deciding factor. I am sure that would be accepted."

"I see," said Gideon; and then he realized that he wasn't exactly bursting with enthusiasm or appreciation, and smiled rather wryly. "Thank you very much. May I ask another question?"

"As many as you want."

"Do *you* want me to take the job?"

Quickly, decisively, Scott-Marle said: "Yes, if I have your assurance that your heart would be in it. Don't misunderstand me." He spoke more hurriedly than usual. "I know what the executive aspect of the work means to you. I know you are not the most tolerant or patient of men where administration is concerned. You like to cut red tape, and at assistant commissioner level it can't always be cut. On the other hand, you're now near the middle fifties. You may feel the time has come when you could hand over the day-to-day supervision of the detective force. If you've reached that stage, I want no other assistant commissioner. If you think you would always be hankering after more active work, I would rather you declined. You would be of ten times more value to the Yard, and incidentally to me, if you stayed where you are."

Gideon was smiling more freely.

"You couldn't be more frank, and I appreciate it. I've often wondered how I would feel if this situation ever arose, and now it's here I don't quite know how I feel. Is there likely to be another chance?"

"In a few years' time, do you mean?"

"Yes."

"I think not. I have a second choice in mind, from outside the Force. It wouldn't be popular within the Force, whereas yours would be, but the man I have my eye on is the best one after you. He's forty-five."

"I see," said Gideon. Quite suddenly his heart felt like a leaden ball inside him. He brooded for a few moments. "Will Monday week be time enough? I'm not sure how much time I'll have to give to the main jobs on hand."

"Monday week," agreed Scott-Marle quietly. "I don't need to say that I will accept and respect your decision, whatever it is." He stood up and moved round the desk. In the moment of silence which followed Gideon knew from experience that Scott-Marle had dismissed the subject from his mind and was thinking of another. Gideon hadn't; his thoughts were still in a whirl.

"Is there any prospect of a quick result over the Pallon girl?" Scott-Marle asked.

Gideon was jolted out of his preoccupation.

"I don't see any, but if we don't find her quickly I doubt if we'll find her alive. The only line we've got is Schumacher, and if we treat him as a suspect it might have exactly the result we don't want. I can't soft-pedal with him for too long, though."

"I told the Home Secretary that you would find her if it were humanly possible." Scott-Marle was half-smiling again, while Gideon was wondering: How the hell did the Home Secretary get into this? "He told me that was precisely what Elliott Henderson had already told the American Ambassador."

Gideon's expression was bleak.

"Very flattering. But if Henderson talks too much, this will leak into the newspapers. We don't want that yet."

"No, I suppose not."

It was hardly a question, yet it carried the implication that the decision to keep the story of the kidnaping secret might be wrong, and it put a needle of doubt into Gideon's mind. He made no further comment, but he was already searching his mind.

"You might call this an American week," Scott-Marle remarked.

"We've had 'em before and will again." Gideon was almost too blunt in the way he said that.

"No doubt. What do you hope to get out of Parsons' visit to Milan, by the way?"

"Improved relations," Gideon answered. "And possibly an indication that Lucci might have had enemies in Italy."

"Do you think he had?"

"I think he might have had."

Scott-Marle nodded, then rested a hand firmly on Gideon's shoulder; in the early days he would have indicated dismissal by saying, "That's all then," or something as brusque. Now he said:

"Don't spend too many hours at the desk."

"One more question," said Gideon.

"Yes?"

"I've assumed this A.C. matter is strictly between you and me for the time being—that no one else knows."

"Some may guess. I've told no one."

"Good," said Gideon. "Thanks."

When he stepped into the passage and the door closed behind him he stood for a moment, then began to walk slowly toward the lift. It was as if that heavy weight was growing heavier in his chest. Two of the staff passed him, neither more than an acquaintance; they seemed to stare.

"Commander."

"Good morning, Mr. Gideon."

Gideon said, "Morning." Then he drew a deep breath and moved along the passage with long strides and an almost aggressive manner as if going in to attack the whole world of crime. In the lift he felt in a kind of no man's land. Back in the C.I.D. building he squared his shoulders, half-grinned, and said to himself:

"I ought to be feeling on top of the world!"

Then he thought, I wonder what Kate will say.

Almost at once he realized that Kate probably wouldn't be at home, and she would in any case be so anxious about Prudence that it would be unkind to add another preoccupation. He wasn't quite sure that his reasoning was sound, but it took the edge off his exhilaration. This was a decision he would have to make for himself. He smiled suddenly at the thought of how Lemaitre would try to hound him into saying yes; Lem was the last man to be told at this stage.

In fact there was no one with whom he could really discuss it, except Kate.

He opened the door of his office.

Lemaitre was saying to a man sitting in the armchair in front of Gideon's desk:

". . . that's the lot so far, Mac. Not enough to bring *me* haring back from holiday."

"Man without a conscience, that's you," retorted the other man. Then he saw Gideon, and jumped up from the chair. "Good morning, Commander!" There was a Scottish accent in his voice, but the greeting was not quite "Guid mairning." He was Superintendent James MacPherson, who had been in Oban on his annual leave and whom Gideon had expected back the following Monday.

"Hello, Mac." Gideon shook hands. "Got tired of being in barbaric lands?"

"Man, there was work to be done here, so where else should a body be?" MacPherson's eyes were as blue as the calm water of a Scottish loch on a sunny day, his hair was the color of new corn, paled a little by gray. His skin had the freshness of a man who spent his life out of doors, and his features were clean-cut. He combined efficiency with thoroughness and an overearnest approach to his job with a bright manner which seemed to reflect unflagging good spirits.

Seeing him, knowing that the news of the discovery of the Rite-Time watches had brought him back, did Gideon a lot of good. Everything except the Rite-Time case faded from his mind; he was able to think about it as if it was the only case on the books.

"Where did you hear we'd found some of the watches?"

"I know Ian Roberts at Oban well, and he picked up a report from you about the smash-and-grab in Frisk Street. Och, the moment I heard those watches were on the market I couldn't do a thing but come back. It cost me a new swimsuit for my wife, mind, and a big farewell party with the family."

"Which you can't claim on your expenses," Lemaitre pointed out.

"Would I dream of claiming more than my fare to London?"

Gideon looked at the file still in his hands, containing many of his own interim reports.

"There were twenty thousand watches stolen in America. We've found no more than fifty of them," he said.

"Fifty-nine," corrected MacPherson. "George, when those watches didn't come on the market almost at once I knew there were two possibilities—either they hadn't come to England at all or else there was a big shipment being held somewhere until the distributors decided it was safe to start selling them retail. Possibly they would be worked on and disguised, but that would mean a very big job and a lot of skilled workmen, so I discounted it. With twenty thousand to dispose of, the odds against individual smuggling were pretty high too, that's why I settled for the big shipment which would be released in different parts of London, perhaps all over the country. Either would mean a wholesaler with a good number of retail outlets."

MacPherson paused, as if inviting commendation.

"I didn't read this in your report," Gideon said.

"I wouldn't put guesses in a report."

"Might be a good idea if you put that kind of guess in," Gideon said mildly. "So you think a big wholesaler is involved?"

"A wholesaler with many retail outlets," corrected Mac-Pherson, "or a factory which sells to several different wholesalers. We now know about Orlova, where Klein bought his, but they might be one of several distributors."

"What will you do now?"

"If you agree I'll get one or two retailers we can rely on to put out feelers—they can order half a dozen as a trial. If they're in three outlets already, it shouldn't be difficult," Mac-Pherson went on. "If Orlova's the only firm which can supply them, we'll have no trouble; if several wholesalers stock them, we'll have more work to do. We don't want to jump the gun."

"Being a bit canny this time, aren't you?" asked Lemaitre. "Why don't you go for 'em, bang, bang, bang?"

MacPherson hesitated, looking at Gideon.

"Any special reason?" Gideon inquired.

"I cannot say there is," answered MacPherson, "and I cannot say there isn't. It's more than a feeling in my bones, George. It has all the indications of a big racket—the number of watches, the apparent delay in selling them, the fact that New York thought it big enough to warn us about. It could be much more than this one consignment of watches, and if it is, we ought to know the size of it before we decide how to work. We certainly don't want to charge Orlova if they're only the little fish."

Gideon waved a hand.

"Go ahead, Mac. Let me know whom you're taking on the job with you. An inspector or a sergeant and a couple of officers should be enough. If there's anything worth talking about I'll be glad to see you any time. Let me have a note each morning."

MacPherson's eyes were bright with satisfaction.

"Pardon me," said Lemaitre when he had gone, "but don't be surprised if Mac starts taking a larger size in hats."

Before Gideon could comment his switchboard telephone rang, and one on Lemaitre's desk rang at the same instant. They plucked up the receivers as if they operated on the same reflexes, and Gideon felt a familiar flare of hope; that there might be good news of Nina Pallon.

"Gideon."

"This is Alec Hobbs," said the man who had seen Schumacher that morning. "I've done everything that can be done for the moment, I think."

His tone told Gideon that he had no news that could be called good.

14

A Voice of London Origin

Superintendent Alec Hobbs was that *rara avis* among the
C.I.D., a public school and university man—Repton and
King's, Cambridge—and one who seemed more fitted to the
Foreign Office or the Conservative benches in the House of
Commons than Scotland Yard. He was a detective because he
had always wanted to be one, and Gideon came more and
more to see him as a very good detective indeed. The difference in their backgrounds had created problems of commu-
nication at one time, but these were no longer important; that
was partly due to Kate Gideon and Hobbs's wife, Helen, who
had become firm friends. Helen Hobbs suffered from Landry's
paralysis, which kept her fast to a wheelchair, but lately she
had opened her home to a group of senior officers' wives for
meetings from time to time, such as that which Kate had at-
tended about Hong Kong.

There were three good reasons for putting Hobbs onto the
Henderson investigation. He had spent a year at an American
university and was a close student of American affairs, including police methods. He was socially Henderson's equal. And
because of his voice and rather ultra-British manner he was
likely to fool Schumacher into underestimating him.

One thing was certain; if he had had good news to report
he would have told Gideon at once.

"What did you make of Schumacher?" asked Gideon.

"I think he's lying somewhere along the line, but I can't
find anything to support it. He was undoubtedly at the Tate,
and also at the National Gallery. He was at the Royal
Academy and at the Victoria and Albert too. I took his photograph to each, and he was positively identified at them all."

"Wasn't the girl identified?"

"Not precisely," said Hobbs. "He had a girl with him. She
was in her late teens or early twenties, and she wore a black
sweater and a red skirt. But only the attendants at the Tate
were prepared to state that she was the girl of the photograph. The others all hedged, saying she might be or might

not be. And that might or might not be worth following up,"
Hobbs went on.

"I'm sure it is," said Gideon almost sharply.

"I've two officers working on it, trying to obtain more
specific descriptions of the girl who was with Schumacher,
and why the gallery officials hesitate to identify the girl of the
photograph. Have you anything in particular you want me to
do?"

"What do you want to do?"

"I would like to concentrate on Schumacher, and try to
find out what he was doing here on his last visit."

"What do you think is the best way to go about it?"

"I think I might be able to break Schumacher down,"
Hobbs said.

"By making it clear we suspect him?"

"Yes."

"Let's keep that shot in our locker," Gideon decided.
"What else?"

"I'd like to visit all the divisions you briefed about the kidnaping, in the hope of getting a line on the people Schumacher met when he was in London before, what hotel he
stayed at—"

"I'll settle for that," interrupted Gideon.

He rang off and stared at the window. Lemaitre was still
talking on the telephone. A shadow passed in front of the sun,
and it was as if one passed in front of Gideon's mind—a
shadow of doubt. First Scott-Marle, now Hobbs, implied
doubt about the wisdom of letting Schumacher think he was
getting away with it.

Gideon pulled the original photograph of Nina toward him
and studied it. Very gradually the image of her mother became superimposed, and somehow he was alive to the pulsating vitality of the kidnaped girl.

His internal telephone rang. It was Fingerprints, with a few
questions to ask about exhibits from last night's burglaries and
car thefts; the picture of a bright-eyed, vivacious girl slowly
faded from Gideon's mind.

Nina's eyes were still closed, but she could hear that
strange roaring sound more and more loudly. It frightened
her. Ever since consciousness had crept back into her, fear
had been in both her heart and her mind.

She did not see Facey, standing at the foot of the bed and
staring at her, and she did not hear him mutter:

"She's moved. She'll come round soon."

"When she comes round, give her some drink and a little food," ordered Schumacher. "We'll want her to talk to her mother soon."

Felisa Henderson stepped across the apartment to the long window which overlooked Hyde Park and so much of London. This was a city she had loved ever since her first visit, at about Nina's age. She could stand here and look down upon the late spring flowers, the lush spring grass, the fresh green of oak and ash and plane-tree leaves. From this height she could hear but not see the traffic in Park Lane and the new road just inside the park, but she could see the underpass at Hyde Park Corner. Beyond that was another park and the unmistakable outline of Buckingham Palace; the brilliant colors of the flowers in the palace grounds were quite discernible. She could see the twin towers of Westminister Abbey and the severe red brick of the Roman Catholic cathedral; and she could see the tower of Big Ben and, stretched along the Thames' embankment, the outline of the Houses of Parliament.

In another direction was Knightsbridge, the little shops where the precious things of the world were hers for the liking, where there were tailors and couturiers, jewelers and shoemakers.

As nearly as anyone from another land could feel both love for and affinity with a city, she had for London.

Now she felt as if she hated every inch of the great sprawling metropolis.

She felt that she hated herself.

If only she could *do* something; if only she could change places with her daughter; if she could just see and comfort Nina she would feel better. This awful waiting and its attendant helplessness were unbearable. She who had everything she could want in the world had lost the one thing that mattered most.

It was as if Nina were already dead. Felisa could not stop herself from going over and over and over in her mind all the things she could have done for her child, and had left undone. She had been the one who had wished Schumacher onto Nina as an unwanted guardian so that she herself could spend a few more paltry hours selecting silks from the exotic East. If only she hadn't!

She heard a sound, turned, and saw the door open. Elliott came in. She knew from his expression that he had no news, but she had to ask:

"Have you heard anything more?"

"No," he said.

"Elliott," Felisa said, "I feel so absolutely *dreadful*."

"I know how you feel, my darling."

"No," she said. "You don't. You can't. No one can." She began to walk about the room.

"Felisa, you must come out for a while," Elliott said.

"You know I can't leave here until there's some news."

"You must," he insisted. "You can't stay caged up here." *Caged.* It was exactly right, summing up exactly what she felt. "We can walk through the park, and if there should be a message it can be brought to us. We can be watched so that they know exactly where we are."

"No," she refused.

"Felisa—"

"I must stay here!"

"Felisa," he said, "it is dreadful for us both and you are making it even worse."

Her eyes became huge, her whole face was twisted in hurt and in anger, but she didn't speak. Elliott moved slowly toward her, and as she glared he said quietly:

"There is nothing in the world I would not do to help you."

Choking, helpless, almost hopeless, she turned away.

Then the telephone bell rang; the bell of the outside line. The shock of the ringing jarred through her. She turned and stared at it, and stretched out her right hand. Henderson did not move to take the instrument, although he knew that the call was probably for him.

She lifted the receiver.

"Hello."

"Who is that?" It was a woman, an English woman.

"This is Felisa Henderson."

"Nina's mother?" the woman demanded.

Felisa caught her breath, and her color ebbed so dreadfully that Elliott strode across and put an arm about her waist. Hastily, she said:

"Yes. Do you—do you know anything about my daughter?"

"I know she's alive and well," the woman declared. "And she'll stay alive and well if you do *exactly* what you're told *exactly* when you're told to do it."

There was a fraction of a minute's silence; then the speaker rang off, and there was only the buzzing on the line. Slowly, as if the very movement brought physical pain, Felisa put down the receiver. Her husband stood very close but did not speak, until at last she said in a tiny voice:

"We must do it."

Elliott asked in a husky voice, "What must we do?"

"Whatever they say."

"What have they said? Who was it, hon?"

She told him with great precision, forming each word as if it were of decisive importance, and when she had finished, she added:

"It doesn't matter what the police want us to do; we must do what *they* want, now."

Gideon's switchboard telephone rang, and as he picked it up he heard the operator say:

"Now hold your horses."

"I tell you it's urgent!" That was a man.

"Who is that?" Gideon asked.

The man said, "Commander Gideon, sir, this is Detective Officer Melluish, speaking from the Bingham Hotel. Mrs. Henderson has just received a call, sir, on the direct line. I recorded it from the extension."

Gideon felt his chest tightening.

"Yes?"

"It was a woman, sir—I think a young woman. Almost certainly of London origin, sir. She said that Nina Pallon was alive and well, and would remain so if Mrs. Henderson did exactly what she was told."

"What was she told?"

"The caller rang off at that juncture, sir."

"I see," said Gideon. "Have you a messenger with you?"

"Yes, right here."

"Tell him to bring the tape straight to my office." A voice of London origin, Gideon was repeating to himself; a shrewd observation. He started to lower the receiver, heard the man speak again, and put the receiver back to his ear. "What was that?"

"I—er—I said I'm due for relief for an hour, sir. May I bring the tape personally?"

"All right. Get a move on." Gideon almost banged the receiver down, and lifted the internal one, dialed a number, and stared across at Lemaitre's empty desk. A man with a marked Oxford accent responded after a long time—Carpenter, another of the Yard's rare birds, whose most remarkable gift was his ear for voices and for languages. He was in fact a professor, and as such he was known to the Yard.

"Professor, this is George Gideon," Gideon said. "I've a tape due here in about half an hour. Will you come and listen to it here, and place the voice if you can?"

"With pleasure," the professor said. "In half an hour."

He rang off.

A great many things were happening at that very moment, all of acute interest to Gideon. Hobbs was in CD Division, talking to the Superintendent-in-Charge and going over the reports received from men on the beat and plainclothes men on whatever job they were doing. Among the reports was that from P.C. Hyde, who had heard of a girl's scream from the milk roundsman, though Hobbs had not yet reached that paragraph.

Barney Barnett was boasting to Quincy about his latest job but had not yet mentioned that he had heard of an American who was working with old Facey.

Kate Gideon, who had slipped out of Prudence's house ostensibly to do some shopping, was actually talking to Pru's doctor, whose manner was disturbingly grave.

Darkie Jackson, who was on the payroll as a "salesman" at the Orlova Watch Company, received word from a pimp in Soho that Superintendent MacPherson of the Yard was back; MacPherson was the Yard's specialist on stolen watches and cheap jewelry, and although the news might have no significance, Darkie felt it worthwhile telephoning his manager, a man with the unusual name of Orlick. Orlick shared an office in Aldgate with a man of mixed Spanish and English blood, named Cordova; the name Orlova was an obvious combination of the two surnames and as good as a trademark. In fact Orlova's registered trademark was made up of two intersecting circles— ⊙⊙ —which was familiar to many retail jewelers and fancy goods retailers. No one in the world knew that Orlick had one murder to his name, that of a youth who had threatened to disclose that Orlick dealt in stolen goods. And Orlick was the only man in the world who knew that Cordova had committed two murders, each a seaman who had tried to blackmail him about smuggling watches.

Each knew that his partner was ruthless.

By some odd freak of circumstance, the police had no idea of the nature and the cold-bloodedness of the partners, and Darkie Jackson had never been on the Yard's books either.

Orlick was a tall, willowy, fair-haired man who looked like a Swede and was in fact one quarter Norwegian. His pale eyes had a curiously set look, and close observers noticed that he blinked very little. Cordova was a fifth-generation Londoner, and yet his dark hair and eyes and his sallow skin left no one in doubt of his Southern European blood. People who heard his Cockney accent for the first time were startled, he seemed much more likely to speak in broken English.

On the morning of Darkie's report about MacPherson's return to duty, the partners sat as they always did, opposite each other at a large pedestal desk in a very small room. Whenever either pushed his chair back to get up the top of the chair bumped against the wall. This caused slight damage, only half-concealed and half-prevented by a strip of transparent plastic stuck to the wall behind each chair.

Orlick took Darkie's telephone call, listened, and mouthed "Darkie" so that Cordova knew who it was. After a while Orlick said:

"Call back in half an hour. I'll tell you what to do."

"What's on?" demanded Cordova as Orlick put down the receiver.

"More trouble," answered Orlick. He had an unemotional way of speaking, as if words came from a machine and not from his mind. "MacPherson is back at Scotland Yard. Already the police are asking for details of Rite-Time watches from the retailers. We released them too soon."

Cordova said thinly, "If this blows, it could blow us with it." After a few moments' deliberation, he went on, "Tell you what. We'll tell the retailers not to sell those watches yet. Say we've reason to think they've been smuggled. We bought them through Anglo-American Trading and they're out of business now." Little trading companies often went out of business when they had served their purpose for Orlick and Cordova. "We'll tell the cops we heard a rumor that Anglo-American got some goods past Customs, and we stopped trading in them right away. MacPherson can think what he likes, he can't prove nothing. You agree?"

"Yes. It could get by."

"Let it soak, then we'll tell Darkie what to do," said Cordova.

About that time Superintendent Parsons of the Yard was sitting in one of the cafes in the *galleria* which led to Cathedral Square in Milan. He was alone. He could not see the cathedral, but could see tourists by the dozen taking photographs, and other tourists feeding the huge flocks of pigeons.

Out on the square it was very, very hot.

In the shade of the *galleria* it was hot enough, but by sitting still and sipping an ice-cold lager, Parsons achieved at least an illusion of coolness. Yet he was not there to get cool. He was there because Percival White had flown into Milan only that morning and was now sitting farther along the cafe—fifty feet away from Parsons, and two or three rows nearer the front. So far White had met no one. He had booked in at a hotel near the zoo, and had come there by taxi. Parsons doubted whether White had seen him yet. A handsome young sergeant in the Guardie di Pubblica Sicurezza was at another cafe, opposite. The Milan police were cooperating fully.

White was youthful-looking, with close-cropped gray hair. He was dressed in an Italian-cut suit and could have passed for an Italian. He was sipping Cinzano and glancing right and left. An endless stream of well-turned-out Italians walked briskly by, many tourists looking hot and tired sauntered in and made for the nearest empty table.

Suddenly White stiffened, and stared toward the entrance from the square. Parsons, looking in the same direction, saw Giovanni Mancelli, who had represented Lucci in London.

Mancelli scanned the serried rows of cafe patrons, saw White, moved toward him, and then stopped in his tracks and looked round. He stared straight at Parsons with a scared look in his eyes. Obviously he had noticed Parsons while looking for White, and suddenly realized who he was. He paused only for a moment but it was long enough to make White look toward Parsons too. Recognition was instantaneous.

Parsons had no doubt about one thing. These two men had met there because they had not wanted to be seen at Lucci's offices. Each was badly shaken by the presence of Parsons, who gave a satisfied smile and ordered another lager. As he did so he phrased a sentence or two for a postcard report to Gideon at the Yard.

One other thing was happening about that time, almost the only thing which would have jolted Gideon (if he'd known about it) out of his concentration on the Pallon kidnaping.

In a sunlit glade, in Windsor Great Park, Frank Mayhew lay at Florence Foster's side, one hand upon her breast.

15

The Virgin

"This is wonderful, just wonderful," Mayhew said. There was a quiver in his voice, and although Florence did not notice it then, his accent had become American, not Australian. Even had she known it she would not have thought twice about it then, for she was ashamed of herself.

It was not shame because of the caressing of his hand; it was shame because she almost hated these caresses and held her body stiff with nervous tension. It was as if the years had rolled away and she was filled with a sense of physical revulsion, as she had been so long ago. It was silly. It was absurd. *It was hateful!* She couldn't be normal. She liked him. Only that morning she had told herself that it would be easy to fall in love with him. In the hotel, on buses, walking in the streets, in the theater she loved being with him, but today he had hired a car, a little Mini-Minor. Sitting side by side in it they were very close. True, they had been as close before and she had felt a real thrill, but in the car they seemed to be so much alone. The people in the streets and in the other cars were not really nearby, this was a little world cut off from the rest.

So her edginess had begun.

In the crowded streets of Royal Windsor, fascinated by the crests over so many shops saying *By Appointment to Her Majesty the Queen,* she had been happy. Walking up the sweeping hill toward the castle, which stood so gray and strong and solid as if it were holding back the centuries, she had asked for nothing more. In the silence of St. George's Chapel, which seemed hallowed—in fact everywhere there were people all was well.

Now they were here.

The car was nearby, half-hidden from the road which swept across the park, the park of old trees and grazing sheep, and gentle-looking deer.

Of course she must let him hold her.

Of course she must let him kiss her.

Of course she must expect him to fondle and caress her. He

was a man, she was a woman. She knew exactly what she was doing, this was what she had expected, what she had almost hoped for.

Wasn't it?

She couldn't be a virgin all her life. There was no shame in this, only shame in the feeling of revulsion. She had to lie still, she had to let him do whatever he wanted. It was natural, didn't she understand? And he was a man she could respect, a good man, a man who would never betray her. This was 1965, she was a modern young woman in her twenties with no one to answer to for her actions.

He was pressing more firmly. He was pressing his body against hers. He was fumbling—

"No!" she gasped. "No, no! I can't!"

She began to struggle in a frenzy, and she did not know that she had astounded him because she was frightened so soon. Surprised, he let her thrust him aside and scramble to her knees. She was getting away, the little bitch was actually getting away! He snatched at her. He caught her arms. He flung her down.

It seemed to her in the last moments of her life that she was looking into the face of a devil.

He covered her body with bracken and leaves.

He did not go back to the hotel, for he was growing more cunning now and preparing in advance for the ecstasy he knew so well how to find.

There was no one at the Rosemount Hotel to care that night; in fact there was no one around at all to care that Florence Foster lay so still under the stars.

"You want to know sumpun?" demanded Barney Barnett in a voice he honestly believed sounded American. "I'm disappointed in you, Quincy buddy. I'm right disappointed."

"Is that so?" Quincy was sitting in the saloon bar of a public house in Fulham, only a mile as the crow flies from the arches at Hammersmith, where Nina lay. "What's my weakness?"

"You've gone soft."

"You mean I've gone straight," retorted Quincy.

"Same thing," sniffed Barney. "The job's a cinch."

"Not for me it isn't."

"Listen, Quincy, I tell you I know what I'm about. I've pulled off thirty-one jobs in the past four years and not been nabbed once. How about that for a record?" Barney demanded proudly.

"*Now* I know who's slipping," said Quincy Lee.

"You calling me a liar?"

"Wouldn't dream of it," said Quincy comfortably. "Maggie's a smart girl."

"Who said anything about Maggie?" Barney demanded truculently.

"I did."

"Forget her," said Barney, in a lordly way. "She's okay for the penny number jobs, but for the big stuff you come to me. I've got it worked out so as to fool any bloody copper *and* Maggie. I've always wanted to pull off one big job and retire —just like you did. I'm not getting any younger, Quincy. Can't go on forever."

"What, not even *you?*"

"Stop your kidding," urged Barney. "I know the place, I know the time, I could lift a hundred thousand quid—close on three hundred grand, Quincy. It couldn't fail."

"Then what's stopping you?" inquired Quincy Lee.

"Only one thing, I swear it."

"What thing?"

"Selling the ice when I've got it. The fences in London are a lot of bloody crooks, that's what they are. Thieving lot've baskets. Now, if I did the job just before you sailed for the great Yewnited States you could sell the stuff on your side. A few months later I'd come over and you could pay me my half. A fifty-fifty deal, that's what I'm offering."

"And would you trust me for real?"

"With my life, Quincy. With my fortune!"

Quincy said almost unbelievingly, "I believe you would."

Barney's eyes glowed.

"So it's a deal!"

"No," said Quincy Lee, almost regretfully. "It's not a deal. I'm not going back to the game, and that's my last word. But I thank you, Barney, I really appreciate it. Let me buy you a drink."

"Slipping, that's what you are," Barney complained bitterly. "I never thought going to America would make you soft. *Some* Yanks are tough, I can tell you that. That reminds me. Remember old Facey? The artist cove. Well, he—"

"Well, bless me heart if it ain't old Quincy back from the dead!" a woman boomed across the little room.

It was Maggie.

She wore a flowered hat and a flowered dress, and her eyes were shiny bright. She skipped across the saloon to their table, and kissed Quincy on the cheek; in fact she kept on kissing him, and between each kiss she uttered a word or two.

"Don't you"—kiss—"let my Barney"—kiss—"talk you into"—kiss—"anything"—kiss. "If you do"—kiss—"you'll have me"—kiss—"to answer to."

"Cut it out, Maggie," Barney protested. "You're putting me in a very embarrassing position."

Maggie gave Quincy an affectionate push and turned her attention to Barney. She did not kiss him but gazed as if enraptured into his eyes, and as she did so she whispered:

"If you walk out on me again I'll grass and don't you forget it. When I say I want to see an old pal I want to see an old pal. You wait until I get you home."

She made her husband both angry and nervous, and he completely forgot about old Facey and the Yank. Had he remembered, Quincy Lee might have passed word to Lemaitre.

"What did the poor anxious mother say?" Schumacher was in the back of the shop in Gulliver Street when Lucy Green rang off after talking to Felisa Henderson. The room was gloomy, but the brightness of Schumacher's eyes showed like luminous rocks beneath ultraviolet light.

"She sounded as if she was a long way away," Lucy retorted. "And—" she broke off, groping for the words to explain what she meant. Schumacher did not try to hurry her, and at last she went on: "She sounded as if it hurt her to talk."

Schumacher smiled slowly, and with deep satisfaction.

"That's what we want," he said as if he were speaking to himself. "She's softening up. I want you to deliver a little note to the lady, Lucy. She'd better have that tonight, and she can sleep on her troubles. By morning she should be ready to crack."

Lucy said shrilly, "I'm not going to deliver any note!"

"You are, honey." Schumacher gave her a little squeeze. "You're so deep in this you'll never get out unless I pull you out, so you do what I tell you." His voice was gentle and he was smiling, but she sensed that he was not smiling about her. "Don't forget you'll get ten thousand pounds when it's over— that's a lot of money to spend even in America. And you want to come to America, don't you?"

It was her dream.

"Of course I do, but I didn't expect you'd have to use violence on the girl."

"If you stay in the business, one of the important things you'll have to learn is that you can't handle a job of this kind

with kid gloves. When you make up your mind to do it you
do it. Now this is what *you* have to do . . ."

A little after seven o'clock that evening Lucy Green
stepped out of the elevator at the seventh floor of the Bingham Hotel and walked toward the Hendersons' suite. She carried a beautiful bouquet of tulips and daffodils. There were
two doors leading into the suite, the first for general use, the
second leading straight to Felisa's room. Lucy tapped at the
first door, and Elliott Henderson soon opened it.

"Good evening, sir," Lucy said. "These are for Mrs. Henderson."

Henderson said, "Oh." He reached out for them. "Do you
know who they're from?"

"With the compliments of Beryl's, sir."

Henderson did not find anything remotely surprising in
Beryl's sending flowers, for Felisa had spent much of the previous afternoon with the court dressmakers. He had hardly
taken the flowers before the girl turned and hurried off, but
he did not give her haste a second thought. He fingered the
small envelope with a coronet and the name "Beryl's" beneath
it, and a printed *Mrs. Elliott Henderson*. As he turned, Felisa
came from her room.

"Who was— Oh, flowers."

"Beautiful, aren't they?"

"Who would send me flowers at a time like this?"

"Who knows that it is a time like this?" asked Henderson
gently. "They're from Beryl's. Where shall I put them?"

"I'll take them," said Felisa.

Both of them thought the same thing: that arranging the
flowers in a vase would give her something to do. Henderson
watched her as she went out, but he did not follow her. She
put the wicker basket on a table, and unpinned the envelope,
taking out the card without thinking.

A few strands of jet-black hair lay in the folded paper inside the envelope, and on the paper was a simple message:

*If you want to see Nina alive again make sure your hus-
band does exactly what he's told.*

Felisa stood staring down at the card and the hairs, so
black and shiny like Nina's. Of course they *were* Nina's. She
did not speak or move, and it seemed a long time before
there was any sound.

Then Elliott came in.

The moment he saw her he knew that there was some new

crisis. He stepped to her side and read the message that trembled in her fingers. When he looked up, she was staring at him. He had never before seen her as a stranger.

"Elliott—if you don't do what this man says, I shall leave you."

He did not speak.

"I mean it," Felisa said. "I shall leave you." When he still did not answer her voice rose. "Must you stand there like a dummy? Didn't you understand what I said?"

"Yes," Elliott answered. "I understand fully, Felisa." He was thinking that he had hardly noticed the girl who had brought the bouquet, and that most of the time her face had been hidden by the flowers. But he had seen her walking away and he had noticed how tiny her waist was, and the shape of her legs, which were almost too thin. He was thinking another thing too—in its way as agonizing as any. He had soon to make a choice between doing what Felisa wanted and working with the police. It was not as simple a decision as it might appear. If he worked with Gideon, and he believed he should, and if Gideon failed to find Nina alive, then Felisa might in fact leave him. He had no illusions about that. In any case it would come between them in a marriage which had been as nearly idyllic as one could be. He was as much in love with her today as when they had married, but he had always known that she worshiped Nina, that Nina was vital to her happiness.

"You *must* do what you are told to," she insisted.

"Felisa—"

"There is no point in arguing."

"Felisa, we have the greatest police force in the world working for us."

"You heard that man Gideon say that only two victims out of five had been rescued."

"Because the relatives of those who died didn't trust the police."

"He didn't say that. You know as well as I do that the police don't often find the victims of kidnaping." No matter how he hated to admit it, that was true. From the tragedy of Lindbergh to this day there was a ruthlessness about kidnapers; there had to be in any human being who could take a child from its parents.

"Yes, I know that," Elliott told her. To lie, to hedge, to prevaricate, all these things were pointless with her; she had the kind of penetrating honesty which could cut through to the heart of any matter.

"Elliott, you must do what they ask."

He nodded very slowly. He had not yet made his decision but to argue and to refuse just now would be the ultimate cruelty. He would have to make his decision on his own, and if he decided to go along with Gideon and Scotland Yard, and if Gideon failed, then ahead of him lay years of desolation.

If he could be sure that by paying whatever ransom was demanded he could save Nina he would not hesitate. But there was no way of being sure. So he had to do what he had done throughout his life: make a decision based solely on his own judgment.

It hurt him to see the sheen of tears in Felisa's eyes.

"Now do one thing for me, honey," he said. "Let me walk you through the park."

She nodded, without speaking.

Hyde Park was filled with lovers, and they were as lovers too, so there was comfort for them. Elliott did not stay out long enough to agitate her, and when they reached the suite again she was much more relaxed.

"Do you think you'll rest if you go to bed?" Elliott asked.

"I think so, darling. Will you fix me some hot milk?"

"Surely," he said. They carried a small electric kettle and saucepan, and there was a refrigerator in the room. He "fixed" the milk with a tablet of sonoril, which was tasteless but should ensure her rest.

It was a little after nine o'clock when she fell asleep.

It was a little after nine o'clock when Nina woke to full consciousness and fear. That was when she discovered that she was bound hand and foot to the bed and was alone in darkness.

Panic was so raw in her that she could not think, she could only struggle, and struggling hurt her wrists and ankles. She shouted, but the walls seemed to throw her cries back at her.

Soon she lay in terror, sobbing.

Her mother lay in stupor, sleeping.

16

Demand with Flowers

There had been no message from Kate, so when Gideon reached home just after seven-thirty on a glowing evening, on the street where every tiny garden had its blaze of flowers and every newly painted door and window was bathed in sunshine, he expected to hear her call out. She did not. The house had the empty feeling he so disliked, but it affected him less by day. As he set about getting cold ham, cheese and pickles, butter and crusty bread he reminded himself that the last 93 bus from Epsom did not reach Putney Bridge Station until midnight, so Kate might not be in for hours. Perhaps it was as well. Here in this familiar house, every worn and shabby ornament or piece of furniture with its own association, he could think more about his own problem, and the Yard's cases receded to the back of his mind.

He wasn't exactly a wealthy man. Any knowledgeable people who visited him here would know that. But the house was his, bought on a mortgage spread over twenty-one years, and paid off seven years ago. They had inherited no money and little furniture, but over the years they had bought a few good pieces, including a Queen Anne court cupboard in the dining room and three Louis Quinze chairs in the front room, and nearly everything had quality. Bringing up a family of six children, seeing them through training for their different jobs, was an expensive business, and both he and Kate had always been thrifty—too thrifty, he sometimes thought—because they wanted to make sure of a comfortable old age. He would get a good pension, of course, but compared with a man like Henderson he thought in pennies against hundreds of pounds.

If he took the assistant commissionership he would get 2,000 pounds a year more than he was now getting, he wouldn't need to retire until he was sixty-five, and his pension would be correspondingly larger. He had given his life, everything he had, to his job, and this was the highest reward. Would anybody but a fool reject it?

Why was he so doubtful? Why had he been almost depressed instead of elated when Scott-Marle had offered him the job? Was it because of his anxiety for Nina Pallon? He wished he hadn't thought of Henderson in any connection, because it brought the American's stepdaughter's plight to the forefront of his mind again.

He cut off another piece of red Cheshire cheese and popped it into his mouth off the knife. Kate would have either protested or stared long-sufferingly seeing him do it. Kate. Was it fair to hesitate when the extra money would mean so much more to her? It could make a lot of difference to the children too; their marriage did not lessen the parental desire to help.

Children. Their youngest daughter was about Nina Pallon's age. Poor kid. What the hell *was* the right thing to do? A whole day had passed without any kind of clue.

The telephone bell rang. He stood up at once, still eating, swallowed the last of the cheese, lifted the receiver, and said:

"Gideon."

"George," said Kate. "I thought you mightn't be home yet."

"Home, had supper, just about to read the paper," he said with forced heartiness; over the telephone it would sound natural. "How's Pru?"

Kate didn't answer. Quite suddenly alarm coursed through Gideon.

"Kate, are you there?"

"Yes, dear," Kate said. "Peter was passing, so I didn't want to sound too worried." Her voice fell to a lower key. "Pru really isn't well, George."

"Is it serious?"

"It could be." Kate wasn't giving him a straight answer. That might be because she couldn't or because she hardly knew what to say over the telephone. "If she rests completely for the next two weeks she should be able to have the baby all right. If she doesn't—"

"My God." Gideon was really shocked. "Is it as bad as that?"

"George," Kate said simply, "I'll have to stay."

"Of course you will. Stay just as long as you have to. I'll be all right here—Rogerson's not coming back for a while." He brought those last three words out without hesitation. "So I'll be standing in for him. I can bring most of the desk work home, I'd be no company for you."

Very softly Kate replied, "Bless you, darling."

"Don't you go overdoing things, now."

"No, I won't," Kate assured him. "Good night, dear."

"Good night," Gideon said gruffly. "Love to the kids." He rang off, and stood beside the telephone with an expression which few at the Yard would have recognized. It had been a long time since any of the family had been seriously ill, and it carried his thoughts back to the illness and death of their seventh child. Their marriage had almost broken on that rock because he had left Kate with the sick child and gone out on a case. Gradually his thoughts changed. "Quicker Pru sees a specialist the better," he said aloud.

He felt that he should have asked who had been consulted; suddenly there were a dozen questions he wanted to ask Kate.

A car drew up outside. He saw its dipped headlights through the panels of stained glass in the front door and heard it come slowly to a standstill. It seemed a big one. He expected to find it was a squad car from the Yard, but if it was, why hadn't someone telephoned to warn him? One set of footsteps approached, and before the caller knocked, Gideon had switched the porch light on, and was opening the door.

Elliott Henderson stood there.

"Forgive this intrusion," he said in his precise way. "I will be very grateful if you will spare me a few minutes."

It was one of those occasions when Gideon's natural ability to close his mind to all but the immediate problem was invaluable. It was not easy to shut out the thought of Prudence, but he did.

"I can give you as long as you like," he assured Henderson. "I'm alone, and you're not interrupting anything." There was not even the sound of radio or television. Gideon turned into the front room, partly Victorian parlor, partly drawing room, switched on lights, and drew the curtains. Most people here for the first time would have looked about them, if only covertly. Henderson appeared not to. "Have you heard from them?" Gideon inquired.

"My wife has." Henderson held out the envelope with the note inside. "She is now sleeping under sedation and will not come out of it for several hours." He watched as Gideon opened the envelope gingerly, and shook the card out; he picked this up by the edges. "I'm afraid both my wife and I handled that."

"Be hard not to," said Gideon. "Excuse me." He went out of the room and picked up the telephone, dialed the Yard, and asked for Superintendent Scott. "Gideon here, Leslie. Have a fingerprint man sent out to my place at once, to do a job here."

"Don't tell me you've been burgled!" the night superintendent joked.

"Do you know if Hobbs is still out?"

"So it's not funny," Scott remarked. "Sorry, George. Yes—
he called in from Kensington and asked if you'd left any message for him. I gave him the message about the tape recording with the professor's opinion that the girl who telephoned
is a Londoner from one of the southwest districts. Hobbs
asked for more tapes to be run off by morning. I'm arranging
that now."

"See if you can find Hobbs, and ask him to call me here,
will you? Henderson has had a written warning."

"Oh, hell," breathed Scott.

Gideon went back into the front room. Henderson was
near the door, standing erect as a soldier on parade.

"They're working on the tape recording of the woman who
phoned your wife, placing the voice."

"You've placed her environment?"

"We think we know that she's a native Londoner from a
southwestern district. That doesn't take us far," warned Gideon, "but if we pick up one or two other facts we might be
able to relate them. For instance, there seems a modicum of
doubt about whether Schumacher was with your daughter all
day. It's possible that another girl was with him in the afternoon, thus confusing us as to the time and place of the kidnaping. These aren't facts, are not even definite probabilities,
but they are distinct possibilities." Gideon's manner was almost didactic.

"Answer me one question," Henderson said.

"If I can."

"If Nina was your daughter, would you be reasonably confident of finding her? Have these fresh possibilities greatly increased the chances?"

Gideon answered bluntly. "Not greatly. A little, I think."

"I know you cannot be influenced by other people's
emotional problems," said Henderson, "but I must be. My
wife is emotionally disturbed, almost to a point of unbalance.
She wants to do a deal with Schumacher, or whoever the kidnapers are. I have promised her that I will. I now have to
make up my mind whether to deceive her or not. The conse-
quences of deception if you failed would be very grave indeed
for both me and my wife." Henderson smiled faintly, and
Gideon waited, admiration and bewilderment mingling in his
mind. He could not imagine any Englishman talking with such
frankness, but he could well believe that it was the only way

Henderson could clear his mind. In a way, Henderson's position was rather like his: he could not talk to Kate. Henderson could not talk rationally to his wife, yet each man had to make a decision which would affect his whole future. "I am not asking you to help me decide," Henderson continued. "I simply want to know what you would do in the circumstances, knowing all the facts. I cannot have your knowledge of Scotland Yard."

Gideon thought, I can't lie to him. Almost painfully he thought, If I could buy Prudence's life I'd pay every penny I've got—and he can pay a million dollars without turning a hair. Next he thought, At least I don't believe they'll ever let Nina go free unless we find them and force them to.

Henderson was clasping his hands and pressing them tightly together.

Gideon said: "I would deal direct with the kidnapers and keep the Yard informed step by step, exactly as I advised before. Something they do or say, or some instruction they give, might be the lead we want. Once we know where Nina is, we should be able to save her. There's one thing it's easy to forget."

"What's that?"

"The kidnapers also are laboring under great emotional stresses and strains. Success is vital to them. They are affected as much by the chance of making a fortune as you are of getting back a daughter. If it comes to the point where we have to admit we can't help, by keeping us informed you won't have weakened your own chances of buying Nina's freedom."

"There's a thing easy for you to forget," countered Henderson. "If I keep you informed, if I reach the point of an exchange of money for Nina, and if you act on information I've given you and Nina dies as a consequence, my wife will know what I did."

"Yes," agreed Gideon.

"But as a police officer you would have to act, wouldn't you?"

"Yes."

"Thank you," Henderson said. "I must try to sleep on it." He turned to the door, and Gideon hurried after him, realized belatedly that he hadn't offered a drink, decided this was not the moment, and reached the front door in time to open it. "Good night," Henderson said.

"Good night, sir."

A chauffeur was standing beside the car, a Rolls-Royce. Henderson climbed in, and did not once look back. The car moved off slowly and Gideon stood there, not knowing whether he had done the right thing. He could have temporized. He could have lied. He could have said that he would consult with his superiors in the morning. That last question had been the decisive one: Henderson might sleep on his decision but it was one he had already made.

The telephone bell rang. Gideon closed the door, walked heavily to the table and the instrument, feeling very tired.

"Gideon."

"George, I think we may have made some progress in the Nina Pallon case," Alec Hobbs said.

Gideon's heart leapt as it had not leapt in years. Hobbs was too careful to raise false hopes, too levelheaded to show his satisfaction without good cause. Gideon had a wild thought, of rushing after the Rolls-Royce. He checked it.

"Good. Let me have it."

"*First* things first. The girl with Schumacher yesterday afternoon was not Nina Pallon. I have now talked to seven people who saw them together. This girl was about the same build, but with much larger breasts. The Pallon girl has a boyish figure."

"Go on," said Gideon.

"*Second*, a milk roundsman in Gulliver Street, Chelsea, thought he heard a scream coming from an art shop yesterday morning, about the time Schumacher and Nina left the Tate. He told a divisional uniformed man, who put it in his report. I have been very busy following that up—we found the milkman and an elderly man through that copper.

"*Third*, I have talked to the elderly man who also thought he heard the scream, which was uttered a few minutes after they saw a man and a girl enter the shop. The old fellow and the milkman had a word or two about it, and decided it was a woman who'd been calling out to attract the milkman's attention. And they both describe a man who was going into the shop just about then, and they think there was a girl just ahead of him and he measures up reasonably well to the description we have of Schumacher—gray-haired, benevolent-looking.

"*Fourth*, one of the constables on traffic duty outside the Tate saw Schumacher and Nina leaving there on foot and walking toward Chelsea, twenty minutes before the man and girl entered the shop.

"*Fifth*, that art shop is now covered back and front."

"I'll be in Gulliver Street in fifteen minutes," Gideon said. "Wait for me."

Gulliver Street was well lit, but there were many dark doorways, many alleys leading off, many cars behind which the police could hide. Gideon pulled in near a car in which two men were sitting, and as he got out one of the men left the car and came to him.

"Mr. Hobbs is in a shop across the road from the art shop, sir."

"Thanks."

"Shall I take you round the back way?"

"Yes."

Three minutes later he was with Hobbs in a small tobacconist's shop, the owner of which was an ex-policeman. Two other plainclothes men were there.

Gideon always had a curious sense of surprise when he saw Hobbs for the first time for several days. Hobbs was a compact man whose close-fitting clothes detracted from his height, and he was only five feet eight, six inches shorter than Gideon and inches shorter than most C.I.D. officers. There was about him a kind of controlled elegance; sometimes he spoke and behaved as if he had a distaste for his job, but nothing could have been further from the truth. He had an unmistakable air of command and control, and within earshot of other ranks, as now, his formality seemed proper for him.

"Glad to see you, Commander."

"Hallo," said Gideon. Then: "Any movement across the road?"

"Not a sign of movement yet."

The art shop was in darkness, like the flat above it; it was halfway between two street lamps, so that the doorway was full of shadows.

"What's it like at the back?" asked Gideon.

"There is an approach from a service alley. Four men are within fifty yards of it. And the man seen there this morning was undoubtedly Schumacher, almost certainly with the Pallon girl. I've talked to the milkman too. His description fits too closely for there to be much doubt."

"Right," said Gideon. "I'm going over."

"I think you should let me go," said Hobbs.

"Not this time." If that girl were there, if anyone else tried to rescue her and failed, it would be forever on Gideon's mind that *he* might have succeeded. He had to do this himself. "Cover me, Alec. Send men round to the back to tell the men there to move in five minutes from now, precisely. Watches checked?"

"Yes," said Hobbs. He had lodged his protest, and now accepted the inevitable. He gave orders to a man who glanced at his wristwatch and hurried off.

Only Hobbs was within earshot.

"George," he said, "the time is coming when you must stop taking so much on yourself. Only you would blame yourself if anything went wrong here tonight."

After a pause, Gideon said, "Have you met the Hendersons?"

"I met Henderson this afternoon."

Gideon surprised himself by saying, "You must meet his wife." He was staring down at Hobbs, seeing the grim smile playing at his lips. Hobbs hadn't meant: "Stop stealing my thunder." He had recognized the compulsion that worked in Gideon, and also the causes behind the compulsion.

He felt a curious kind of affinity with this man, and the vividness of the feeling astonished him. He wondered what Hobbs would say, and almost chuckled when Hobbs used the kind of retort most likely to come from Lemaitre.

"Well, don't box it up, will you?"

"Not if I can help it." There was still a minute to go. "Kate thinks Hong Kong is quite a place."

"So does Helen. Those group meetings are exactly what she needs." Hobbs spoke with quiet emphasis.

"Yes." Gideon's thoughts had flashed to Kate and Prudence and their anxiety, and suddenly he frowned. Hobbs was bound to wonder what caused the frown, so he went on gruffly, "Good thing it wasn't tonight. Kate's over at Epsom, some kind of scare over our first grandchild-to-be."

Hobbs said almost angrily, "Why do we have to live with that kind of anxiety?"

"God knows," grunted Gideon. After a pause, he went on, "Time I was moving."

He left the shop and walked fifty yards up the street before crossing the road. As he walked, he was aware of a metamorphosis which he had known occasionally in the past. Depression and anxiety lifted. He felt the kind of excitement which he had known when he had first seen action and, in these later years, when he had played an active part in a big case. Here was his chance to act, not simply to think and to direct.

It passed swiftly through his mind that as assistant commissioner he could never play a part like this.

Then he reached the doorway of the art shop.

17

Early in the Morning

The shop was still in darkness and no sound came from inside. Gideon stood at the front door, a hand in front of him, until precisely one minute before the men from the back would move in. Then he turned the handle, pushed stolidly but without force, and felt bolts resisting top and bottom. He drew back two feet, then thudded his great weight against the door, shoulder foremost—two hundred and fifty pounds of tough bone and muscle. There was a sharp, explosive crack above his head. He drew back and hurled himself forward for a second time. The door gave way at both bolts. A shove, and he was through.

He flashed his light round, seeing grotesque figures of all shapes and sizes round the walls, paintings framed and unframed. In a far corner was another door, open. He strode toward it, and snapped on several light switches. The shop, the back room and a narrow staircase were all lit up.

He heard no sound but that of his own making.

Even then, before he had started to search, he felt the first pang of disappointment. Anyone here must have heard the noise and would be moving in alarm—or *lying still in fear?*

Sounds came, from the yard.

The back door wasn't bolted, but was secured by a Yale lock. He spared time to snap it open and call, "Gideon here," then swung round and headed for the stairs. Each tread creaked. The boards were as bare as Gideon's hopes. It was like shadow boxing.

There were three doorways leading off the landing, but no light. Each door was open. Gideon had a moment of dread that Nina might be here, already dead. He switched on lights to show dilapidated rooms lumbered with old canvases, old frames, a few new paintings ready to hang, and in the corner of one room an easel by a table smothered with wrinkled half-empty tubes of oil paint, a jar of brushes, all a painter's stock in trade. Most of the paintings were unpleasant, a few positively obscene.

There was no sign of Nina.

Apart from the artist's studio there was no sign of occupa-
tion except in what had once been a kitchen, downstairs. This
was now a washhouse-cum-boxroom-cum-rubbish dump. Here
were cracked cups and saucers, tea, coffee, condensed milk, a
tin of biscuits, a tin kettle, a brown earthenware teapot. Gideon felt almost sick with disappointment when Hobbs came
in.

"So they've flown."

"Yes," said Gideon. "Did you get a set of Nina Pallon's
fingerprints?"

"Yes."

"You can check for them, anyhow." Gideon made the best
of it. "Schumacher's too!" Hobbs had been just as thorough as
Gideon had expected.

He was contemplating Gideon very straightly, and gave a
curious impression: that he was growing in physical stature.
For a moment Gideon suspected that some comment had
been on the tip of his tongue, but he had kept it back.

It came out.

"You got away with this one. Why don't you call it a day
and get a night's sleep?"

Gideon felt only slightly annoyed, whereas another man
saying the same thing might have made him angry.

"We'll have a look round first," he said, and actually swiv-
eled his gaze as one of the men who had come in after Hobbs
bent down to pick something up. Gideon saw it glisten. The
man examined it, then turned to Gideon and Hobbs.

"What've you found?" Hobbs asked quietly.

"Looks like a used ampoule," the man said. He was young,
fair-haired, diffident. He raised the glistening thing closer to
his eyes. "That's right, sir. Morphine for injection, half a
grain."

Hobbs said with quiet satisfaction: "It looks as if they
doped her, Commander." He raised his voice. "Don't handle
that as if it were a beer bottle—there will be prints on it."

Fingerprint men from the division were already moving in.

Another man called, "Here's something else, sir."

Gideon had to force himself to allow Hobbs to go up the
stairs first. The caller was standing on the landing, holding a
pair of black sandal-type shoes. They looked tiny in his big
hands.

"They're marked Italia Shoes, New York, sir."

"Size?" demanded Hobbs.

"Three and a half C."

"Nina Pallon wears size three and a half," Hobbs stated flatly. There was a long pause before he went on: "Would you like me to tell Henderson?"

"I'd like you to work on this end, all night. If you have to, wake the whole neighborhood. We want the time they left, transport, descriptions—"

Hobbs was giving that amused smile of his. Gideon stopped in mid-flow, and gave a bark of a laugh.

"The lot," he said. "I'll see Henderson."

A few people were still sitting about the Bingham Hotel, including a Yard man, who did not show any sign of recognition, which told Gideon that Schumacher was in his room. Gideon went up to the seventh floor, unannounced, and tapped on the main door of the Henderson suite. Almost at once Henderson opened it.

He had a gift for covering his feelings.

"Come in." Only his eyes showed the light of hope and that soon faded. He glanced at the plastic bag in Gideon's hand, then back into Gideon's eyes. Bleak faced, he asked, "Have you bad news?"

"Not good, not bad," Gideon said. "Would you recognize Nina's shoes if you saw them?"

"Yes."

"Sure?" Gideon had expected some hesitation.

"Only yesterday morning I told her that I thought she was wearing the worst possible shoes for a day at galleries and museums," replied Henderson. "May I?" He took the bag, opened it, and took out the shoes; each now had smears of gray powder, to bring up prints.

Gideon could almost feel the other man's agony as he said, "Yes. They're Nina's."

"Then we've found the place where she was kidnaped," Gideon said. "We will know a lot more before the night's out. There were fingerprints, but none of Schumacher's, although we have plenty of witnesses that he was seen to go into the place with her."

Henderson hardly seemed to hear all this.

"Nina?" he asked. "Not good—not bad news."

"We think she was drugged," Gideon told him. "We found a half-grain ampoule which had contained morphine, and if she was given the whole dose it would keep her unconscious for at least twelve hours." To help ease Henderson's burden, he reasoned: "They would hardly put her out for so long if they intended to kill her, which is on the credit side. So is the fact that from the moment the drug took effect she would know nothing—no pain, no fear."

Surely that must help this man.

"What time was she kidnaped?" Henderson asked.

"About eleven o'clock this morning."

Henderson said very quietly, "If she was drugged then, she is just about able to feel both pain and fear again."

She felt no pain; a little discomfort, that was all, especially at her wrists and ankles, where she was bound.

But her fear was a hideous thing, because of the black darkness, the now less frequent roaring and the throbbing which never seemed to stop.

"I feel very bad because I cannot really feel grateful to you," Henderson said. "I will later. I realize that it's almost a miracle that you've found out so much already." He raised his hands, and gave a taut little smile. "I needn't ask, but I have to. You're keeping at this every minute, aren't you?"

"Every single minute," Gideon assured him. "And *I* needn't ask this but I have to: you won't make a deal without letting me know, will you?"

"You have my word on that."

"Thank you," said Gideon. Then he asked, "Shall I take the shoes?"

"Do you need them?"

"We will later, but not now."

"I think I ought to show them to my wife when she wakes," Henderson said.

Gideon went home to his empty house, and was not disturbed during the night. He expected to sleep badly, but in fact slept soundly. In a peculiar way he felt that this was partly due to Hobbs, who had handled himself, the investigation and his relationship with Gideon so well.

Superintendent Alec Hobbs did not even think of sleep.

It took an hour and a half to find out that the art shop was owned by a Sydney Jackman, who lived in a small house in Fulham, and owned a great deal of dilapidated property in Southwest London. He was a little man with straggly gray hair and a forlorn appearance, particularly when called out of bed in the early hours of the morning and taken by a police car to the Gulliver Street shop. By then twenty households within sight of the shop had been disturbed, but nothing useful had been discovered.

"It isn't my fault if the shop is misused by the tenants," Jackman complained. "They pay their rent, and if they behave themselves that is all I care about."

Hobbs said, "Come with me, Mr. Jackman." He took the owner for a quick tour of the premises, including the nastiest of the pictures. "You could be in trouble for allowing this kind of filth to be displayed to the public. You know that."

"But I didn't know they were here!"

"Some people might believe you," said Hobbs, as if skeptical. "Who is the present tenant?"

"A Mr. Smith!"

"Smith," echoed Hobbs. "How long has he been here?"

"He took it for a month. He said he had an American client coming to see some special paintings. He paid in advance, I hadn't got anything to complain about."

"You hadn't then," said Hobbs coldly. "You might have now. Who was he, Jackman?"

"I tell you his name was Smith. That's all I know."

"Had you ever seen him before?"

"No, never!"

Hobbs said harshly, "If you're lying, you will be in serious trouble. I'm not concerned about dirty paintings either. A girl was kidnaped and drugged here today. Anyone aiding and abetting the criminal would be an accessory. Do you want to think again?"

"I don't know anything," insisted Jackman hoarsely. "I swear I don't know. I can tell you what the man looked like, I'll do everything I can to help you, but I can't tell you things I don't know."

"I had a feeling he was telling the truth," Hobbs phoned to Gideon at seven o'clock next morning. "Leslie Scott has everything in hand. A dozen men are checking on artists. Did I tell you there was some yellow ocher oil paint, Reed and Ward's first quality, in two of the fingerprints on the ampoule?"

Gideon, sitting by the side of the bed, unshaved, pajamas rumpled, said, "No." His eyes brightened for the first time since Hobbs's call had waked him.

"There was. And one of the more obscene paintings had been touched up very recently with yellow ocher which was still wet—probably done yesterday morning. The prints aren't Schumacher's, so there was another man in that shop yesterday morning."

"Keep looking for an artist," Gideon said.

"It's all in hand. Sorry if I woke you," Hobbs went on. "I'll take a few hours off and be in about noon, if that's all right with you?"

"Come in when you're ready," Gideon agreed. "I'll see that everything ticks over."

"Thanks," said Hobbs, and the word stretched into a yawn. "Sorry."

Gideon put the receiver down and got moving. Had Kate been present she would have seen the man of twenty-five years ago, who simply could not wait to get on the job. He shaved and showered in ten minutes, made tea, dressed and drank the tea in five, and was in his car and heading for the Yard at twenty-five past seven. The night-duty men at the gates, the desks and Information seldom saw him before they left at eight o'clock, and all snapped to attention. All of them had the slightly dazed look of the tired; it was early in Gideon's morning but late in their afternoon.

"Didn't expect to see you," said the Information inspector. "It's been a hell of a night."

"Anything big?"

"Nothing to bring you in early, just the mixture as before."

Gideon asked, "Do you know whom Superintendent Hobbs has briefed?"

"All the names are on your desk."

"Thanks." Gideon went up to his office, and was half-exasperated to find Lemaitre not there already, although he wasn't due until nine o'clock. Gideon glanced through reports on his desk, including the names of the dozen detectives who were checking the movements of artists. There was a description of the man sometimes seen at the shop, Jackman's "Smith." He drew up an instruction sheet to be sent to all London divisions by teletype; this would reach the divisions shortly after eight o'clock, and all the police in London would be on the lookout.

The description of the girl seen working at the shop wasn't good enough for general circulation yet, but there was no doubt that she must have been passed off as Nina by Schumacher. Before long he had to make up his mind what to do about Schumacher. He had enough on the man to charge him; but there was no way of being positive that if Schumacher were held it would lead to Nina. When the identity and perhaps the character of the artist were known, it would be easier to decide.

Gideon pulled himself up with a jerk.

"The truth is I'm scared of pulling Schumacher in," he said in muted tones. "Why should I be?"

Was it because Henderson and Henderson's wife were influencing him? Did he *want* to give the Hendersons a chance to pay the ransom, so that no one could say that by following proper police methods he had led to the girl's death?

That was another thing: why had he felt so sure that her life was in danger, even from the beginning?

Footsteps sounded in the passage and turned toward the door. Gideon expected a tap on it but instead the door was pushed open and an elderly man came in, whistling; he was one of the messengers. He was halfway toward the desk before he saw Gideon, and came to a standstill as if petrified.

"All right, what is it?" Gideon demanded.

"I—I didn't know you were here, sir."

"I should hope you didn't. What is it?"

"Teletype message just in from New York, sir, for your attention." The man, a near-retirement police constable, handed Gideon one of several papers from a folder. "Will that be all, sir?"

Gideon nodded dismissal, smoothed out the paper, and read:

Mayhew parent received p.c. today from Kensington stop Advise extreme caution with Schumacher in new circumstances stop Have just learned from Los Angeles police department he was once suspected of part in kidnaping of teen-age girl found murdered after ransom paid stop Telephone or teletype all possible information. Nielsen.

It was as if some evil genius was protecting Schumacher. If he, Gideon, had known about the suspicion of kidnaping, Schumacher's interest in the Hendersons would have screamed a warning. But were the California police any less culpable than he?

The truth was, he should have had Schumacher watched.

18

So Much at Once

If Rogerson were coming in, Gideon would have gone to his office and talked over the tactics with the Assistant Commissioner. He couldn't do that with Scott-Marle. With a sense almost of shock Gideon realized that until this moment he had not thought of the Commissioner's offer since before Hobbs's call last night. Here was the most important thing in his professional life, and he hadn't given it a thought!

To himself, he said, "So it can't really be that important."

That was a fleeting reflection, gone almost as soon as it came. The outside telephone rang. This must be about the artist—no one else was likely to know he was here.

"Gideon."

"What's the matter, George, can't tha' sleep?" It was Ormeroyd from the North, and he knew nothing about the kidnaping. Gideon switched his thoughts to the factory sabotage case, but it was not so easy as usual. "I rang to leave a message, and they told me you were in," went on the Yorkshireman. "I'm leaving Glasgow this morning. I'll be at Macclesfield this afternoon, God and the weather permitting. It's raining cats and dogs up here."

Gideon glanced at the window and saw that the sky was overcast.

"Just want to talk about the weather, Jake?"

"Touchy this morning, aren't you?" Ormeroyd scoffed. "George, the damage at the biscuit factory in Glasgow was the same kind as the damage at York—no doubt about it. And some of the damage was done the same night so it couldn't have been by the same person."

"Organized sabotage in small factories, is it?" Suddenly this was the only case in Gideon's thoughts. "What does it look like? Spite?"

"No," Ormeroyd said, so positively that Gideon knew he had something of importance to report.

"Then what?"

"In every case so far the damage has been done to machines which are busy with export orders," answered Ormeroyd; then, as if he really savored what he had to say next, he went on: "And most of the export goods go to the same country. Care to guess which?"

Gideon was in no mood to play guessing games, but half-a-minute would make no difference and would humor Ormeroyd.

"Russia?"

"No, it's not anti-Red. The reverse in fact."

Gideon exclaimed, "The United States?"

"Right on the nose, George. Someone wants to damage our export trade to the U.S.A. in their own small way. I thought you might have some ideas."

Gideon spoke almost without conscious thought.

"I'll send someone over to the Faculty of British Industries and have them check if any other manufacturers are having trouble with goods for America. That what you want?"

"Yes. Good old George."

"Telephone late this afternoon and we might have something for you," Gideon said. "If I'm not here, talk to Lem."

"Right-o," Ormeroyd said, and added with a chuckle in his voice, "What's the weather like in London?"

"Bright and sunny," said Gideon. "No Yorkshireman would recognize it." He rang off before Ormeroyd could answer back, savored the moment, then considered the best man to deal with the FBI. He thought of Hobbs, then rejected him as impossible while the Pallon case was on. Then he thought: FBI for Faculty of British Industries, FBI for the Federal Bureau of Investigation. He made notes:

1. *Best man for our FBI.*
2. *Advise their FBI (they to check imports from G.B.).*
3. *? Do (2) through Nielsen.*

As he finished he had another thought: that the job Ormeroyd was on could develop into one of the kind that developed only once in a decade. He must be very, very careful whom he chose for the job, take a man off another job if needs be. It must be someone who could work well with Ormeroyd and with whom Ormeroyd could work. Would Hobbs be right, even if he were free? Suddenly he thought: Ormeroyd himself ought to be in charge of it. That was a facer—

He picked up a red pencil, and marked *Self* on the notes he had just made, put them in the Pending tray, and brought his mind to bear on Schumacher again. He was not immediately aware of it, but the interruption from Ormeroyd had drawn something of the emotional tension out of his attitude toward the kidnaping. He should talk to Schumacher very soon, and in view of the warning from Nielsen, there might be a lot to be said for arresting the man this morning.

He heard footsteps outside. This time there was a timid tap at the door. On his "Come in" the messenger entered most circumspectly, carrying a letter basket piled high with mail and reports. This was the usual morning delivery, reports from divisions and reports and requests from the county and country borough police forces. Lemaitre usually sorted these out for him.

"Thanks. Put it there, will you?" He pointed, the messenger put the basket down, and hesitated. "Want something else?" he demanded.

"I—er—I just wondered if you would like some coffee, or tea, or anything, sir." The man was sixty or more, gray, nervous, anxious to make amends for a trifle, which doubtless loomed enormous in his mind.

"Not a bad idea. Coffee, cream, toast—fix it right away, will you?"

"Yes, sir!"

Gideon smiled at such eagerness in a man so old, and promptly thought, Old? I'm within six or seven years of him. He began to sort through the mass of letters and papers, looking for reports on Schumacher. He found two, close together. The Yard man on duty at the hotel until six o'clock that morning reported: *S. in his room since 11:15 p.m.* The hotel detective reported: *No calls to or from S. room since last report.* There was a third report near the bottom of the pile, which covered Schumacher's known movements between three o'clock on the afternoon of the kidnaping and midnight last night. Attached to this, which came from Information, was a negative report about the girl believed to have gone round to the art galleries with Schumacher.

"That artist's our best bet," he said aloud. Then he heard loud footsteps outside again, as if the messenger had found fresh confidence. In fact the door burst open, and Lemaitre stood gaping.

"Blimey!" he exclaimed. "Might as well kill a man as frighten him to death." He let the door bang behind him; then his eyes lit up. "Got anything on Nina Pallon?"

"Not enough," Gideon answered, and told him. He was just

finishing when the messenger came in, with everything Gideon had ordered plus three pork sausages under a dish cover.

"Thought these would keep hotter than bacon, sir."

"Good idea," Gideon approved. "Good thing you discovered I was in early." Relief showed in the man's eyes as he went out.

Lemaitre gathered up the papers.

"I'll sort these out while you eat that. Kate back?"

"No."

"Didn't think she was or you wouldn't be stuffing yourself. Want to see anyone who asks to see you this morning?"

"Yes." Gideon almost swallowed the word as he bit into a piece of toast, realizing that he was very hungry; he hadn't had a good meal since yesterday's breakfast.

As Gideon was eating, a middle-aged chambermaid at the Rosemount Hotel knocked on Florence Foster's door, and tried the handle awkwardly, for she balanced a tray of morning tea on her left hand. There was no response and the door didn't open. The chambermaid had been at the job for nearly thirty years, and memorizing the habits of guests was second nature to her.

"That's funny." She knocked again, then took her passkey from her apron pocket, unlocked the door, and called, "Coming, miss!" She stared at the bed, which was undisturbed, at two letters from Wiltshire which lay on the floor, at a room just as she herself had left it the previous morning. A nylon stocking which she had put back over a chair arm had slipped off again; that was the only difference. She took the tea away, and at a service pantry at a half-landing found the chambermaid from the floor below sitting down and sipping a cup of tea.

"It's a funny thing, but my Miss Foster's been out all night."

"Tell you another funny thing," said the other maid, half-leering, "but my Mr. Mason didn't come home either. How about putting one and one together, Daisy?"

"Not that girl," Daisy declared. "She isn't the kind."

"They're all the kind," declared the other chambermaid.

"Well, I'm going to report it," Daisy said.

Michael Dunn was getting his own breakfast. He felt almost guilty at feeling so hungry when Cynthia hardly ate at all. He was really worried this morning, because she had coughed so much during the night. Now she lay limp and pale, and he did not know whether she would have the strength to make the train journey to Bournemouth by herself. He had planned to drive her to Waterloo to catch the 10:30 train.

When he went in to see her her eyes were open.

"Hallo, Cyn darling," he said with forced cheerfulness. "Feeling a bit better now?"

She moistened her lips, and a weak voice came from the wasted body. "Mike—I'm afraid."

"Don't be a goose."

"I—I don't think I can get to Bournemouth."

"Of course you can! If necessary, I'll carry you there."

"Mike," Cynthia said, "I think you ought to send for the doctor. I've got such an awful pain in my chest."

Maria Lucci was drinking coffee and watching her son Antonio as he nibbled at a roll and butter. He had never been a hearty eater, and since his father's death he had touched hardly a thing. Maria had expected him to be upset, but not so upset as this. She did not know whether to be glad or sorry that the school vacation would soon be here. At school there were lessons and games and other boys to take his mind off his grief.

"Antonio, my son, you must finish quickly," she said. "You do not want to be late at school."

Quite out of the blue, he cried:

"I don't want to go to school! I hate school! All the boys hate me. They hate me! And they say beastly things about my father!"

It was as if a knife had plunged into his mother's body, and for a few moments she was silent, simply staring at the boy. Then, standing up with great dignity, she said:

"The things they say about your father are not true. I, your mother, promise you that. Even today I am going to see the police, who are finding out the truth. Say this to your friends, Antonio. They are wrong. You have good reason to be proud of your father."

She did not know whether that helped her son, but in a way it helped her. She had in fact an appointment to see Colonel Nocci, head of the Pubblica Sicurezza in Milan. Now she would fight even harder to make him try to clear the name of her son's father.

At eleven o'clock she was shown into Nocci's office, in a new building near the Fort. Nocci stood behind his square, shiny desk, looking a little like Il Duce in the far-off days, but it was the presence of the other man that most impressed her. He was the English detective, the man who had told her of Benito's death, and whom she had seen at the cemetery.

The lieutenant smiled at her gravely.

"Already you know Signor Parsons from London," he said. "Signor Parsons believes it possible that your husband did not commit suicide, signora."

"I am sure that he did not," declared Lucci's widow.

"Then we need your help, to try to prove that," said Nocci. "His partner from England is in Milan. We wish you to see him, and . . ."

Frank S. Mayhew alias Mason was eating breakfast and reading the *Daily Express* in the big cafeteria at Lyons Corner House at London's Marble Arch. He was enjoying bacon and eggs, buttered toast and coffee, and he was feeling quite pleased with himself because there was no report of the finding of Florrie's body.

"They probably won't find it for weeks," he reassured himself.

He glanced up at the railed-off passageway that led to the food counters. Two teen-age girls were walking along there, on their own. Both had short skirts, high-heeled shoes and yellow-blonde hair, but there any resemblance stopped. One was thin, with tiny, pointed breasts; the other was plump and stocky, with big but well-shaped curves, big hips and jutting breasts. Mayhew could not keep his eyes off her. The girl sensed something and glanced his way; she had fine, bold, brown eyes.

She tossed her head and turned her gaze away.

Mayhew moistened his lips.

"Now, she's really something," he said to himself. "She really is a lay."

There was a jeweler's shop in the Edgeware Road, near the Corner House, and during the night two men had burgled it, and got away with 7,000 pounds worth of watches and jewelry. Divisional police had been there for two hours, and one of the men working on the Rite-Time watches investigation had been over. Forty Rite-Time watches were in stock, but were marked: *Not for sale yet.* They had been supplied by the Orlova Company and, according to the manager, Orlova had telephoned to ask him to keep them back.

"Something to do with tax," the manager had said. "If they were smuggled in, *I* didn't know anything about it."

The officer, named Frobisher, was standing just behind the two girls. He saw one of them glance toward a man sitting at a table, and turned his head. A man was sitting alone, staring at the girl, but his back was towards Frobisher, who did not give him a thought. He was too preoccupied with his own discovery.

After a good night's sleep Jerry Klein had a big breakfast. His wife had felt much happier about him, for the fears of the early part of the week seemed to have been dispersed. Jerry himself was beginning to feel secure. Darkie had not been to see him again, nor had any policemen been to question him. He was more determined than ever to refuse to have anything more to do with hot goods.

He was sitting in a tube train when a man came and sat next to him and jogged his elbow, making him let go of his *Daily Mail*. It was because the man did not apologize that he looked up.

He almost froze.

"What a remarkable coincidence, seeing you here," said Darkie Jackson. "I've got some instructions for you, Jerry. Don't sell any of those Rite-Time watches until I give you the okay. They could lead you into a lot of trouble. And if the bloody coppers stick their noses in again, tell them I told you not to sell. Understand?"

It was after ten o'clock before Nina Pallon was given some dry biscuits and lukewarm tea. The man who had jabbed the hypodermic needle into her was with her while she ate, but he did not say a word. In desperation, she asked:

"Why are you doing this?"

No answer.

"Are you holding me for ransom?"

No answer.

"Please tell me! I'll give you anything, anything at all, if you'll let me go."

Her voice was almost inaudible. Her head ached with awful throbbing which beat time with the dynamo. Hardly a minute seemed to pass free from the roaring sound, which now seemed not only above her head, but inside it.

"Let me out of here!" she cried.

He pushed her back on the bed. He took the arm he had

freed and tied it to the little bed again. He got up, went out, and closed and locked the door.

"*Let me out, let me out, let me out!*" Nina cried.

There were twenty men within fifty yards of her, but none could hear because of the other noises, and the thickness of walls and floor.

Felisa Henderson sat up in bed about that time, with a silver breakfast tray in front of her, and everything but the coffee untouched. Elliott was in the sitting room, on the telephone. It would not be long before he would have to talk to his business associates and his office, he could not stay with his wife indefinitely.

Remembering his "You must eat something, honey," she lifted the lid off a silver salver, which held the hot toast.

But for that, she would not have had the message.

It lay between two pieces of toast, soiled by crumbs, a folded note which she knew could mean only one thing. Her fingers quivered as she picked it up and unfolded it.

19

Calculated Risks

There was a single sentence on the piece of hotel notepaper, printed faintly in pencil. The sentence read: *Call Sch'er on the house phone. He will know what to do.*

Felisa put the note down, stared at the window for what seemed a long time, heard the ting! of the telephone in the next room, started, picked up the note and put it under the sheet. Almost at once Elliott came in. He looked no different from usual, brisk, alert, well-groomed, handsome. Perhaps his eyes were glassy and the lines at his lips were noticeable, but that was all.

"That was Birmingham." The emphasis on the *"ham"* was very noticeable. "Everything is fine over there. I've told them not to harass me for a few days."

Business, even at the end of a telephone, was his life, his whole life.

"At least you lifted the cover off the toast, honey!" he said. "Aren't you going to eat any?"

"I'll eat a little." Felisa buttered a piece of toast, and cut off two narrow fingers. It nearly choked her, but she ate it. All the time she stared at Elliott, so intently that she thought he must feel there was some special reason. He was prepared to cut himself off from business for *her* child. What would he do if she told him about the note?

She knew what he would want to do: tell the police.

He had promised to deal with "them" direct, but she could not rely on him unless he was convinced it was the right thing to do. She was convinced; he still had doubts.

"Elliott," she said, "you have a conference with the cotton brokers in the city, haven't you?"

"I did have. I've told Rieman to cancel it." Rieman was his London business agent.

"You shouldn't do that." Every word Felisa uttered seemed to come out with an effort. "You told me that some buyers and brokers are coming here from Manchester for the conference."

"I'll see them when we have Nina back."

Her eyes were dull, as if from the aftereffect of the sedative, yet Elliott had noticed with relief how clear they had been when she had wakened. Something had happened to change that, and he wondered whether it was full recollection of the situation or whether a message had reached her—on the breakfast tray, for instance.

He had lifted the covers himself.

"I think you should go this morning. You have a telephone in the car and I can reach you at the Cotton Exchange. I shall be all right, Elliott. I won't become hysterical again."

"You really want me to go?"

"I know you'll come back right away if I need you."

"Be sure of that." He went across to her, kissed her cheek, and stepped back from the bed. "I'll leave in half an hour. Can I get you anything before I go?"

"I'll have some more hot coffee," Felisa answered. "Then I'll have a shower, Elliott. Elliott—" her voice was suddenly thick with emotion.

He said quietly, "Yes, honey?"

"I want you to know I think you've been wonderful."

"Wonderful?" He could hardly bring the word out. "If I could only find—"

He swung round quickly, and went out. With the closed door behind him, he stared at the telephone; forcing himself to think. She was anxious to be rid of him, and must have a strong reason; it could only be connected with Nina.

Should he let her do what she thought was best? Or should he make her tell him what had happened and pass the story to Gideon? If he didn't know what had happened he couldn't pass it on, but would that ease either his mind or his conscience? What mattered was to assure their future; that was fundamental. If he made her talk, if he told Gideon, if Nina died—

Before he left for the City, Felisa was dressed in a sheath of black trimmed with mink. She seemed almost impatient for him to go.

Five minutes after Elliott had left, and when she had watched the Rolls-Royce glide along Park Lane, Felisa went downstairs to a house telephone and dialed Schumacher's number. These calls, not from outside, were on an automatic system and did not go through the hotel exchange. She expected the man to answer at once; but there was no immediate reply.

"He can't be out!" she said to herself almost in panic. "He can't be!" She replaced the receiver, forced herself to wait for a minute or two, and dialed again.

Schumacher was sitting in the solitary armchair in his small room, the morning newspapers by his side—all five of them. None carried a word about the kidnaping, and he felt more secure than he had last night. When the bell first rang, he ignored it, but his lips formed the words:

"There she is."

The ringing stopped, but started again after a short interval. He took his time answering.

"Mr. Schumacher?"

"Hello?"

"Yes." Schumacher smiled, a taut, almost wolfish smile. "Is that Mrs. Henderson?"

"Yes. I had a message asking me to contact you—"

"I don't think we ought to talk too much over the telephone," Schumacher interrupted. "I would very much like to come and see you. Is your husband with you?"

"No, he won't be back for two or three hours. Have you any *news?* Tell me, please."

Schumacher said very carefully:

"Of a kind. We really mustn't talk about it over the telephone, Mrs. Henderson. I will come and see you in ten minutes if you will leave the door of your own room unlocked."

"I will."

"Mrs. Henderson," Schumacher said, "I want you to know that the situation is nearly as distressing for me as it is for you."

He rang off, stood still, and smiled tensely. He knew that he was being watched whenever he went into the foyer, and believed that some of the hotel staff were spying on him, but it was only a dozen steps to the fire-escape staircase. He waited for nearly ten minutes, went out and walked up two floors, then glanced along the passage toward the Hendersons' suite; no one was in sight.

The door was unlocked. As he stepped inside, the smile seemed to be wiped from his face.

Felisa Henderson, watching the door as a cat watches a mouse, saw him come in. She was astonished to see the expression of distress on his face, to feel the pressure of his cold hands as he gripped hers, and to hear the tremor in his voice as he spoke.

"There is only one reason for me to do this, Mrs. Henderson. For Nina's sake. Nothing would make me act in such a manner—except the hope, the belief, that I can reunite you and your daughter."

Does she believe it? Schumacher wondered; and he answered himself: Sure she does. I can see it in her eyes. And he was right.

"Does she believe me?" Percival White asked himself.

He was looking into the somber brown eyes of Maria Lucci, who stood in front of him with a stillness which gave her short, almost tiny figure great dignity. She wore a black dress and shiny black beads, which showed up the pallor of her neck and face. She was near the window of a beautifully appointed apartment which overlooked the cathedral, and the almost ghostly beauty of the carvings and the statuary. Beneath them, Milan throbbed with people and with traffic. Unknown to White but known to Maria, Parsons and young Sergeant Birra were in the next room, where they could hear every word.

When Maria did not speak, White said again:

"It was a great shock to me. I had no idea that anyone was getting money from those girls."

"You knew what the houses were used for," Maria said.

"Yes, I did, but we only owned them. They were let on a long lease to the managers. I'm not a saint, but—"

"No, Mr. White, you are certainly not a saint," Maria said bitterly. "You are a very evil man. You paid these men to lie about my husband. You are the one who caused his death."

White took a step toward her.

"I didn't know," he insisted. "I swear to you I didn't know. I came to Milan to try to find out, and—Mancelli tells me that when those witnesses came to Milan they *did* see your husband."

"It is not true."

"Mrs. Lucci, it won't help if you don't face the facts," said White. "They did come to Milan, they did see your husband, and they have sworn on oath that they brought the money from England and paid it over to him. If they're lying, it's not because of me. Why don't you believe me? I want to help. I want to know the truth, whatever it is. Don't you want to know the truth?"

"I want the name of a good man cleared," Maria Lucci said firmly.

Ten minutes later, when White had gone, she poured coffee for the two policemen. Parsons was slightly ill at ease in this unfamiliar luxury, but Birra, who had been born in the slums of Genoa, behaved as if he had never known anything different.

"You ask me to talk to him and to accuse him," Maria said. "Now that I have done this, please tell me what you think. Is he an evil man?"

Birra said, "If he's a liar, he's a good one."

"If he's not a liar, we still have to find out whether these two managers gave the money to anyone else in Milan. Whom did your husband trust, Mrs. Lucci?"

Very slowly, she said, "He trusted too many people. But in the London business, there was White, and there was also Giovanni Mancelli."

It looked as if it hurt her to say that.

"The P.S. people are now checking on Giovanni Mancelli," Parsons wrote to Gideon. "They're planting a man in the Lucci offices here—Mancelli is in charge now. Interesting, isn't it?"

As Felisa Henderson also wondered how much to believe, Schumacher was speaking very earnestly. He had a most plausible manner, and was remarkably convincing, but Felisa realized that she wanted to believe him, for he told her that her daughter was alive.

"I haven't seen Nina, but I've talked to her, Mrs. Henderson. There's no doubt it was she, I could never mistake her voice."

Felisa asked gratingly, "Is she safe?"

"She—she says she is well, but—" Schumacher hesitated, and so turned the screw and caused even greater pain. "I hate to say this, ma'am."

"Don't spare my feelings."

"Ma'am, she—" Schumacher broke off again, with a catch in his voice, and it was easy to believe there were tears in his eyes. "She is badly frightened."

Felisa caught her breath.

"They've said they will kill her if you don't pay the money for her release, and—and she said she believes they mean it," Schumacher went on. "There's no doubt she's very frightened, Mrs. Henderson."

"She must be terrified." Felisa spoke as if to herself, then raised her voice. "What—what else did they say?"

"They asked me to act as liaison," Schumacher answered, with such simplicity that it was completely disarming. "I must tell you that I knew nothing about all this until this morning, when a man called me, and told me he wanted me to speak to Nina. The call came right out of the blue, I hadn't a moment's warning." Schumacher's hands were spread out in front of him as he protested his loathing of what he had been compelled to do. "After I talked to Nina, they told me what to say to you."

"What do you have to say?" There was a harsh note in Felisa's voice.

"It's—it's so ridiculous, ma'am. The amount of money isn't—"

"How much did they ask for?"

"A million dollars," Schumacher muttered. "A million."

The amount did not seem to give Felisa a moment's concern.

"Did they say anything else? How they wanted it, where it was to be paid, what guarantee they would give of my daughter's safety?"

"They said you were to give it to me and that if I took it to a place they would name later they would release Nina to me. They said that if the police were to follow me, or to trace them, they would cut Nina's throat. That's all they said except—"

Felisa hardly knew how to control her voice.

"What else could there be?"

"They asked for a down payment, Mrs. Henderson. They said they wanted a hundred thousand dollars today."

"Today!"

"That's right. I told them it would be impossible, but they appear to think that a hundred thousand dollars was chicken feed to you, that you have twice as much as that available in jewels alone." He spread his hands again. "They simply wouldn't take any notice when I told them you couldn't part with your personal jewelry, it was unthinkable."

"When do you need the money?"

"By five o'clock this afternoon."

"It will have to be before then," Felisa stated flatly. "It will have to be before my husband returns from his conference." Now she was looking steadily into Schumacher's eyes, and for the first time he wondered whether he had in fact deceived her. "But how do I know you are telling me the truth? How do I even know that my daughter is safe?"

Schumacher half-closed his eyes.

"They will telephone you at a quarter past eleven, and Nina will be able to talk to you."

This time there was no long-drawn-out period of anguish.
At a quarter past eleven the telephone rang, and when Felisa
answered it a man spoke in a voice so nasal that it was
difficult for her to understand.

"Have you talked to Schumacher, Mrs. Henderson?"

"Yes. Is my daughter—"

"Don't rush me," the man said. "You know what I want?"

"Yes."

"Can you fix it?"

"Yes."

"That's the ticket," the man said. "Hang on."

Into the silence that followed came what sounded like a
gasp, even a stifled scream. Felisa's hand tightened on the receiver so that it seemed her bones would break. Schumacher,
watching, muttered under his breath, *My God, my God, it's
terrible.*

As the sound of his voice died away, Nina's came, distant,
hoarse but unmistakable as she said:

"Felsa, oh, Felsa!" No one else in the world ever left a syllable out of Felisa, it was the way Nina had pronounced the
name when she had been a child. "Get me out of here, please
get me out. It's awful, it—"

The man said, "Don't try any tricks, missus," and the line
snapped dead.

That was at twenty minutes past eleven.

At five minutes to twelve, Hobbs came into Gideon's office
with the tape of the conversation. A very tall, very thin, almost gaunt man rose from the chair opposite Gideon, rising
slowly, as if he were uncoiling himself. He watched as Gideon
took the tape and fitted it to the machine. Lemaitre came
over. Hobbs stood, relaxed and yet eager, showing no hangover from his night work.

"Ready, Professor?" asked Gideon.

"Yes."

Gideon pressed the starting button. A whirring sound
seemed to last for a long time before the man's voice became
audible. Every syllable that was uttered, every sound including a background throbbing and a roar that faded slowly,
came clearly into the office.

At last the man said, "Don't try any tricks, missus," and
there was a click on the receiver being replaced. After a few
seconds of silence Lemaitre said sweepingly:

"We don't need an expert to tell us what part of London *he* comes from. Proper Cockney." He looked at the professor as if defying him to argue.

"Yes, I think so," the professor agreed, "but with overtones which suggest that he no longer speaks Cockney regularly. The nasal vowels are impossible to imitate, of course, except with long practice. Is that all you need me for, Commander?"

"No," said Gideon. "I want you to get a dozen copies of that tape made at once, and have them sent round to the divisions—someone might recognize the voice or the background noises. The thudding sounds like a dynamo. Did anyone identify the other sound?"

"I think it was the roar of a train," Hobbs said.

They heard the tape again, and this time it was impossible to miss the chug-chug of train wheels on their steel lines.

"We want the address of every place in London where we might hear that noise," said Gideon. "It could be a house near a main line, it could be a house near the tubes when they come close to the surface. It might be railway arches. Get cracking, Lem." He turned to Hobbs. "Any luck with the search for our artist?"

"Hundreds of them are being questioned," Hobbs said, "but we've turned nothing up yet. That's routine, now. I'll help Lem get started in this new search."

It would have been so easy for Hobbs to say the same thing in a way that would have put Lemaitre's back up. Instead, Lemaitre cracked:

"Come on then. What are you waiting for?"

The professor smiled at Gideon, but did not speak.

20

Big Business

Satisfied that everything possible was being done to find Nina, Gideon turned to the reports on his desk. The most urgent had already been dealt with but some important ones were outstanding, and he wanted to make sure that preoccupation with the kidnaping did not make him overlook any significant factors. He read each report, but found nothing new. There was an interim one from Parsons, saying that White was in Milan and had seen Mancelli. That was all so far. There were no reports from MacPherson over Rite-Times, or from Oliver on the West German marks case. His secretary had made a 2:30 appointment for him at the head office of the Faculty of British Industries, in Tothill Street. He was to see the director of export sales, a man named Fielding. Fielding was occasionally interviewed on television about the British export drive—a balding, lively man with a convincing manner.

Gideon's exchange telephone rang, and he lifted it mechanically.

"Yes."

"Mr. Prosser of Kensington on the line for you, sir."

"Put him through. . . . That you, Jack?" As he spoke Gideon thought of Nielsen's note about Mayhew posting a card to his mother from Kensington.

"Morning, George. Got a little thing I think you ought to know about." Prosser was too old in C.I.D. service to trouble Gideon with trifles. "We've got a man and a girl missing from the Rosemount Hotel in Kensington Gate. They booked in separately and on different days, but they've been around a lot together."

"Well?" Gideon saw the door open an inch and a hand appear. He watched it as Prosser went on:

"The girl's about five feet two, very good figure, and the man . . ." He paused, as if for effect, and Gideon saw Oliver's face at the door. He beckoned Oliver, who looked as if he had just come from a funeral. "If he weren't an Australian," Prosser said, and stopped on a note of triumph.

"Sorry, I didn't quite get that," said Gideon.

"You didn't—" Prosser's voice registered his disgust. "I'll say it again, slowly. The man who is missing answers the description of Frank Mayhew, except that he's an Australian."

Gideon didn't speak.

"George, what's the matter with you today?" demanded Prosser.

"How close is the description?"

"Nearly as close as the initials F. M. When I showed the photograph of Mayhew to the porter and to the maid who does the man's room, they identified him pronto. But they're sure he doesn't talk like an American, and the porter says he can tell an Australian any day."

"Prints?" demanded Gideon.

"Not yet. It's no crime for a man to stay away from his hotel all night, or to have a floosie with him."

"Check the room for prints, and search it," Gideon said briskly. "If it's definitely Mayhew— What name is he using?"

"Mason—Frank Mason. That's what I mean—F. M."

"If he's Mayhew, we want a general call out at once," Gideon said. "Ring me back, Jack. And thanks."

"Right." Prosser rang off, and Gideon stared not at Oliver but out the window, wondering why a man of Prosser's age and police experience felt it necessary to get approval before taking positive action. Gideon pushed the question out of his mind and turned to Oliver, who had an unlit cigarette between his lips. Gideon tossed him a box of matches, and Oliver caught them. The head offices of the joint stock banks and of the major foreign travel agencies with banking facilities should have some figures about the West German marks by now. Oliver lit his cigarette and tossed the matches back. He was overdoing the poker-faced gloom so much that Gideon expected big news.

"How many million?" he demanded.

Oliver's face seemed to fall apart. Gideon, pleased with himself, was almost free from major preoccupations for the first time that day.

"You're a crafty old so-and-so," said Oliver. "Really thought I'd shake you this time. Two and a half."

Gideon ejaculated, *"Million?"*

"Yes."

"You've shaken me." Gideon said. After a pause he went on: "How wide are they spread?"

"Very wide indeed," Oliver answered. "All the big cities have some, so have most of the smaller towns. Can't get a clear picture yet, but it looks to me as if they've been distributed during the past few months. All the big branches of the banks and the travel offices with *bureaux de change* have a few thousand at this time of the year, and smaller places usually carry a few. It looks as if there was one big consignment through the London Clearing House, accepted as genuine. You know what's worrying me, don't you?"

There was one obvious answer, but Oliver had been deflated enough for one session.

"What?"

Oliver took the cigarette from his lips, rested it carefully on an ashtray, and pressed the tips of his fingers together.

"This isn't a widespread passing of forged notes by a few dozen crooks who hand it in over the counter. This is big business, the distribution *must* have started in a big way too. None of our main banks suspected the genuineness of the notes, and they must have received them from sources they regarded as unimpeachable." Solemnly, Oliver asked, "Do you agree?"

"Yes."

"In other words, George, these reached London through the official channels of one or more big German banks."

"Yes."

"So one or more of the big German banks was either (a) deceived by the forgeries or (b) connived at the forgeries."

Gideon's exchange telephone rang. He lifted the receiver, and said, "Hold on." Then he covered the mouthpiece with his great hand.

"Well?"

"It seems to me I ought to concentrate on finding how they got into the country and have a complete picture of that before we take any action about calling in the notes," said Oliver. "Someone is going to be left holding the baby over this, George. Either the Bank of England or whichever of the Joint Stock Banks brought the marks in—*or* the suppliers from Germany. If we handle it clumsily, we could land our own people in the soup. If I get a dud pound note I'm liable to be landed with it unless I know where I got it from. Even if I can get it replaced it can take a long time. Against that," Oliver went on, "if we don't call in all the forged notes, the banks might continue to deal in them. This is a headache whichever way you look at it."

Gideon said: "Go over to the Bank of England and see Sir George Richmond. He's in charge of foreign exchange. He knows what we've been doing and he's right on top of his job.

Tell him exactly what we've found, and ask him how he would like the job to be handled now." Gideon put the telephone mouthpiece to his lips, said, "Won't be a jiffy," covered it again and went on to Oliver. "We've got to know before the close of banking business today, or there will be chaos."

"And this way we won't burn *our* fingers." Oliver smiled with ungrudging admiration. "I say, don't ever leave us chaps to manage on our own, will you?"

In the few seconds that followed, everything faded from Gideon's mind except that remark and the implication behind it. Oliver had meant it as a joke, yet he had also meant it seriously. *"Don't ever leave us chaps to manage on our own, will you?"* As assistant commissioner he would have to.

Suddenly he thought angrily, "How bigheaded can I get?" He snatched up the telephone, and growled, "Gideon."

It was Prosser.

"George," said Prosser, "the man missing from the Rosemount Hotel is Frank S. Mayhew. Three separate witnesses have identified his photograph."

Gideon was already lifting the internal telephone as he said, "Haven't a photograph of the girl, have you?"

"Yes. It's on the way to you. She's a Florence Foster . . ."

There followed one of the great ironies of the Yard's work; an irony which was part and parcel of everything Gideon and the Yard had to do, unavoidable because it was done in ignorance as well as in hope, but so time-wasting, so prodigal with the Yard's resources, which were already stretched nearly to their limit, that they carried much bitterness with them.

That morning the Yard began the search for Florence Foster. A thousand photographs were printed and distributed, twenty thousand men in the Force began the search for the girl as well as for Mayhew alias Mason, every station and substation was involved. The newspapers were brought in, television and radio were called in to help, tens of thousands of man-hours were spent on the search for the girl who lay buried under the leaves and bracken, beneath the fleecy white clouds and the patches of dark-blue sky in Windsor Great Park.

It was a Windsor policeman who started the final phase in the hunt for Florrie. He remembered seeing her getting into a Mini-Minor in Windsor High Street.

"Not often they come that size and shape," he told a C.I.D. officer at the police station. "Breasts like balloons, and they're more noticeable when they're short, too. That's the girl all right, poor little basket. And that's the chap—he was standing by the car holding the door open, proper polite. The car went toward the park and Ascot, sir."

"Sure?"

"Dead sure."

The C.I.D. man set everyone he could spare onto tracing the movements of the car, and a red Mini-Minor was not yet common enough to escape notice. He sat at the telephone, directing operations, not realizing that in his way he was doing what Gideon did from the Yard.

A woodcutter who had been sawing some of the branches pruned in a thicket the previous autumn recalled a Mini-Minor parked sixty yards away from where he was working. He well remembered the man and girl going into another thicket.

"None of my business what they get up to so long as they're out of sight," he said.

"Did you see them come out?"

"Well, no, I only saw the car driven off. I'm not sure they were both in it, I took it for granted."

Half an hour later he stared down at Florence Foster's body, now cleared of leaves and bracken, and he was almost sick.

"She's dead, George," the Windsor superintendent told Gideon.

"How?"

"Just the way you'd expect. Raped and strangled."

"She fight?"

"Must have, desperately."

"Any trace of the man?"

"His prints were on her handbag."

"Right." Gideon rang off, and immediately sent for three superintendents and three chief inspectors. He told them that no one must rest, no one must relax, until Frank S. Mayhew was under arrest. All divisions were to be put under pressure, all airports, bus stations, seaports and railway termini were to be under twenty-four-hour surveillance, every hotel and boardinghouse was to be warned to look out for the man whom it was so easy to like and to trust. Even during this briefing Gideon kept thinking about the other missing girl, Nina. So far there was no word about her, and the stations now alerted for Mayhew were already alerted for her.

Why did no one seem to recognize those other background noises?

Alice Clay saw Mayhew's photograph on the television screen later that day.

"He's a devil," she said to herself. "An absolute devil." Then she jumped up. "But I mustn't sit here watching TV, I'll be late for the club."

The Reverend Ronald Stephens would have been a very happy man had he seen the way she reacted.

Before that, just before Gideon briefed the six men, Felisa Henderson talked to the manager of Carter's, one of the jewelers from whom she bought gems of fabulous beauty and fabulous worth.

"It is a temporary matter," she told him. "I need thirty-five thousand pounds in cash by one o'clock, and my husband is out of town until this evening. If you require a security, then the Bondi necklace and—"

"Mrs. Henderson, I shall be only too happy to help you," the manager replied. "Perhaps you will permit one safeguard."

"What safeguard?"

"That you collect the money in person or permit me to bring it to you."

"If you will bring it to me I will be very grateful," Felisa said. "When may I expect you?"

"I will be at your hotel in half an hour."

There was nothing unusual in visitors from famous salons calling on wealthy women, even though this one stayed only for a few minutes, to hand over the money and to obtain a receipt. His call was noted by the detective on duty and reported, but no special action was considered necessary at the Yard, and Gideon wasn't told.

Ten minutes after the Carter manager had gone, Schumacher entered Felisa's room. Even when he saw the money in a small briefcase which lay open on the bed, his eyes did not flicker.

"So you succeeded," he said huskily. "I only wish it were not necessary."

"Do you know where you have to take it?"

"Yes, surely."

"Where?"

"Mrs. Henderson," said Schumacher earnestly, "I am quite sure it is better for you not to know. You can trust me implicitly."

Felisa thought bitterly, I can't, I feel sure I can't; but I have to.

Aloud she said, "When are you to give it to them?"

"This afternoon, at a time not yet decided."

"When you hand it over," Felisa said, "you must make one thing absolutely clear."

"And what is that?" inquired Schumacher.

"They will get nothing more until I have seen Nina, and know she is not hurt."

"Be sure I will make that very clear to them," Schumacher promised.

When he closed the door, Felisa stood watching it, half-afraid now that she had done the wrong thing. What would Elliott say? Supposing Schumacher just went off with the money, or "they" went off with it? Quite suddenly her calmness was ripped to shreds and she whirled into a panic of her own making.

She swung round to the telephone to call Elliott.

21

Rush

Abel Schumacher walked down the fire-escape stairs to his own room, carrying the briefcase in his left hand. There was spring in his step, buoyancy in his mood. He unlocked the door, stepped inside, closed it softly, and then tossed the bag into the air with a muted cry: *Bonanza!* He all but did a jig to the bed, taking off his jacket as he went. He picked up the briefcase, squeezed it, hugged it. Then he turned his back on it, went to the wardrobe, and took out another suit of clothes, baggy and in need of pressing, and much too big for him. The lining was several layers thick, and these layers were divided, rather like the sections of a money belt or a billfold. He carried the trousers to the bed, and took out one of the wads of 5 pound notes. He counted this; there were twenty—100 pounds in all. He put one wad in the first lining layer close to the waist, one in a second, one in a third, then filled the next three sections. In all, he filled fifteen lots of three, so 4,500 pounds was in the waistband of the trousers. The jacket was fitted with deep inside pockets, and when he had filled these over 20,000 pounds was hidden in his clothes, more than half of the full amount.

He spread two pages of a copy of the European edition of the New York *Herald Tribune* on the bed, and spread the rest of the notes on it, then folded it across. It made a bulky newspaper but it was still a newspaper. He sealed it with Scotch tape, then folded it inside two more sheets. Tucked under his arm, this did not look too conspicuous.

He was at the door when the telephone bell rang.

The sound made him jump violently, and he twisted round. It was a call through the hotel exchange. He swallowed hard. The bell rang again, and he went toward the instrument, clenching his teeth. He lifted the receiver.

"Hallo."

"Abe?" It was Lucy Green.

"I told you not to—"

"Abe, the shop was raided last night."

He felt as if an electric shock had run through him.

"Did you hear?" Lucy almost sobbed.

"Yes. Was he—" Schumacher couldn't finish.

"It was empty," Lucy said. "Abe, when can I see you? I'm ever so scared."

"Tonight at six o'clock," he said quickly. "Piccadilly Circus Station, North Regent Street subway." Before Lucy could speak again, he put down the receiver. When he wiped his forehead with the back of his hand it was wet. He went into the bathroom and dried off with a towel. Five minutes later he went along to the staircase. At every landing there was a service lift, but he did not press for the car.

So far he had got away with it, but this was the danger period, and he was acutely aware of it. If he were seen he would be followed, and even if he shook a trailer off, the airport and all traffic termini would be alerted.

What he did not know was that one of the detectives now detailed to watch the back of the hotel saw a man who looked like Mayhew enter a cafe close by. The detective took time out to telephone his division, and was delayed by a busy line. He was away from his post for those crucial minutes during which Schumacher was making his escape.

Schumacher walked through the storerooms for meat, vegetables, fruit, eggs, nearly every food the hotel needed day by day. Three warehousemen were pushing hand trucks toward the hoist to the kitchens, another was wheeling a truck from the street loading platform, which was on a lower street level than the front of the hotel. Schumacher waited in an alcove which smelt earthily of potatoes until the man had passed, then climbed into the van. It was nearly empty, and dozens of Hessian sacks were piled up at the far end. He moved some of these, then sat on the floor behind them. A dozen more sacks were tossed in, one actually draping over his shoulder. Men shouted words he hardly understood before one slammed the doors at the back; he heard an iron bar dropped into a slot. The van swayed as the driver climbed to the wheel, quivered as the engine started.

Twenty minutes later the van stopped near Covent Garden market. The driver opened the back doors, and clambered in for some of the sacks. As he staggered off with an armful, Schumacher followed him, stepped out of the van onto another loading platform, and walked towards an intersection. A man near the van called out:

"Hey, Harry! Who's yer mate?"

"*Mate?*" another man echoed, but before the driver realized what had happened, Schumacher had turned the nearest corner. He did not even hear the driver of the van say, "Well, he couldn't't've took anything, except a few old sacks."

The fourth taxi that approached Schumacher was free.

"London Airport, in a hurry," he ordered as he climbed in.

"I've missed the terminal bus."

As the taxi moved across central London toward Victoria, it passed within two hundred yards of Lucy Green, who was sitting in a tiny shop with a Hawaiian decor, drinking espresso coffee served by a colored waiter from Jamaica. Twelve minutes later it passed within a hundred and fifty yards of the arches where Nina Pallon lay helpless and afraid.

Schumacher did not intend to see Nina, Lucy Green or Facey again.

He intended to fly to Paris on the first available plane, using a false name and a false passport, then to fly from Paris to Buenos Aires, via Dakar. In the Argentine $100,000 would last a long, long time.

The tape recording of the brief conversation between Schumacher and the girl Lucy reached the Yard five minutes after Gideon had left to see Sir Arthur Fielding of the Faculty of British Industries. Lemaitre listened to it, and almost smirked with satisfaction.

"She's nice and jumpy, anyway. And we'll pick 'em up at Piccadilly tonight if Gee-Gee gives the word."

"Why wouldn't he give the word?" asked the professor, who had verified that the girl's voice was the same as that they had heard before.

"Depends whether we've found Nina," Lemaitre said.

Five minutes afterward Gideon's telephone rang; it was Elliott Henderson.

Two things happened within minutes of each other, near the time that Gideon was talking to Henderson about Schumacher and the ransom.

Quincy Lee, who was staying with his only sister in a little house in Bethnal Green, opened the front door to a sharp knock and was surprised to see Maggie Barnett on the doorstep.

"Well, what a sight for sore eyes," he said. "Come in, Maggie."

"I'm coming in all right. I want a word with you," said Maggie ominously.

Quincy, puzzled but unperturbed, took her into the front parlor and called out to tell his sister he wouldn't be long. The aroma of rich beef stew filled the house.

"Now, what's on your mind?" he demanded.

"I want an honest answer to an honest question," Maggie said. She looked aggressive and sturdy as she stared at

Quincy. "Are you or are you not doing a deal with my husband?"

Quincy looked her straight in the eyes.

"No," he said, "I am not. Nothing would make me, Maggie. My nose has been clean for twenty years. I told Barney so flat—it's no use."

Maggie, still half-frowning, sounded puzzled.

"It's a funny thing," she said. "Ever since he heard you were home, he's been acting Mr. Bighead. Has he said anything to you?"

Quincy answered quietly. "You know what it is, Maggie, don't you? He wants to prove how smart he is, how easily he can look after the both of you."

"I'd like to see him!" She gave an explosive and rather happy little laugh. "Well, that's all right, then." Suddenly she asked, "He hasn't borrowed any money from you, has he?"

"He knows he'd be wasting his time," Quincy answered. "Is he flush or something?"

"He said he was going to get my portrait painted by old Facey, and went on about Facey doing a job for an American. I don't think he knows any Americans. He said anything to you about it?"

"No," answered Quincy.

He went round to the nearest pub for an hour before lunch, and a divisional plainclothes man, off duty, was already there. The treatment meted out to Quincy had a prodigal-son savor. In return for a beer he told the story of Barney's longing to have his wife's picture painted, and the divisional man, aware of the call out for a painter, asked what artist he had in mind. Two or three other customers joined in the laughter, and one remarked that old Facey hadn't been around for a few days.

The divisional man thought this worth reporting.

His divisional C.O. thought it worth telephoning Gideon; he settled for Lemaitre.

About the same time, the retired police constable who kept the news agent's and tobacconist's shop opposite the now empty art shop suddenly remembered where he had seen one of the men who had been in the art shop lately; it had been in Petticoat Lane, Aldgate, doing lightning portraits for ten shillings a time. Immediately, the ex-P.C. telephoned the divisional station, and soon this information also reached Lemaitre, who checked with N.1 Division and made sure that Facey sometimes did lightning portraits—in Petticoat Lane among other places. Then Lemaitre put through a call to Gideon at the Faculty of British Industries' office.

Gideon stepped into the impressive-looking office of the director of exports of the Faculty of British Industries and found three men there, not one. They all stood up. Fielding, who looked as if he was about to step before a television camera as a favorite uncle, shook hands and said:

"My chairman and vice-chairman wouldn't allow this occasion to pass without meeting you, Commander Gideon." The chairman was vaguely like the Duke of Wellington of a hundred fifty years ago, the vice-chaiman was a bronzed and youngish man, once a renowned cricketer. Gideon was used to the effect he—and any senior police official—had on other people; even the most sophisticated stood a little in awe. "Do sit down, Commander."

"Plain 'Mr.' suits me," said Gideon.

"But not your reputation," replied the chairman. "What crimes have been committed in our name?"

"Before we find that out, there's a call for Mr. Gideon— from a Mr. Lemaitre," Fielding said.

Gideon thought with a rush of elation touched with dread: *They've found her.* He could not imagine Lemaitre interrupting this session with lesser news. He took a telephone, held on for what seemed a long time, then heard Lemaitre's voice. The subdued tone of his "Sorry to worry you, George," drove all elation away, and Gideon steeled himself against bad news. "Henderson's just been on the blower. His missus did a deal with Schumacher, gave him what she called a down payment of thirty-five thousand quid, and . . ." Lemaitre related the whole story with a bluff downrightness which incidentally conveyed his opinion of Felisa Henderson. "We might be onto that artist, though." He passed on a precis of the two reports, and went on with a brighter note in his voice: "Maybe Schumacher will be at Piccadilly Circus at six o'clock."

Gideon said bleakly: "The girl will be, but he certainly won't—he's got what he's after, he won't take a second bite at the cherry. We've got to make sure he can't get out of the country by air or sea. Arrange a watch on all airports, and—"

Lemaitre's voice carried a squeak of protest. "But, George—"

"Have Piccadilly Underground Station watched too," ordered Gideon. "Is anything else in?"

"Not a thing."

"I'll call before I leave here." Gideon put the receiver down slowly, partly because he was so preoccupied with the news, partly because he needed a few seconds for the transition to the immediate business. For a moment or two his mind was a complete blank about it; then he thought: *Ormeroyd*, and the reason for his visit clicked into focus. He was aware of the three men watching him.

"Sorry," he said. "I won't waste any time with preliminaries, gentlemen, I'll come straight to the point. In the course of investigation into suspected cases of sabotage of machinery we've come upon indications that a well-organized plan might be in operation, affecting exports to the United States. Cashmeres, biscuits, silks and shoes are among the commodities affected. We don't know whether we've discovered all there is to it or whether we've only just touched the fringe. If it's widespread it's got to be stopped, quickly, and you're the best people to help."

He looked at each man in turn, and did not doubt that each was alarmed. The chairman even showed signs of positive consternation.

Fielding asked in a sharp voice, "Are you saying that this is an organized campaign?"

"I couldn't prove it in court," Gideon said. "I wouldn't be here if the circumstantial evidence wasn't pretty strong." When no one spoke, he went on: "I'm hoping you can make a check among some of your members, get a sampling, say, of those who export to the U.S.A. And if you could get your exporting members to look out for indications of sabotage in machinery allocated to export orders, it might give us some answers." He paused. "If it's nothing much, we won't do any harm. If it turns out to be big, we might save a lot of trouble."

Their continued silence annoyed him. These people weren't simpletons, so why should they behave as if they were?

"Don't you agree, gentlemen?"

The chairman said gruffly, "Yes, indeed. Forewarned is forearmed." He looked at Fielding. "You go on, Arthur, will you?"

Fielding smoothed down his thinning brown hair.

"Only yesterday we were told by the Society of British Industries that there were so many reports of damaged machinery and of damage to goods in transit to America that I suggested—half in jest—that it was almost like sabotage. The incidence of damage is always far too high."

Gideon was beginning to understand their attitude.

"How high?"

"Nearly ten percent," Fielding answered.

"Where does it occur?"

"I should perhaps make it clear that we are an advisory board, with the scientific and technological development of an industry our main concern. In practice, of course, we are more than that—we are the eyes and the ears of British Industries, just as the Society might be called the limbs and the body. On these specific matters we have to be guided by our associate organization. From that, I gather that the loss occurs at any stage from the time it leaves the factory to the time it reaches the American port," Fielding answered. "It's spread pretty evenly over all kinds of consumer goods. We—"

"This is what we'll do," the chairman interrupted; until then he had given the impression that he wasn't really listening. "We'll telephone fifty companies in the London and Midland areas, and have a word with the chairman or the managing director—keeping it quiet, eh, Commander? Just a spot check. If there is sabotage at the factories on an organized scale, it shouldn't be too much trouble to catch some of the saboteurs. Well, Commander? But before we took action, or asked you to, we'd have a quiet word with the union chiefs concerned. Associated Engineering Union, eh, Victor?"

Victor was the vice-chairman.

"And two or three others, yes. We can't get this job done without them—as you well know, Commander. When should we get a cross section reaction? Tomorrow, eh, Victor?"

"I don't see why not."

"Good. Commander, we'll have a comprehensive picture by tomorrow—no, it's Saturday. Monday satisfactory for you?" The chairman actually put a monocle to his left eye.

"Monday will suit us, my lord," Gideon agreed.

"Good, good. Catching some saboteurs red-handed might be easier than tracing pilferage and sorting out deliberate from accidental damage on trains and ships. We're most grateful to you. Eh, Victor?"

"*Very.*"

"Arthur?"

"We certainly are."

"You'll keep in closest touch with the Commander, won't you?"

"I will indeed," Fielding said crisply. "Can we call on you for help at short notice, Mr. Gideon?"

There was only one possible answer.

"Yes. The more you've got for us to go on the better."

"Oh, of course. Better for us to find out as much as we can first, anyhow."

Ten minutes later Gideon left the building. He had not forgotten that he had promised to call Lemaitre, but preferred to do it from his car radio.

"Excuse me, sir," said his chauffeur, on the steps of the building.

"What is it?"

"They told me you were on your way down. Mr. Lemaitre says they've identified the artist positively and know where he is, sir. He wants instructions as soon as possible."

Gideon turned from the foot of the steps leading to the FBI building and began to *run;* it was years since he had done so. The people in the crowded streets evaded him, and many turned to stare. He threaded his way along the narrow pavement until he reached his car, parked under the watchful eyes of a police constable.

"Not going to be there much longer, sir, are you?"

Gideon, puffing, did not answer, but squeezed into the car, lifted the radio telephone, and gasped:

"Gideon. I want Superintendent Lemaitre."

"Gideon," the uniformed man breathed.

"George," said Lemaitre. "Thank God I got you. It's old Facey—remember him. It was old Quin—"

"Never mind the details. Where—where is he?"

"You okay?" demanded Lemaitre. "Huffing and puffing—"

"Where is Nina?" roared Gideon.

"They think she's in one of the arches at Hammersmith—above a cabinetmaker's place. Facey's there, for certain, and he took a big tool chest in the evening Nina disappeared. Wouldn't let anyone help him carry it up the ladder to his loft. Must have wanted to do it himself when they'd gone home. Haven't made any direct approach yet but the divisional chaps from Hammersmith and Chiswick are surrounding the place. Hobbs wants to know if he should close in."

Gideon said, "Not until I get there or until there's an indication of crisis. What does Facey do at the arches?"

"Paints a bit, makes picture frames—"

"Get someone there to ask him prices for picture framing —get a talker, someone like Singleton. Then get all the dope you can on Facey—what he's been doing lately, whether he's been in trouble, whether he's ever shown homicidal tendencies."

"I can fill in the rest," Lemaitre interrupted.

"Have it for me when I reach the arches. Tell Hobbs I'll be at the corner of the street leading to them, I forget the name, in twenty minutes or so."

"But how—" Lemaitre almost screeched.

"One more thing," Gideon interrupted in his loudest "no nonsense" voice. "Tell Henderson to go to the arches."

He put down the receiver as Lemaitre said, "I give up." He was breathing quite normally now, and spoke as his driver got in beside him.

"Get me to Mansion House Underground, I'll go by tube to Hammersmith. See that there's a car there—no, wait a minute. See there's a car at Turnham Green Station, that's the nearest spot, waiting for me. Get a move on."

"Yes, sir." The driver swung out into an empty roadway. "The constable thought you'd be in a hurry and held up all the traffic, sir. Gives us a clear run."

"*He* thought of that, or did you?"

"He did, sir."

Gideon grunted, and the car sped on.

He was lucky. Two minutes after he reached the platform at Mansion House Station an Acton train came in, and it stopped only twice before Earl's Court. Even then the journey seemed slow, but Gideon knew he would reach Hammersmith in half the time it would have taken by road.

He had time to think and had time to wonder why he had always felt there was an acute danger to Nina Pallon.

When he strode out of the station at Turnham Green, he found two police cars and graying, wise old Harry Naylor, one of the oldest divisional superintendents on the Force, waiting for him. Hobbs would be at the arches.

"Anything new?" demanded Gideon.

Naylor said, "Yes, George. He smelled a rat."

Gideon felt himself go cold.

"Facey?"

"Yes." They were getting into Naylor's car. "There wasn't time to send a Yard man so I sent one of my younger chaps, who wasn't likely to be recognized. Facey wouldn't let him search the place he calls a studio, but as he stood on a loft ladder the girl called out. Facey panicked, pushed our chap off, and the fall broke his leg. Then Facey slammed the hatch. He's up there with the girl."

Gideon asked, "So we're absolutely sure she's there?"

"He's admitted it. He says he'll kill her if we don't let him go free. He's given us a time limit of an hour, and twenty minutes has already gone."

"Is Henderson there?" Gideon asked gruffly.

"He's with Hobbs, and Hobbs has told him the odds," Naylor answered.

22

The Arches

"Underneath the arches," Gideon said under his breath, and the old music-hall song took on a sinister overtone. He turned the corner that led to them, a viaduct which carried the Great Western line of British Railways. There were seventeen arches in all, built of solid blocks of stone and cemented into place by the English and Irish navvies of a century ago. There was hardly a crack in any of the walls, but there was grime—thick black grime, ingrained so deeply it was now part of the cement and part of the stone itself. The grime came from the chimneys of a hundred thousand trains which had crossed here over the years; and from the smoke from the hundreds of thousands of chimneys from the homes of the neighborhood.

As Gideon entered the cobbled service road, a train roared over the viaduct, drowning all other sounds, even the voices of three newspapermen who rushed toward the car as it slowed down.

The sound muffled Nina Pallon's sobs too; hysterical sobs born of her fear and the shock, and the look in Facey's eyes.

The roar drowned his words, but she saw him mouthing at her; he looked as if he hated her.

"What's on, Commander?"

"Is it true there's a kidnaped girl in one of the arches?"

"What makes it rate your personal attention, Mr. Gideon?"

"Who is she?"

Gideon climbed out of his car. He had respect if not always liking for the press and often needed its help; surliness for its own sake was folly.

"Yes, a girl named Pallon is missing, believed kidnaped. She's the daughter of Mrs. Elliott Henderson, an American visiting this country. There'll be an announcement later." Now Gideon was striding toward a knot of men, including uniformed policemen, standing about halfway along those grim, grimed arches.

"Any ransom sum named?" a man called.

Gideon pretended not to hear.

Fifty yards away the police had erected a barrier by parking, broadside on, a van marked *The Arches Cabinet Works.* The cobbled roadway was so narrow that nothing else on four wheels could get through. Two policemen were at the entrance, two others just in front of it.

"Commander!" One of the newspapermen hurried. "We'd like one or two good photographs."

"You can get good ones from here," Gideon said, and raised his voice. "No one but authorized personnel is to come in, eh, Superintendent?"

"No one," Naylor confirmed.

They passed the barrier, which led from the walls of the arches at one end to a high brick wall leading to a disused railway track on the other. Several men and two youths, three wearing white carpenters' aprons, stood near the high double doors which led to the cabinetmaker's arch. The doors needed painting but the name of the firm showed up clearly enough. Someone said in a whisper:

"That's him. That's Gideon."

"Who's Gideon?" asked a boy.

"The boss at the Yard. Didn't you know?"

Inevitably a thought flashed across Gideon's mind: I could be. I could be top man in the Criminal Investigation Department just for the asking.

Then Henderson and Hobbs appeared in the small wicket doorway let into the main doors. Sight of the American's face drove every other thought from Gideon's mind. Without thinking, he found himself shaking hands; as if Henderson needed and Gideon tried to give some kind of reassurance.

Hobbs went off.

"I know the score," Gideon said to Henderson. "Allow me three minutes." He stepped into the huge arch, rather like a high-domed aircraft hangar bright with fluorescent lighting. Along one wall were carpenters' benches, along the other were handsaws and two lathes, everywhere the floor was littered with shavings and sawdust. Stacks of planed timber in a great variety of sizes stood in the middle of the big shed, and the aromatic odor of newly worked wood mixed with the stronger odors of stains and polishes.

A dynamo was throbbing: *boom, boom, boom, boom;* that was the sound they had first heard over the telephone and later on the tape recorder.

Hobbs and two plainclothes men were at the foot of the wooden ladder, like a ladder leading to a hayloft. At the top of the ladder, the hatch was down; it looked as tight as if it were dovetailed. Other policemen were here from the Yard and from the division, and one was in front of a two-way radio set which stood on one of the workbenches. A middle-aged man with a graying beard, which made him look both old and old-fashioned, approached Gideon and Naylor.

"Mr. Higginbottom, Commander—the manager here," Naylor introduced him. "He's been most helpful."

"I only wish I could do something more than pray," Higginbottom said. He sounded wholly sincere. "I've thought of nothing else since I realized—"

"Is there a fire escape?" asked Gideon.

"There is, but Facey has blocked it from the attic," Hobbs said.

"Is there any way in from the top?"

"The railway line has no service pits or manholes up there," Higginbottom volunteered.

"Any approach from the arches on either side?"

"Both walls are four feet thick, it would take hours to break through. I wish I hadn't to be so negative," Hobbs said, "but Mr. Higginbottom is quite sure."

Henderson, within earshot, neither moved nor spoke. Gideon, glancing at him, saw the anguish in his eyes.

"Who talked to him?" Gideon asked Hobbs.

"I did. Facey says he'll open the hatch in half an hour—that's in ten minutes' time. He added that if we try to shoot or throw tear gas inside, he'll close the door, and set the place on fire."

"Think he means it?" Gideon demanded.

Hobbs said very quietly, "Yes, I do. If there's any forced entry, though, this time it's my job."

There was no point in arguing; if Hobbs felt as sure as that he had good reason. Gideon turned to Henderson. His mind was scarred with the other man's agony, but it was also alert and pulsating, searching for some way of saving the girl.

"Please," Nina managed to say in a voice which did not shake. "Let me go. Don't keep me here."

Facey was staring at her.

"If you let me go my father will do everything he can to help you. I'm sure he will."

She felt sure of that, and yet she felt quite hopeless, because there was no way of reasoning with this man who seemed to hate her for what she was, not because she had done anything to deserve such hate. He stared stonily at her.

He had not shaved for days, and his gray beard was like a barricade about his deep-lined face.

"Please listen to me," she began again.

He did not stop her from talking, but he did not seem to hear. Suddenly, when she was in the middle of a sentence, he stood up and went to the bench. On it was a large can marked *Turpentine Substitute—Inflammable.* Next to this were small tins of paint. On the bench and on the floor beside it were piles of shavings which would burn like tinder.

"Why don't you listen to me?" she cried; and then her voice broke. "Please, oh, please."

Only forty feet below Nina, Gideon was thinking, They're expecting a miracle from me. Both Henderson and Hobbs seemed to be waiting on him. Miracle it would be if the girl was saved, yet his thoughts still raced and he considered one possibility and rejected it, another and rejected that.

"Gideon, let me talk to him," Henderson said.

"That may be the only way," agreed Gideon. It would certainly be the only way of making Henderson feel that he had tried. "We ought to consider how best—"

The radio operator exclaimed, "Mr. Gideon!"

Gideon was glad of a chance to look up.

"Yes?"

"Mr. Lemaitre on the line."

Gideon moved across, hands outstretched for the headphones. He clipped them on. Lemaitre's voice, although sounding disembodied, carried a note of eagerness.

"George, I got some dope on Facey. Dunno what you can do with it, but it's got some meat. Disappointed artist, never had a chance, sorry for himself, got a hate complex for all connoisseurs—"

"Hold it!" Gideon beckoned Henderson and Hobbs, and repeated, "So Facey has a hate complex for art collectors and connoisseurs. That it?"

Henderson's eyes were glittering; he had never seemed so dominant or of greater stature, although he stood quite still, hands clenched by his sides, as the radio officer clipped a set of earphones on him so that he could listen in. Hobbs was frowning in concentration, as if trying to divine what was going on.

"I talked to Facey's wifey," Lemaitre went on. "They brought her in from Division. She knew he was involved in some game with Schumacher. He came over three months ago and they laid something on. She thought it was a big art theft, and she's been shaking in her shoes every time she's opened a newspaper."

"What does she say about Facey?"

"She says he's crazy," Lemaitre answered bluntly. "I told her what the situation was, and she's terrified in case he kills the girl. He's got a hate complex for—"

Henderson's eyes were like glass.

"All right, Lem," Gideon interrupted. "Anything more specific?"

"Wouldn't call it specific, but the impression Mrs. F. gave me is that this was to be Facey's big chance to get his own back on the big shots of the art world who go for the Old Masters and the modern abstractionists and let the good painters of the day starve. Mind you, it's only—"

"Thanks, Lem. Have a word with Hobbs, will you? Hold on." Gideon pulled off the earphones and handed them to Hobbs, as Henderson handed his to the radio officer.

It was only a minute to the moment when Facey was due to open that door in the ceiling.

"He hates art collectors. He thinks his work has been ignored. Got the angle?" Gideon asked Henderson.

"Yes."

"I'll lead in and give you your cue." Gideon moved toward the wooden ladder, which was solid enough to hold two men his size, whereas Henderson was not much more than half his weight. He climbed up with Henderson a step behind him, but almost at once Hobbs pushed a big stepladder into position. The ladder had a platform at the top, and Henderson moved to this.

With a few seconds to go, a deep hush fell upon the arch. Every man down on the floor was staring at the hatch door, and Gideon was within inches of it. He craned his head back until his neck hurt, watching that door.

Almost to the second, it moved.

Almost to the second, a gap appeared, two inches at one side. Without warning, a blazing ball dropped through the gap. It passed within inches of Gideon's head, touched his shoulder and brought the stench of burning cloth, bounced onto a tread and dropped to the shavings and the sawdust below. It burned so fiercely that Gideon knew it was a screw of paper or cloth soaked with inflammable liquid.

He slapped at his shoulder, where a flame licked up at his cheek, and put the flame out. Hobbs had his jacket off in a trice, smothering the flames, and called, "Fire extinguisher. Quick."

"I warned you!" Facey's voice sounded clearly above the scuffling of men rushing about yet trying desperately to make no noise. Hobbs's coat was smoldering. "I told you I'd burn the place down if you came and tried to get in."

"Facey, don't talk so much," Gideon interrupted.

"Talk!" screeched Facey. "I'll show you if it's talk! If you bloody cops aren't away from the arches in ten minutes, that's the end. Understand me, that's *it*. And don't think you can fool me." The shrillness of hysteria wailed in his voice. "I can see the alley, I can see the road, I can see the High Street from here. *Understand me?* I can see if you bloody narks are trying to trick me. Clear out. Understand? *Clear out,* or I'll burn the place down and this arty little bitch with it!"

The strange thing was that Nina felt calmer than she had been since she had come round enough to realize what had happened. She could not move but she could see and hear Facey. She could also hear the man with the deep voice. She felt as if she was resigned to the coming of death.

Gideon seemed to be quiet for a long time, far longer than the circumstances warranted. Henderson's eyes were screwed up with the agony of waiting; a man below said in a grating whisper:

"For gossake say something!"

"Hush!" ordered Hobbs.

For a few moments the only sound was the hiss of the foam from the extinguisher.

Gideon asked in a casual-sounding voice, "How many of your paintings are up there, Facey?"

"Plenty of them!"

"Going to burn them too?"

"Why shouldn't I? Go on, tell me, why shouldn't I? No one will buy them. They buy all the stinking abstract muck they can lay their hands on, they pay daubers like Picasso fortunes for little bits of canvas not worth spitting on, but me—"

"How many, Facey?"

There was a pause.

"Who's that?"

"Commander Gideon."

Facey gasped. "Gideon. That's a good one, that is. That makes me tops, that does! What do you know about pictures, Gideon? Going to become a collector on a copper's pay?" His laugh was a series of squeaks. "Why, you couldn't afford to buy—"

"I know I couldn't afford to buy anything of yours," Gideon said quietly. "When I saw your pictures at the Gulliver Street shop I knew they weren't for me. But someone else— who knows art— What would you value them at, Mr. Henderson, you're an art buyer."

Facey caught his breath again.

Henderson spoke in a voice as matter-of-fact as if he were in an art shop.

"I wouldn't like to set a price on them—not a market price, that is. They'll appreciate in value, of course, but no one could say how quickly."

"Would you buy them?" Gideon asked.

It was almost possible for Gideon to believe Henderson's quiet "If I had the chance, yes, of course."

There was a sobbing noise from the attic floor; whether Facey or Nina it was impossible to say.

"For how much?"

"I wouldn't want to pay more than five hundred dollars each," Henderson said, "unless I could have a lien on all he's done. But I don't see how—"

Gideon leaned back, placed the palms of his hands flat against the hatch cover, and thrust with all his might. The cover swung upward. He caught a glimpse of Facey crouching down and listening, saw the man dodge back, saw the hatch cover wobble, as if undecided which way to go. He thrust up again with one hand, sent it crashing back, gripped the edge of the hole and hauled himself up and over, met by a stench of turpentine.

Facey was scratching a match along the side of a box.

Gideon flung himself at the man. The match fell, the box fell; the match went out as Facey was sent thudding to the ground under Gideon's weight. Gideon felt the frail body go limp, twitch, and lie still, and he realized that Facey had banged his head and was unconscious.

Gideon stood up slowly.

Henderson was climbing in, Hobbs behind him. Nina, lying on her back on a narrow bed, was craning her neck to see. She recognized her stepfather. Radiance that was like a benediction shone from her eyes, and radiance of another kind shone in Henderson's.

Gideon had never known a greater moment of serenity.

Hobbs said in a dry, unemotional voice, "What an incredible man you are. I'll go and call off the hunt."

23

Homecoming

Two plainclothes men carried Facey down the steps; he was still unconscious. Gideon took a final look round the studio-workshop, the narrow bed, the heap of clothes on which Facey had slept. Close to that were four pictures, two against one wall, two against another. They were all of nudes—middle-aged nudes with raddled faces and big pendulous breasts. The photographers were already busy, and one joked:

"I could sell these to the Beautiful Body magazines."

Henderson reappeared, climbing through the hatch.

"Hallo," said Gideon in surprise. "I thought you'd gone."

"I've talked to my wife, and Nina is being looked after by your police doctor." Henderson paused. "Gideon, I don't know what to say. I haven't the words." Strangely, he looked nearer breaking down now than he had at any time.

"Don't try to say anything," Gideon said. "Just be thankful we got her."

Henderson moistened his lips.

"Thankful, yes." He looked at some of the paintings, and winced. "The man must be mad."

"Lot of sane people like this kind of muck," said Gideon. "The devil of it is, he could have earned a good living, sketching and painting among his friends." He changed the subject. "I'm afraid we've had no news of Schumacher and the money."

"Schumacher I would like you to catch," said Henderson gruffly. "The money"—he broke off, as if biting his tongue on the words—"doesn't matter." His eyes were glowing.

Gideon wished he could be present to see Felisa Henderson's eyes when she was reunited with her daughter.

The strange and the wonderful thing to Elliott Henderson was the way Felisa looked at him, over her daughter's head, and how brilliant her eyes were through the shimmering tears. It was as if she was trying to make him understand that all she felt for Nina she could forever share with him.

Michael Dunn opened the door of the flat above the shop, stood for a moment, and listened for some sound: some coughing or asthmatic breathing, or the rustle of movement as Cynthia struggled to get up. The silence was both welcome and puzzling. He went across the living room, noticing that everything was spick and span, the newspaper folded, the flowers—tulips—beautifully arranged. She shouldn't have worked so, it must have worn her out. His heart began to thump as he approached the bedroom, out of love for his wife, out of gratitude that she should have made such an effort for his homecoming.

As he opened the door he expected to hear her breathing, but he did not. Could she have gone out? It seemed unthinkable—

There she lay: sleeping.

He approached the bed, still puzzled by the silence, filled with heartache because of what the exertion must have cost her. She was not in bed, but on it, fully dressed even to her shoes, one of which lay by her foot; the other dangled, half on.

He reached the bed, his puzzlement growing, because of the silence and her stillness, and the way she lay, one arm halfway over the edge of the bed, head forward, lips parted, eyes closed.

He touched her. She was cold.

He placed the palm of his warm hand upon the bareness of her arm and she was *cold*.

He breathed, "No." After a pause, he breathed, "No, no!"

Then he saw the bottle of sleeping tablets by the side of the bed, almost empty. The screw cap was on, the cottonwool was inside the bottle but all but two or three of the tablets, twenty or thirty at least, were gone.

"Oh, my God!" He rushed to the telephone, and as he reached it saw the note propped up against it. In Cynthia's handwriting were the words *"Mike darling."* His hand trembled as he picked this up. His teeth grated against one another. He wanted to open it but he picked up the reciever. The ringing sound seemed to go on and on, but when it stopped a man answered in a familiar voice.

"Dr. Soames speaking."

"Doctor! It's Michael Dunn. My wife—my wife's unconscious, she seems to have taken all those sleeping tablets—"

"I'll be there in ten minutes," Dr. Soames said crisply.

With the letter clutched in his hand, Michael Dunn put the receiver down heavily and then moved hesitatingly, fearfully, back to his wife. He knew she was more than unconscious. that she was dead.

He tore open the letter, and the tearing seemed to go on inside him.

Mike darling, I can't go on. I know I've got cancer, and I can't go on. You've been wonderful, so, so wonderful, but I can't live like this any longer, it hurts so much. Forgive—please forgive.

When he opened the door to the doctor tears were streaming down his face.

"Honey, what's eating you tonight?" demanded Jill Pommeroy, half an hour after Pommeroy had come home from the office at Kismet Cosmetics. The furnished apartment was bright and airy, the touches Jill invariably gave to a room or a home were everywhere. "You look as if you've discovered that the company's going to close down."

Pommeroy said heavily, "It won't close down, hon. But I've discovered that one of our suppliers has been defrauding us."

"You mean, cheating?"

"Yes, he—"

"The heel!"

"Jill," Pommeroy said, "he's been putting in false invoices and collecting on them to pay for his wife's illness—that's what it looks like. But I'll have to report to the other side, and they'll tell me to have this man booked. I'll hate doing it."

When Gideon got back to his office, late that afternoon, he found Lemaitre and others in a positively festive mood, largely from relief at Nina Pallon's rescue, partly because there had been a crop of arrests on cases which had been outstanding for a long time. Gideon, still feeling the glow from what he had seen at the arches, forced himself to make notes of what had been agreed at the FBI offices, and then sat back as Lemaitre finished talking to Hobbs on the telephone.

"Hope it's not too bad," said Lemaitre. "Eh? . . . Yes, trust Gee-Gee when he gets going." He rang off. "Hobbs burned his hands a bit, and he's going to have them dressed, then go home. He'll be there if you want him."

"I won't want him. Are the burns bad?"

"He said not, but he'd say that if he'd lost all the skin off his fingers."

So Lemaitre felt that way about Hobbs.

"There's one thing you chaps seem to have forgotten," Gideon said dryly. "We haven't got Schumacher, and he's got thirty-five thousand pounds. I've a nasty feeling that he got out of the country before we put the watch on the airports and seaports."

"Almost deserves to get away with it," Lemaitre said glibly. "He sold us a dummy all right. But you needn't be so pessimistic, George. We'll find him through the Green girl when we pick her up at Piccadilly."

His internal telephone rang, and soon he was talking again.

Gideon had a strange, almost shivery sensation inside him. Lemaitre was his second-in-command. Lemaitre was a good detective and the only man here with an all-round knowledge of all aspects of C.I.D. work. He was the best available man to take over the Commander's position, for by a series of accidents other men who might have succeeded to the job were not available. And Lemaitre, the perfect second-in-command with his perennial optimism offsetting his habit of jumping to conclusions, his absolute reliability and unstinting loyalty, his attention to detail, his phenomenal memory and detailed knowledge of the Force, was the most valuable of all men—to Gideon.

What would happen if he were to take Gideon's job? Would the facile optimism which characterized him let him handle it well? As well as Hobbs, for instance?

Never mind Hobbs!

What the hell am I thinking? That I'm irreplaceable? Gideon's reaction was almost vicious in its intensity, but his innate integrity made him admit that if he did take the A.C.'s job he would have to spend a lot of time guiding the new Commander, and that Lemaitre could never be the right man even if he were the best available.

Wouldn't he, Gideon, do better to stay where he was and help the new Assistant Commissioner to find his feet?

A messenger came in with the evening newspapers. There were front-page photographs of Frank Mayhew, alias Mason, and good photographs of Florence Foster, his second English victim.

WILL THERE BE A THIRD?

cried one headline.

Lemaitre, his newspaper rustling, looked up.

"We've got a second leader, George. Says in effect, what the hell's the Yard doing to let this Yankee killer stay free?

Bound to happen, I suppose, but we don't get a hap'orth of public credit for Nina P." When Gideon didn't answer, he went on: "Tell you what—Mayhew will probably start a wave of sex killings; after two or three crop up there's usually a rash of 'em."

"Cheerful, aren't you?" Gideon grumbled, but at heart he knew that theoretically Lemaitre was right. Though he felt out of patience with the other man, he managed to conceal it.

Parsons was feeling out of patience with Colonel Nocci, but knew that he must not show it. In a way he did not blame the other man for his attitude, and he had half-expected it. They were in Nocci's office; it was very warm but the P.S. man did not seem to notice the heat. His facial likeness to Mussolini seemed very marked, and his heavy jowl was shadowed with dark beard. Yet his manner was one of sheer reason.

". . . it is, I repeat, a fact that you at Scotland Yard appear to blame Italians for all your vice, my friend, but some Englishmen have been guilty of procuring young girls for the delight of other men, and also of living off these girls. The habit is not exclusive to Italians."

"I never said it was," Parsons said equably.

"But in this matter, although you have no definite evidence against Mancelli, you prefer to believe he is guilty—as I find it easier to believe that Percival White is guilty. On this question of murder—is murder yet established?"

"No," Parsons admitted.

"It is not one of Scotland Yard's triumphs," remarked Nocci slyly.

"Unless we can get a confession no one's likely to score a triumph." Parsons eased his damp collar. "If those two managers perjured themselves—"

"And being Italians in London, they almost certainly did."

Parsons felt a flare of anger, and knew that Nocci saw it. He bit back a sharp comment, and as he stared at Nocci and saw the hint of a smile in the Italian's eyes he had a mental image of Gideon, deliberately needling a man so as to find out what he was really made of. How would Gideon behave in these circumstances?

He thought he knew; and his mood changed.

"Do you know what you ought to do, Colonel?" he said, half-smiling. "You ought to come over to London and tell Commander Gideon and the Commissioner what you think about the attitude of the London police to Italians in Soho.

You ought to see our records on West End vice too. You'd think we had imported every pervert from Italy. In fact, you would find half the people with Italian names were third- and fourth-generation Englishmen. You'd learn a few other things —just as I'm learning them over here."

Parsons paused, completely composed again.

"And what more would I learn?" inquired Nocci.

"That, like you, we want to find the criminal, whether he's English, Italian, American, or from Timbuctoo. In this case, we thought—"

"Who thought?" demanded Nocci.

"I thought and Gideon listened," answered Parsons. "I told him I thought Lucci could have had a raw deal. So Gideon said, spare no expense, go to Italy and prove it."

Nocci was smiling.

"He did not say: 'Prove that the villain is Percival White'?"

"He just wants a villain."

Nocci laughed.

"We shall do our best to find one for him. But not tonight. My wife is anxious to meet a man from the famous Scotland Yard. If you will be good enough to join us at dinner, we can at least show you one thing that London cannot."

The one thing was Milan Cathedral, its countless little spires and figures shimmering in the moonlight. It was seen from a patio which seemed to merge with the stars.

That was an hour or two later than the time when Lucy Green waited nervously at Piccadilly Station, badly scared, but unaware that Schumacher was in fact nearer Milan than London. It had not occurred to Lucy, in her simplicity, that he had simply used her for the kidnaping and now cared nothing for her.

Two big men came up to her, one on either side. She thought they were wolves, working in a pair.

Then one of them said, "Lucy Green?"

"Supposing I am?" She was truculent out of even greater fear.

"We have just charged a man named Facey with abduction," the man said. "We want you to come along with us to tell us what you know of the kidnaping of Nina Pallon."

Lucy stood there unbelieving, too numbed at that moment to realize how great was her need for fear.

Usually, Gideon would have been on his way home by a quarter to seven, but with Kate away there was no hurry, and he made inroads into the inevitable accumulation of paper-work. He had made a note:

"Commendation for the D.O. who passed on Quincy's story about Facey. Thank Quincy. Check how Hobbs is."

He was still writing when his exchange telephone rang. It wouldn't be about Lucy Green; she was over at Cannon Row, weeping, he had been told, but talking more and more freely. She had already said that she had first met Schumacher three months ago and agreed to help him and Facey, but denied that she had known that kidnaping was involved. If she and Facey would name Schumacher, there would be a good case for asking Interpol to help and for applying for extradition wherever the man was found. Gideon lifted the telephone without thinking although it flashed through his mind that if anyone tried to get him as late as this it was either a forlorn hope or an emergency.

"Gideon."

"There is a call coming through for you from Milan, Mr. Gideon," the operator said. "It might be a little while yet."

Gideon said, "I'll wait for it." Parsons wouldn't telephone unless he had news or, more likely, unless he had uncovered an angle which needed urgent attention in London.

It was ten minutes before the call came through.

"George, I think we're on the way," Parsons said. "Nocci planted a man in Lucci's offices, and the chap found a girl whom Mancelli put in the family way. Remember Giovanni Mancelli?" That was rhetorical, and Parsons hurried on as if he had to get every possible word into every moment of tele-phone time. "Every time the managers visited Milan, they spent an evening at Mancelli's apartment. It's a very plush apartment. Between you and me, Nocci feels we've ridden him rather hard. If you could face those managers with the fact that they went to see Mancelli, they might crack."

"Who would you put onto them?" asked Gideon.

"George Gideon, who else?" asked Parsons.

The fact was, Gideon admitted when Parsons had rung off, he wanted to see the men. He had too little opportunity of working outside the Yard, and Soho was his manor, his square mile. One could say what one liked about a police-man's lot, but it was right for him.

As assistant commissioner, would he really be a policeman? Had Rogerson ever been directly involved with any investiga-tion since he, Gideon, had been at the Yard? One reported to the A.C., took his advice on administrative matters, or used him to help put pressure on the Secretary's office, the other departments, or even the Home Secretary. But the A.C. had never been involved.

Still, two thousand a year was a lot of money.

Police both in uniform and plain clothes saw him, and the word soon spread that Gideon was on the warpath. It reached the prostitutes, some of whom had known him in his days as superintendent of the division, and it was carried fast and far.

It reached the ears of the two witnesses, Segura and Biagnini, who had given evidence against Lucci, and who knew that they might be charged with any variety of vice crimes soon. Gideon went to Segura's flat first. It was close to the Grandi Hotel, in the very heart of Soho.

Segura was rather like the popular concept of Julius Caesar, and Gideon had a fleeting thought that the eunuchs of the Eastern world's harems must have had this kind of look. Behind his austerity, however, there lurked fear, which showed in pale-brown eyes.

He had never met Gideon, but obviously he knew of him.

"Mr. Segura," Gideon said briskly, "I've just had a telephone call from Superintendent Parsons, who is in Milan. He's already seen Mr. Giovanni Mancelli."

He broke off.

He saw the dread in Segura's eyes, and went on with cold, calculated precision:

"I want to know what happened in Mancelli's apartment each time you visited him in Milan."

It was easy. It was, so often. Once a crack was made, resistance often broke down completely. First Segura and then plump and ingratiating Biagnini, the other manager, blamed Mancelli. Each blamed each other too, and swore the other had poisoned the brandy.

There was some cement-dirt on a pair of Segura's shoes which was exactly the same as the scrapings from the air shaft at the Hotel Grandi.

The ash from the Italian-made cigarettes which Biagnini smoked was identical, under chemical analysis, with the ash found by the one-way mirror set in the ceiling of the room where Lucci had died.

Parsons had not known what to expect when he visited Nocci's home. He had never met Nocci's wife. She was a short, rather plump, merry-eyed woman, and she spoke broken English fluently and attractively. Parsons was laughing with her, replete with pizza and spaghetti and meat balls—

"What else I give Inglisi, si?"—when the telephone bell rang. Nocci answered the call, and was back almost at once.

"Gideon," he announced.

"Hey, George, what's on?" asked Parsons eagerly. "Did you get a confession?" He was aware of Nocci watching. "Both on a charge . . . ? Couldn't be more pleased! . . . Thanks for calling, George. If I know Colonel Nocci, he'll pick Mancelli up tonight. And I'll go and see Madam Lucci."

He did, and when he told her the news, the expression in Maria Lucci's eyes was very like the expression in Felisa Henderson's when she had learned that Nina was safe.

Soon after making the call to Milan, Gideon was driven in a divisional car to Fulham. When he turned into Harrington Street he saw lights in so many windows in his neighbors' houses that he felt gloomy at the thought that he was returning to an empty house. Then the driver said something about a good day, and distracted him. It wasn't until he was actually out of the car, answering the driver's "Good night, sir" that he realized there was a window open at his house, and that the passage light was on, although the night was not yet dark. He strode along the path, thinking, Kate's home! and his spirits rose. There was nothing he wanted to do so much as talk to her about the A.C. offer, no other way in which he could really clarify his own thoughts. It was often like this: as if Kate divined the times when he so needed her.

He opened the front door.

"Daddy, is that you?" It was Priscilla, his second daughter, hurrying from the kitchen, hands white with flour. In that moment he saw how like Kate she was. He had not seen her for months, because since her marriage she had lived in the Midlands. It was good to see her eyes light up, to feel her warmth as she gave him a long, hard kiss. When she backed away, she asked, "Surprise?"

"Lovely surprise!"

"Mum telephoned me about Pru and I haven't been to see you for ages, so I told Dick I'd come and look after you for a few days, and do some shopping, and go and see Pru— She isn't going to lose her baby, is she?" From high spirits to gloom or alarm, that was Priscilla, unchanged by marriage and the years. Were her changes of mood so surprising? Hadn't he been on top of the world about talking to Kate, and wasn't he acutely disappointed now despite the warming presence of his daughter?

"Don't see why she should when so much can be done these

days," he made himself say. "She'll be all right." Priscilla linked arms with him and they went to the kitchen. "What's cooking?"

"Roast beef. Mum said if I got a good joint of topside you'd like it hot and there would be plenty to cut at cold. Hungry?"

He had eaten at the Yard.

"Famished!" he told her. "Let's see if you can make a Yorkshire pudding as good as your mother's."

24

Capture

Saturday was always an unpredictable day at the Yard. Some Saturdays comparatively little crime would be committed, on others some smart man, or even a gang, would like to catch the Yard napping. That Saturday was one of the quiet ones. Gideon brought his paper work almost up to date, and then paused to consider the Assistant Commissioner's job. He was still contemplating it with mixed feelings when the door opened and the messenger who had bounced in earlier in the week came in, poker-faced.

"A cable for you, sir—just come in."

"Thanks." Gideon took and unfolded it, thinking, Nielsen? as he did so. There were three words: *Congratulations Thanks Nielsen.*

"I wonder what he'll say if we catch Schumacher," Gideon mused.

"What's that, sir?"

"Nothing," Gideon said. "That's all for now."

The messenger went out, and almost at once the exchange telephone rang again. Gideon, still thinking about Schumacher and Nielsen, heard a man say:

"George, it's Mike Paterson here." Paterson was the superintendent of KL Division in north London. "I think one of my men's cornered your Yankee sex killer."

Paterson's man was Detective Officer Gorlay, in his early thirties, ambitious, sometimes overeager, but with natural powers of observation which would help him to go a long way on the Force. He was at the corner of a street in Tottenham, not far from White Hart Lane, which was quiet in the early summer, all footballers gone. There were two bed-and-breakfast hotels in the street, and when Gorlay had called in to inspect the registers he had carried with him a photograph of Frank S. Mayhew.

The middle-aged man who ran the hotel with his wife said in a whisper, "Yes, that's him. I'm sure it's him."

Gorlay felt a surge of excitement, but did not interrupt.

"He came here yesterday morning and paid a week's rent in advance. He hadn't any baggage with him, you see—he said he'd had to leave home in a hurry, said he'd had a quarrel with his wife. But it didn't fool me. I can tell a liar, I always could, there aren't many better judges of character than I am. I knew I'd seen him before, I said as much to my wife, but it was his picture in the paper I'd seen . . ."

In time, Gorlay had managed to ask, "Is he in his room?"

"Oh, yes. He hasn't stirred since he came back after lunch —only went to the cafe round the corner, he didn't have time to go anywhere else. He's kind of furtive . . ."

Gorlay had telephoned his superintendent.

He was at the corner when two police cars arrived, one from each direction, three plainclothes men in each. Gorlay had not been on the Force long enough to be used to the quiet yet almost brisk efficiency whenever there was a job like this to do. Two men went to the back of the house, one to each corner, two stayed with Gorlay. It was like a military operation. The senior officer was Detective Inspector Chaff, whom Gorlay knew only as a man of few words, most of them biting.

"Want to make the charge?" Chaff asked.

Gorlay was almost too surprised to answer.

"Come on, make up your mind."

"Yes," Gorlay said, and gulped. "Yes, please."

"Don't muck it up," Chaff said, as if afraid that was inevitable. They went into the hallway, where the proud proprietor was almost beside himself.

Chaff didn't say a word to help; he did not intend to. As Gorlay walked up the stairs, he tried to remember every rule in the book. Walk by the wall so as to prevent stairs creaking. Knock lightly, so as not to startle or frighten the man inside. Try the handle very quietly, and push. If the door opens, fling it back and get inside quick.

Chaff and another man were just behind him.

He tapped with his knuckles and tried the handle with his left hand; it needed only trifling pressure to tell him that the door was locked. He prepared to put his shoulder against it as he had been taught, and he was completely unaware of the fact that he stood exactly as Gideon had at the arches.

"Who's that?" a man called. His voice was high-pitched.

"I've come to check the gas, sir," Gorlay answered. "There's a leak somewhere in the house."

Silence followed; silence in which Gorlay's tension built up, the two men behind him moved forward, he thrust himself forward for an attack on the door. Before he put his shoulder to it, the sound of movement came from inside the room. A bolt moved back, the door handle turned, the door opened.

"I haven't smelled gas—" Frank S. Mayhew declared. "I don't—"

He broke off and backed away, his mouth dropping open, all the color draining from his face. Gorlay felt quite sure it was the rapist as he said flatly:

"Frank S. Mayhew, it is my duty to charge you with . . ."

Mayhew stood there, gibbering; it was almost pathetically simple.

"Yes, we got him," the KL superintendent said. "It was easy, George. He keeps muttering he couldn't help it, something made him. Want him at the Yard?"

"Keep him there. We'll send a doctor over," Gideon answered. "I'll get the Back Room busy, you'll have all the newspapermen in London buzzing round you soon. Give them all the information you can, let 'em have pictures of you and this chap Gorlay. We'll go to town on this one."

When he rang off, he thought wryly, So it was easy. Such words came with almost dangerous facility. The whole strength of the Yard had stirred itself, thousands of pictures had been circulated, nearly fifty thousand men had been on the lookout for the man, and not one, not *one*, had seen him. The hotel owner had been alerted by police activity, of course, but the irony was that so much time, money, organization and manpower had to be used to catch a solitary man with a twisted mind, to avenge two girls, and to make sure that others were safe.

Every now and again some crime brought home to him the true burden of his responsibility. With Mayhew on a charge there would probably be an abrupt end to sex crimes for a while; the fear of being caught was still the greatest deterrent. But there was no end to the war against criminals, only periods when the main fronts were quiet. This morning there was good cause for satisfaction, and at the moment only two cases preoccupied him enough to drive his personal problems into the background.

The first was the Rite-Time watches job.

The second was the sabotage of the export of goods to the United States. The possible extent of that, with corresponding political as well as economic significance, made it worrying. He must talk to Scott-Marle about it on Monday.

There was a lot he had to talk to Scott-Marle about.

When his internal telephone rang he was deep in thought and did not answer immediately. If Prudence was going to have a rough time with her baby she would need more money than she had. His son-in-law was earning about enough to keep going, which was all right for the youngsters, but in an emergency he and Kate must be ready to help out. And their youngest boy was still a heavy expense.

The bell rang again; he had forgotten the first ring.

"Gideon."

"There's a Mrs. Klein here asking to see you, sir." It was the front hall sergeant. "She won't tell me what it's about only that it's urgent and she has to see you."

Klein? thought Gideon. Klein? The name rang a bell. Klein? No, he couldn't place it, but there was no harm in seeing her; he wasn't too pressed for time. He made another note to telephone and find out how Hobbs was as he said:

"Take her along to the main waiting room. I'll be there in a few minutes." He rang off on the sergeant's "Very good, sir," and leaned back. Klein, Mrs. Klein. He pushed his chair back and stood up, went out along the half-deserted passages, and was at the door when the name dropped into place. Jerry Klein, the Soho jeweler who had had the Rite-Time watches stolen. He drew back from the door and stepped into an office next door; it was empty. He pulled the inter-office telephone toward him and dialed MacPherson's number.

MacPherson answered at once.

"Mac, go along to the waiting room annex and listen to what a Mrs. Klein has to say to me, will you? Don't come in, two of us might overawe her."

"Jerry Klein's wife?"

"I don't know yet," Gideon said.

He went back to the waiting room, and opened the door. A fine-looking Jewish woman with magnificent brown eyes and a beautiful complexion was waiting for him. She was nervous. Her hands were raised apprehensively in front of her bosom; she wore a brown suit of which Kate would approve, and a small hat, perched decoratively on a mass of nearly black hair.

"Hallo, Mrs. Klein," Gideon said. He smiled, and held out his hand. "How can I help you?"

"I'm sorry to come here worrying you, sir. I know you're busy, but I just had to." Words spilled from the glistening lips. "I'm so worried I hardly know what to do. My husband's a jeweler, he sells costume jewelry and watches and a few good jewels, and his shop was raided the other day—a smash-and-grab raid, I mean. And ever since he's been frightened, ever so frightened. And a man came to the house and made me and the children go out until Jerry came back. I didn't want the children worried, so I did what he wanted but when I came back Jerry was white as a sheet, and he had a nasty cut on his hand. The man's been to see him again, and I think he's trying to make Jerry buy stolen watches. He has in the past. I can't help it if that gets him into trouble, but I can't stand by and see him frightened . . ."

There seemed no pause in the flow, which would be meat and drink to MacPherson. This could be the break they needed over Rite-Time, and it was by no means the first time that a frightened wife had given the Yard vital information.

". . . and you'll do everything you can for my husband, won't you?"

"If he was forced to taken stolen goods into stock, and can prove that in court, you haven't much to worry about," Gideon reassured her. "I think you'd better have a word with the superintendent who is investigating the smash-and-grab raid. Have you plenty of time?"

"Oh, yes, sir, my mother's looking after the children. She doesn't know where I've come, no one does, but I just had to, and I've read about you in the newspapers, I always believe in seeing someone at the very top."

25

Gideon's Wife

When Gideon left the Yard, a little after one o'clock, Mac-
Pherson was as hopeful as he was ever likely to be, and confident too, which suggested that he had unearthed some other
facts which he was not yet ready to report. Gideon put
thought of the case out of his mind, although the picture of
glowing-eyed, vital Mrs. Klein did not fade entirely until he
was halfway home.

Priscilla wasn't in, but a casserole of lamb was in the oven,
simmering, and a big bowl of fruit salad and a jug of cream
were in the refrigerator. A note on the table, which had been
laid, read:

> *Gone over to see the Gordons, I'll be back for supper,
> don't wash up. Silla.*

He laughed.

He cleared out the casserole to the last morsel, made deep
inroads into the fruit, made himself a cup of coffee, and sat
back for half an hour with the newspapers, but at the back of
his mind he kept thinking of Kate, wishing she was there for
him to discuss things with. Suddenly he remembered Hobbs,
and he called his private number. It was a queer thing, but he
would like to talk to Hobbs.

A woman answered, and Gideon thought of Mrs. Hobbs,
the lovely woman, paralyzed so that she could not get out of
her wheel chair unaided.

"Hallo, Helen," Gideon said. "George Gideon here. How is
Alec?"

"How nice of you to call," said Helen, and then with obvious anxiety, "You don't need him, do you?"

"He's free for the weekend, anyhow—I couldn't call this
morning to find out how his hands are."

"Not very good, I'm afraid," answered Helen Hobbs. "I
managed to persuade him to have an injection, and told him
he should sleep for the rest of the afternoon."

"How bad *are* these burns?" demanded Gideon.

"They could be worse, but the doctor says it will be two weeks at least before he can drive a car. George, he's tired too. He's been driving himself too hard." She might well mean: You've been driving him too hard. "Is there any reason why he shouldn't have some sick leave?"

Gideon answered quietly, "No reason at all. We can get along. I'll look in one day next week, when he's on the mend."

"He'll love that," Helen said.

When he had rung off, Gideon reflected almost ruefully that something always prevented him from getting to know Hobbs better. Then he thought, Those burns must be bad. I'll send one of our medics to check with his.

The news about Hobbs further clouded his mood until he went out and ran the mower over the lawn. There wasn't much growth on it yet, but in a month it would need cutting twice a week. There wasn't much to do in the garden at all; with the family away, Kate had time for the garden, and she had green fingers. And he couldn't think of anything in the way of odd jobs in the house. So there was plenty of time to think of the nagging problem: What did he really want to do as a policeman? What ought he to do, as a family man?

Gradually he realized something he had not seen before: there was conflict here between what he wanted to do and what he ought to do. As soon as he recognized that for what it was he realized that the issue was not simple. What *did* he want for himself? The prestige which only the assistant commissionership could bring him? Or the sense of involvement with the Yard's work which he could get only as commander?

Suddenly he thought, It's no use, I'll have to talk to Kate. I'll go over and see her tomorrow.

Kate opened the door of the tiny bungalow, one of a thousand other tiny houses almost identical in design. When she saw Gideon her eyes lit up. For a moment Gideon forgot everything else, and he knew that Kate did, too. They went in, and the everyday world closed about them. Gideon had been here only three times before. He felt absolutely out of place, for his head nearly touched the ceiling and he seemed like Gulliver in a modern land of Lilliput.

The thing that most troubled him was the silence.

"How's Pru?" he asked.

Kate said soberly, "She isn't too good, George. She's sleeping now, the doctor gave her an injection. He says she should be all right if she rests, but he comes in every day, so he's not too happy about her."

"Where's Pete?"

"He's doing some weekend work, to bring in more money. He's a good lad, dear." That was said almost defensively. "And they mean everything to each other."

Gideon conquered the impulse to say, But he can't really afford to keep her. Now that he was there he could hardly do what he had really come to do: talk to Kate about his own indecision.

"Can I see her?"

"Of course."

He was startled by Pru's pallor and by the thinness of her face as she lay on the double bed in a room only just big enough for it and overcrowded with a small wardrobe and a dressing table. When he went into the kitchen, where Kate was preparing the vegetables, he felt sure what to do: Although the children were married they were not really off his hands, and probably never would be. There wasn't any real likelihood that he would ever be able to bring himself to say, They made their bed, so let them lie on it. The odd thing was that he was almost tongue-tied with Kate.

"Grass could do with cutting," he said suddenly. "Think the noise would disturb Pru?"

"George," Kate said, "what's worrying you?"

"What a question to ask!" He was overvehement and knew it. "Prudence looks as if—"

"It isn't Pru. Has a case gone wrong?"

He didn't answer.

They were so close to each other in the tiny kitchen that he had only to stretch out his arm to touch her, but he didn't. She hitched up a high stool, and sat on it.

"There's something," she declared, and then alarm flared up in her eyes. "None of the children have been hurt. Tell me!" She was up from the stool in a flash. "George—"

"No one's hurt badly," he said. "Hobbs has some burns, but nothing serious."

She gave a funny little laugh.

"For a minute you scared me." She went on, "George dear, what's worrying you?"

He made himself smile, and then realized how absurd it was that he should have to, in the circumstances. He ought to be elated, he ought to feel as proud as a man could.

He said, "Scott-Marle's offered me the A.C.'s post." He realized that he hadn't given a thought to poor, doomed Rog-

erson since first hearing, and decided then and there to go
and see Mrs. Rogerson that day. This was with one half of his
mind; with the other he was concentrating on Kate, seeing
bewilderment chase the pleasure out of her eyes. It was so
like Kate that after a moment or two she should say:

"And you don't want to take it?"

"Not really."

"You don't have to, George, do you?"

"No."

She didn't need to ask why he didn't want to; she was
enough at one with him in mind and outlook to understand
his reasons. She simply took the fact for granted; he did not
want the job. In accepting that she pricked the balloon of
prestige and made him see how very much he wanted to stay
in his present job.

"Then what's worrying you, dear?"

He said: "It's worth two thousand a year more, and a much
bigger pension. And it looks to me as if we can still use the
money. When there isn't one emergency, there'll be another.
Not much doubt about that, is there?"

Quietly, half-smilingly, Kate answered:

"The time might even come when we'll be the emergency
and the children will have to help us—but I don't think it's
likely. Darling, *I* don't want a thing more than I've got, and
even if I did we'd be able to afford it, most of the time they'll
look after themselves. I don't really know why you're dither-
ing. And I'm not really sure you'd make such a good A.C."

Gideon stared at her.

Then he burst out laughing.

It was a strange Monday morning for Gideon—a kind of
anticlimax.

On his desk were the usual reports and some simple memo-
randa—including one about the forthcoming Sports Meeting:
Commander George Gideon will present the prizes. Another
said: *Reason to believe Barney Barnett is trying to work out
a job with Quincy Lee.*

Lemaitre had scrawled "Nuts" across a corner.

"What's this about Lee and Barnett?" Gideon asked him.

"Quincy told me half the boys in London want to work
with him, and he's not interested," Lemaitre said. "Even if he
was, Maggie would scare him off! Don't give it a thought,
George. We'll get Barney again one of these days, wife or no
wife. See the report on Lucy Green?"

"Not yet."

"She's come clean," Lemaitre told him with satisfaction. "We ought to get Interpol busy on Schumacher. That reminds me, Henderson rang up. Will you and Kate have dinner with him and his wife tonight?"

"Kate can't," Gideon said at once. "And I'm not sure I should. I'll call him later. Anything else you've forgotten?"

Gideon went through the morning briefing quickly. Mac-Pherson didn't report. Oliver was deeply involved with the West German marks problem, which was no longer the Yard's baby, for the main investigation must now be on the Continent. There was the usual weekend crop of crime, the inevitable arrests. One of them was from Brentford, about a charge to be made that morning against a printer named Dunn, who appeared to have defrauded Kismet Cosmetics of several hundred pounds to help his wife, who had since died. The divisional superintendent had come up to see Gideon about it, an elderly, very conscientious man named Killin.

"What's on your mind?" Gideon asked.

"The local people don't want to prosecute but they've had instructions from the head office in the States to get their pound of flesh. I happen to know you're in close touch with New York, George, and I wondered if you could put in a word."

"Getting softhearted, aren't you?" Gideon said. He felt almost like Lemaitre, who was busy at his desk.

"It's a very sad business. His wife was everything to him."

Gideon thought of Henderson.

"Can't do a thing with New York," he said. "But there's no reason why you shouldn't pull all the strings you can to persuade this man Dunn to have a summary hearing. He ought to be bound over as it's a first offense—it is, isn't it?"

"Yes. I daresay I can fix that. He's had to apply for legal aid, and I know who'll look after him. Just wanted your approval, George."

To the Yard it was such a trifling case.

To the man Dunn it could be his whole future.

At eleven o'clock Gideon entered Scott-Marle's office. The Commissioner already had a brief report on the sabotage inquiry, and Gideon saw a letter from the chairman of the Faculty of British Industries on his desk; so that was moving.

Scott-Marle looked less aloof than usual.

"A very satisfactory ending to the Henderson and Mayhew cases," he said. "You ought to congratulate yourself." When Gideon didn't answer he asked, "What do you want to talk about?"

"The A.C.'s post," said Gideon.

"You're a week early, aren't you?"

"I'm pretty clear about what I want to do."

"Well?"

"I think I'll stay as I am," announced Gideon.

There it was; decision made and the Commissioner told about it. Gideon felt a strange kind of relief, and at the same time had a feeling that Scott-Marle was looking at him in disapproval. He felt as if he had to steel himself to justify the decision.

Scott-Marle said quietly: "There's just one thing that would have prevented you from being the best assistant commissioner I could hope for—the fact that at heart you would always have preferred to be commander. I think you're right, but I'm very sorry that you are."

Why was it some men had to say such warming things so coldly?

"Thanks very much," Gideon said.

"Now there's a new problem," went on Scott-Marle, as if that was that and there was nothing more to be said about it. "This matter of sabotage of goods for America. I don't like the look of it at all."

"Shouldn't think you do," said Gideon gruffly.

"I've a letter and some figures from Lord Olling. The number of cases of suspected sabotage is surprisingly high. Much of it happens at sea and after arrival in the U.S.A. What I'd like you to do is this . . ." Scott-Marle was asserting his authority as he seldom did, almost as if he disapproved of the decision in spite of what he had said. "Put Hobbs on to this job with Ormeroyd, and make sure they have all the help they require. He's the right man to deal with the FBI principals, don't you think?"

Old school tie, thought Gideon: but Scott-Marle was quite right.

"Yes, although he'll be off sick for a bit."

"So I understand, but this is a long-term investigation. Then I would like you to see Lord Olling and Sir Arthur Fielding again, to get the fullest possible picture, and go over to New York to discuss it with the FBI people there—and with the New York police. It could develop into an inquiry for their FBI and will probably become one for Interpol— like the West German marks affair. But we started it here, and we don't often get the chance to show big business what we do for them. No reason why you shouldn't go to New York, is there?"

Gideon's heart was racing.

"Not that I know of," he said.

"If I were you I'd go over by ship, and that will give you time to study the facts before you get to New York. It ought to be fairly soon—in the next month, for certain—so that you can be back in time to help the new Assistant Commissioner when he's appointed."

After a long pause, Gideon said:

"Commissioner, all I can say is 'thank you.' "

Of course, he would take Kate. Prudence would be all right, she had only ten days to go now. It would be wonderful for Kate, as well as for him, a new world of experience. It would mean digging into their savings, but what were savings for?

Just before twelve, his private line telephone bell rang, and he wondered if it was Henderson. When he heard Kate's voice, a shock of alarm ran through him. Then he thought, She's just being Kate.

"George," Kate said, "Pru's lost her baby. She's all right, and there shouldn't be any complications, but—isn't it dreadful? Dreadful. My darling Pru—"

The time to tell her about New York was not yet, but when the time came the news would be great solace for Kate.